Maxx;
Morgan,
Maxx - you
see yourself in
many "!" of my cha
Enjoy! i
XOXO
Mya
Malley

MAGGIE

By

Mya O' Malley

S

Maggie
By Mya O'Malley
www.myaomalley.com

ISBN- 13: 978-0-9978596-1-4
ISBN- 10: 0-9978596-1-X

Cover Art by Jena Brignola

For Alexandra

CHAPTER ONE

Naomi

THERE IT WAS again. She might have missed it, for it had happened so quickly. Naomi figured she would keep this little secret to herself for now. Yet another amazing thing she could add to her list of reasons why she had fallen in love with her new home.

A gigantic sigh escaped her lips. So this was what it felt like to own her own house. Who said she needed to wait around for the perfect man in order to fulfill her dreams? Nope, she took the horse by the reins and fulfilled one of the most important items on her grown-up to-do list. So what if she didn't have the furniture she desired most? This charming 1700s saltbox house had come already furnished, so she took advantage of the fact that she could save some money for better purposes.

Glancing out the large window in her dining area, Naomi took in the vast graveyard beyond; the gray sky compounded the dreary feel of the scenery. Fall was in the air, from the dancing amber leaves to the crisp wind. Some might be spooked to have a cemetery practically in their backyard, but she didn't mind. As a matter of fact, she quite enjoyed being this close to so many spirits. It was oddly comforting. Oh, the tales they could tell, the lives they had led. If only she could communicate with them—she would have a million questions about the plentiful experiences during each of their lives. Naomi supposed her vivid imagination was one of the reasons she had gone into the field of writing to begin with.

Tales of this area being rich in history had been the selling point for her. Taking another peek outside, Naomi rubbed her hands together. She couldn't wait to dive into some extensive research about her own house and the mysterious souls who were laid to rest beyond her window. It also served another purpose: taking her mind off her recent worries.

Sharp rapping on the door jolted her from the dark thoughts. Amy must be early again. Early and late, the two best friends couldn't be more different. It wasn't that Naomi purposely arrived late everywhere she went, but somehow life just seemed to get in the way. Like the time she was hurrying for her job interview when she was eighteen, and she got stuck at a never-ending freight train, which seemed to be transporting endless supplies to the entire northeast. It wasn't the first or last job interview she had been late for. Or how about when she and Amy had gone on a double date and her cat escaped seconds before she was leaving the house? What was one to do, let the cat run away?

"Hi, I see you're early as usual. Come on in, I'm not ready yet."

"What happened this time? Zelda's missing again?" Amy smirked, eyes searching the kitchen for the black cat.

"Need I remind you that you're early? And no, she's in the living room." Sure enough, as if she heard her name being called, Zelda strutted into the kitchen, rubbing her long, fluffy black fur all over Amy's tan pants.

"Oh, great. Zelda, you know how much I love you, but really, my best slacks?" Amy sighed as she grabbed the pet hair roller Naomi kept on the kitchen shelf just for her friend, to remove the cat hair.

"How does the cat hair not bother you? Every time I see you, you've got Zelda's black fur flying off you," Amy exclaimed, waving her arms through the air.

"Give me a second and we'll get going," Naomi called as she was running for the stairs. She stopped short.

Again. A flash of a shadow. It was there. Then it was gone. It hadn't been the first time she had witnessed the peculiar phenomenon and she was sure it wouldn't be the last. Naomi figured it could be her imagination, but then again, it could also be due to the fact she lived on this eerie piece of property. Naomi had never witnessed evidence of ghosts prior to living here, so her gut told her something was amiss. No bother, though; thoughts of a resident spirit intrigued her. At least it wouldn't be boring here.

Amy. Shoot. She sprinted into her bedroom to finish getting ready.

This would be the last, the *very* last blind date she would allow Amy to drag her to. Geez, she and Amy were only twenty-eight years old; what was the rush, especially since she and Nick had only recently split. Nick. He hadn't been right for her, and his jealous ways had finally provoked her to end their tumultuous two-year relationship. Anxious thoughts came to mind before she pushed the troublesome images away.

The last guy Amy had subjected her to had been allergic to cats and had "politely" informed her that if the relationship were to continue, she would need to find a home for her cat. Imagine that! She had abruptly stood and excused herself from the remainder of the date, leaving an open-mouthed Amy with both the man and her own date. Giggling at the memory, Naomi could practically hear her friend shrieking into her cell phone, complaining that she should have at least tried to make it through the end of the date and that the rest of her evening had been quite awkward as Naomi's date had stayed on—and even ate half of her appetizer.

"I'm ready," Naomi called, out of breath from sprinting down the stairs.

"Oh my God, look at you! Where's your brush?"

Naomi's long, dark-brown hair was forever unkempt.

3

"Oh, just a sec," she called as she made her way to the bathroom. Glancing in the mirror, she didn't think her hair looked half bad, but she smoothed it down with her brush nonetheless.

"This is…" Naomi began, as they headed toward Amy's car.

"This is the last time," Amy finished her sentence with a chuckle. "I've heard it before."

"But this time I mean it." With a huff, she settled into the car.

"Heard that before too." Amy turned the ignition and they headed to the nearby river town to meet up with their dates.

It was kind of cool the way Amy arranged for them to meet up with their dates together. Most didn't seem to mind the set-up and Naomi knew the reason why Amy insisted upon these double dates. Naomi wouldn't go on her own. Dating just wasn't high on her list of priorities; she was free for the first time in years and was kind of enjoying the solitude.

Amy was a master at stirring up these dates; some she found on internet sites, while others she found during the course of her day. At times, Naomi wished she were as outgoing as her best friend, for she found herself tongue tied if an attractive man was nearby and usually clammed up and avoided eye contact. Not exactly a magnet for men.

"Now this one I have a really good feeling about," Amy started as she turned the wheel, steering the car into the parking lot of the restaurant by the river.

"Oh, if I had a dollar for every time I heard that one." A small huff escaped Naomi's lips. Amy had basked in the role of matchmaker long before Nick had even come into the picture. *Nick.* The negativity that surrounded thoughts of him was suddenly intense, as if a heavy dark cloud had found its way into her head. Too heavy, she pondered, and much too dark. Naomi considered herself to be a strong woman, but when her thoughts wandered to Nick, she had a hard time shaking that feeling of dread.

"Yeah, yeah. Open mind this time, right?" Amy coached as they walked up to the entrance.

"Who picked this place? I'm a struggling author, remember?" Glancing around at the perfectly landscaped property with a stunning view of the Hudson River, she sighed.

"I did. I told you I think this one is special, and don't worry. The lunch menu won't kill you; it's the dinner prices that get you." With her shoulders back, Amy reviewed the pertinent information regarding Thomas. He was a divorced insurance salesman with a five-year-old son. She wasn't sure if she was up to the roll of being a stepmom, but then again, she was getting ahead of herself here, wasn't she? It was a date, just a date.

Settling down at the table in the back of the room, they waited. "See that, all the pressure you put on me and *they're* late." A few minutes later, a handsome— scratch that, *very* handsome—man with wavy black hair walked through the door. "Whoa."

"That's not him," Amy stated through clenched teeth. "But it's nice to see that you're still interested in a man. Keep your head in the game. Look, here's my date." Amy waved the guy over to the table.

Naomi's eyes followed the dark-haired guy as he found a seat alone at the bar. She didn't even notice Amy's date until he plopped himself down across the table from her.

"Naomi! Earth to Naomi."

"Oh, sorry. Hello, nice to meet you." She met his extended hand with her own and noted how limp his handshake was.

And sweaty.

"Naomi, this is Peter. Peter, my friend, Naomi."

"Nice to meet you," Peter responded with a nervous half smile.

It was never a good sign when someone showed up

late for a first date. Obviously her own date couldn't care less about first impressions. She bit her fingernails as she attempted to participate in the conversation between Amy and Peter. Boring. This chitchat was plain boring. One of the endless reasons she hated getting to know someone new. It took so much time and effort. Plain exhausting is what it was. Almost better to be alone.

Ten minutes later, her date arrived dressed in a business suit. Hmm. Naomi liked her men a bit more casual.

"Hi, everyone. I'm Thomas. I apologize for being late. I was with an important client." Thomas puffed his chest out as he ran a slender hand through his short hair.

Naomi addressed him with a cool stare. *Tool.* This guy had the word tool practically dripping off of him. Naomi tried not to glance at the clock on the wall, but it loomed over her. Tick, tick, ticking. Thinking that she'd rather be home reading a good book with Zelda curled by her feet, she forced a stiff smile.

Somewhere over the course of the conversation, she heard something that caught her attention. Not very good at faking conversation, she noted Amy's icy stare as she responded to Thomas's comments with the most enthusiasm she could muster, which was not much. It wasn't that she was being rude, but when someone just went on and on about how much money he made, his ex-wife and so on, she zoned out. But she did hear mention of the word *pet.*

"I have the most adorable cat, she's all black…"

"You have a cat? Ooh, I don't like cats," Thomas frowned, shaking his head. Tightening her fists, her first instinct was to bolt straight out the door. But Amy seemed to be enjoying herself just fine, and she didn't wish to ruin her friend's date. However, she could take a break. A much needed break.

"If you'll excuse me? I need a drink." Jumping to her feet, Naomi headed straight for the bar. Giggling to herself, she heard Thomas asking if she was actually going to drink at lunchtime. Well, yes, she was, but normally she didn't. *Something about you, Thomas, has made me realize I could use a drink.*

She had almost forgotten about the handsome man still seated at the bar. He had a glass of red wine in his hand, twirling the stem of the glass with his fingers. His eyes were glued to the television set.

"I'll have what he's having," Naomi clutched her purse as she placed her order with the bartender. The handsome man raised his eyebrows, his eyes locking with hers. Naomi swallowed.

"I hope you like a good merlot. That's what this is." She didn't care if he was drinking gasoline, she realized.

"Oh, yes, I do."

"My name's Ryan. Nice to meet you."

The bartender gently placed her merlot in front of her. As she reached for her purse, Ryan told the bartender that he was buying.

"Well, thank you. You didn't have to do that." Naomi felt her face flush.

"It's my pleasure. I didn't catch your name."

"Naomi. I'm Naomi."

"To you, Naomi. I hope you have better dates ahead," Ryan announced, touching his glass with hers. She gulped. It was a great thing to toast to, but how did he know about the status of her date?

CHAPTER TWO

Naomi

DAYS FLEW BY as her mind was directed to thoughts of Ryan. Since the afternoon they had met, she couldn't tear her mind away from him. He worked as a history professor at the college up on the hill overlooking the river, currently teaching online from his home. That day, they had sat for hours, until the bright afternoon sun faded and the darkening night welcomed them. Much to Amy's displeasure, she had stayed with Ryan, eventually grabbing a booth for dinner. Days later, Amy got over herself when she realized how smitten Naomi had become with Ryan. They had spoken every day and met for coffee. Today marked Ryan's first visit to her new house. Humming a favorite show tune, she dusted and fussed, wanting to make a good impression. Zelda weaved in and out of her legs, speaking to her in the way only a cat can. Plans for dinner at the Italian place across the street would follow his visit.

Movement caught her attention for the briefest of moments. A chill swept over her as Zelda howled and took off upstairs. Okay, maybe this ghost business did give her the creeps. Maybe just a little.

Glancing at her watch, she bit her lip as she realized Ryan was due at any moment. She even had those telltale butterflies in her stomach. Yes, she was in trouble.

Zelda's black form came whizzing back into the kitchen, settling down at her feet. Ryan even adored cats. How could she have lucked out so?

She heard the sound of a vehicle pull into her driveway as she leaned over and squeezed Zelda. "Wish me luck, my beautiful girl." Naomi placed a quick kiss on top of the cat's head. A soft meow met her gesture. Peeking out her window, she spotted Ryan stepping out of a small black truck.

Without waiting for him to knock, she opened the door. "Hi, Ryan," she reached up on her tiptoes, kissing him hello on his cheek. She loved how it felt to reach up to his height.

"Hi, Naomi." Whistling, he walked into the kitchen. At first she was flattered, but then realized his appreciation was not directed toward her. Glancing down at her new blouse, she sighed. Fifty bucks. This top cost her fifty dollars, and he hadn't even noticed.

Ryan took a brief look around, shaking his head and grinning approvingly as he regarded her home. Zelda practically leaped at the sight of him. At first, Naomi wasn't sure if it was a positive reaction, but when Zelda allowed him to reach and lift her up, she heard the soft sound of satisfaction. Zelda rarely purred for anyone besides her. How very odd.

"Okay, can I just say that I would have loved to bring my students here for a field trip?" Ryan was off, heading for the dining room. He peeked through the curtains.

"I mean when I used to have an actual class, not just online. Hey, between this house and this old cemetery, how do you ever get any rest?" His wide eyes met hers.

"Excuse me?" What a strange comment.

"I wouldn't sleep. If I lived here, I would explore until I found every bit of information ever written on this place and the grounds."

"I...I'm glad to hear you say that because I feel exactly the same way. I just moved in not too long ago, but I hear the graves out there date back to the early 1700s."

"You bet. This cemetery is known for its history. Mind if I go out and take a look?"

"Um, sure. I haven't gotten a chance to go out there yet." Ryan tugged on her hand, pulling her toward the door.

"Oh!" Naomi nearly lost her footing as she struggled to keep up with Ryan's pace. Zelda let out a high-pitched sound and bounded after them.

"Looks like someone else would like to join us," Ryan laughed, his gaze on Zelda.

"Yes, I'm sure she would, but Zelda here is an indoor cat, whether she wants to accept it or not." What was with Zelda lately? Back in her old apartment, she never tried to sneak outdoors. Ever.

"Hold on a second." Naomi reached for her jacket and giggled. Ryan was already helping her into it.

"Stay." Naomi knew commands were meant for dogs, but she believed that cats were every bit as capable as a dog when it came to learning, even smarter in some ways. They were just stubborn. With the chill of late autumn in the air, Naomi shivered slightly until Ryan's large arms closed around her, warming her. With a contented sigh, she took in the scenery around her property as they walked. Technically, the graveyard was not on her land, but for all intents and purposes, it might as well be since her yard extended right onto the first set of gravestones.

"Look at this," Ryan gushed as he bent to clear leaves from the headstone. "1706. Isn't that amazing?"

It was, but it kind of gave her the creeps, too. "Yes, let's keep walking." She hugged her arms around her torso. He reached for her once more, but all of his attention was focused on the property before them.

Hand in hand, they walked until she couldn't stand to see one more grave. The reaction surprised her. Yes, she was looking forward to researching the history here, but a sense of sadness overwhelmed her. She couldn't shake the feeling of dread. His enthusiasm didn't fade however.

"Let's take a picture to remember today," Ryan said, a broad smile on his face.

A selfie in the graveyard? Fine. She would take their picture. Fumbling to grab her cell from her coat pocket, they posed with the headstones behind them.

Ryan reached for her cell and checked out the picture. He had a wide grin plastered on his face while Naomi's half smile showed her distaste for the setting of the photo.

"Great picture, but you should have smiled."

She opened her mouth to respond but then thought better of it.

"Ryan, let's head back, huh?"

"Okay, but only because I want to explore more of your house."

Well, then.

"Don't we have dinner reservations?"

"Ah, we have plenty of time. What is it; are you scared?" He gazed down at her, mischief playing in his dark eyes.

"No, it's not that. This is fun, really."

Fun? Probably not the best description for this outing, but it was wonderful walking arm in arm with him. Apprehension plagued her again as they headed back, trudging past one headstone after the next.

Naomi could see Zelda pacing back and forth through the dining room window inside the house. The sight didn't ease her anxiety.

Once they were settled back in her warm kitchen, Ryan grabbed her hand and moved forward into the living room. "Look at the architecture. They don't build them like this anymore. Can I see upstairs?"

"Yeah, I guess." It was a good thing she had tidied up around here before he arrived, although she hadn't expected him to go upstairs.

"Wow, these stairs... I can almost imagine ghosts of the past, men, women, and children walking up these very stairs. " She could see it now, too. The narrow stairway upon which children may have run up and down, mothers bringing laundry up the stairs, fathers walking down to breakfast.

"Let's hope the men weren't as tall as I am," Ryan commented as he ducked slightly at the sight of the low ceiling ahead. He made his way through the bedrooms which were narrow by today's standards.

"This house is freaking spectacular." He stood, hands raking through his dark hair. Without warning, Ryan reached over and pulled her in close.

"Oh!" His lips met hers. Once the initial shock of his actions wore off, she lost herself in the sensation of his kiss. Kissing various men wasn't something she had an awful lot of experience with, but she'd kissed enough men to know this was different. Different from Nick and amazing. She didn't care if she needed to come up for air. She could kiss him all night. His energy was contagious.

"*That* was also spectacular." Ryan chuckled as he moved a strand of hair from her eyes.

"Um, yes, I would have to agree."

"Hey, we'd better get going, or we'll be late for dinner," he stated, leading her down the steps.

"Careful," she warned as his head touched the ceiling.

"Ouch." He spun around, laughing at himself. Naomi followed him down the stairs, thinking that Ryan exuded a ton of spirit and energy; she just might have found her match.

"TELL ME HOW a stunning girl like you happens to sit right next to me at the bar, *and* you end up being single? How does that even happen?" He buttered a piece of pumpernickel bread. For such a fit man, he certainly liked to eat. Each time they had met in a restaurant, coffee house included, his appetite was insatiable. Must be all that energy he had. She didn't dare eat that way. She would have loved to, but she had become health conscious lately. Exercise and everything in moderation; boring, but necessary.

Truth be told, she was wondering how she had lucked out, meeting up with him as well. The circumstances upon which they had met were unlikely. "I don't know, I guess the timing was right?"

"I'm very lucky to have met you." He leaned in and kissed her quickly on the cheek. "But seriously, tell me about how whoever you were with could just let you go."

How did he figure that? She wasn't entirely comfortable speaking about Nick. Not yet. The hurt was too recent, too raw. "I guess it just didn't work out. How about you?"

"Oh no, you're not getting off that easily. Talk to me, Naomi. Tell me something you've never told anyone else."

Intense.

Yes, that would be the word she would use to describe him. Intense, energetic, curious, but there was also a gentle, generous side to him that made her wish to spill everything about her ex-boyfriend, from the verbal abuse to the fear and even the good times they had once shared in the beginning. But her story with Nick had faded to an ugly gray in time.

"I can't believe I'm going to talk to you about this, but his name was Nick." Shaking her head, she swallowed. "I guess you could say that I thought we had fallen in love. That is, until I witnessed his other side." A faint sheen of sweat formed on her lower back.

"I'm listening," Ryan moved in closer, taking her hand in his own large palm for support.

"Jealousy. About everything, including what I wore, to who I was with and every little thing in between." She sighed deeply, her hands shaking.

"You don't have to do this; we can stop." His dark blue eyes were serious. There was the intensity again.

"No...I want to. This is something I should have done long before today. It feels good to open up to someone." Even Amy hadn't been privy to most of the finer details of her relationship with Nick. She supposed she had been filled with shame at the thought of finding herself trapped in a situation she truly thought would end in disaster. It was a textbook case. How could an intelligent woman have ended up with such a man?

"I could go on and on, but let's suffice it to say that things got pretty bad before it ended." It was as if he understood her, the way he encouraged but then backed away, sensing that she needed to tell this story in her own time.

"How about we skip to the last part? How did you finally break away?" He studied her with his piercing eyes.

That particular question gave her pause. "It's strange, but it just kind of faded away, not at all what I had expected of our relationship. He was staying at my old apartment almost every night; he had practically moved in. We had a fight. I guess you could say it was the fight of all fights…" Her mind drifted back, back to that late summer evening, when they went out on a double date with his buddy John and John's girlfriend. *Why were you looking at him all night? Do you find John attractive or something?* A feeling deep in the pit of her stomach almost made her gag.

"It just…ended. I yelled at him to get out. He came back the next day and grabbed his stuff."

Naomi paused a moment, feeling a release of emotions. "We argued once more, but then he took everything. He threatened that I hadn't heard the last from him. That he would never let me go."

"And?" He studied her face, rubbing small circles on her hand with his thumb.

"And… a few text messages; some nasty, some apologetic. Then nothing. I haven't heard from him in weeks." Her mind drifted back to his dark threats. Naomi shook her head.

Ryan placed his hand on his chin and gazed at her. "That's surprising from what you tell me. Do you think something could have happened to him? You haven't heard from him at all?"

"No. Like I said, not for weeks now."

It wasn't something she had considered before. Could something have happened to him? How many times had she heard Nick threaten that he would never let her get away, no matter the circumstances? It didn't make sense that he would give up so easily.

"Well, then. It seems he's moved on. Good." Ryan kissed her cheek tenderly.

"I suppose." Naomi bit her lip and shifted in her seat.

The release she had initially felt at spilling her story about Nick was now replaced with creeping apprehension. She was fooling herself. Nick never gave up, but he just may be clever enough to have Naomi believe he had let her go.

CHAPTER THREE

Naomi

LITTLE THINGS. IT was all about the little things. How could she have even predicted what would set him off, make him angry with her? At first, she found herself apologizing for the slightest misstep, always trying to keep the peace. She still loved him then; at least, she thought she did. If only he weren't so angry with her all the time. Moments of tenderness would almost erase the pain.

Almost.

But then it was as if someone lit a flame under their relationship. Companionship and love had deteriorated before her eyes, causing her to wonder how much of it she could have changed if she'd just tried harder. Now, she knew better.

Now that she was away from the relationship, Naomi could see clearly. Whatever had gone wrong between them had been caused by Nick's irrational behavior, which was, she found out later, deep-rooted. Nick had suffered from rejection throughout his childhood. He was raised by his aunt and uncle after his father passed away. Nick's mother had died when he was a small boy and his father's death occurred when Nick was just twelve years old. His aunt and uncle weren't prepared to deal with the emotions of a young pre-teen, so they punished him and worse. The neglect he spoke of was heartbreaking. They never bonded with him, and from what Nick shared, it was a constant battle in his house until he went out into a cold world alone at the age of eighteen. Sad, it was a sad story, and Naomi had urged him to seek help. Problem was, Nick felt that counseling was for weak people, that he was fine. Denial was one of his major issues. Denying his own bad behavior had become more problematic as their relationship progressed.

Past issues, past hurt. She needed to leave it all behind and take it as a learning experience. Never again would she ignore the red flags that signaled relationship disaster. Considering herself lucky to be out of the situation, she took a deep breath. Ryan was different. She was sure of it, as sure as the sky above her was clear blue today. Surely that meant good things, right? Starting her day off with a walk in the park with Amy and a date later that night with Ryan, she figured she was on her way to forgetting and healing.

Writer's block had become more and more of an issue the past few days as Nick had plagued her mind, dragging her down. Deciding that she would move past this unfortunate relationship and grow from it, she sat by her computer. Words usually flowed from her fingertips; her characters often spoke to her. Yes, they actually communicated with her. Now they all remained ominously silent.

"Oh, the heck with this." Brushing her journal to the side, she put her computer to sleep and paced the room. Sometimes just getting out and experiencing life got her juices flowing. Gazing out her dining room window, she bit her fingertips. Wind whipped the small branches of a nearby tree as she studied the graveyard beyond. What if one of her characters was out there in the cold outdoors, their story untold? Grabbing her jacket, she turned to leave, then thought to grab her journal and a pen. Rarely did she go out without pen and paper. She never knew when an idea would come to her and didn't wish to forget anything.

Zelda pounced as she opened the door, sprinting ahead, racing to the edge of the property.

"Zelda!" What had gotten into her? It was no use. The

cat knew how to get home and would return in her own good time. Naomi just hoped she didn't surprise her with a bunny or other small creature as her childhood cat, Daisy, used to do.

Crunchy leaves gave way to a wide dirt path, one that extended to the headstones beyond. The unmistakable odor of burning wood came from a neighbor's house. It would have been nice to have Ryan beside her, but quite honestly, as much as she enjoyed his company, she doubted that she would be able to concentrate with the exuberance that constantly spilled from him. When she was in her writing mode, it was best that she remain alone. A familiar chill seeped through her as she meandered through the property, stopping here and there to read a headstone. Naomi was good at brushing her fears aside, and when it came to writing, she would do anything to get her story, visiting a graveyard included.

It gave her a sense of purpose to focus her attention on these stones. If these souls wouldn't speak to her, then she would speak to them. Leaning over, she glanced at the names and paused to mutter to some of them. *Were you in love? Was it a grand story? How many children did you have? Do you hold any secrets you took with you to the grave?*

Whipping out her pen, the wind flapped the pages of her journal as she steadied them with her hand. She brushed her hair from her eyes, then jotted down some names, some general observations. A peculiar sensation passed over her, as if she were being watched. Glancing around, she shuddered as she noticed the sky was darkening. It was time to get back—she would have to say good-bye to her potential muses for the time being. Off in the distance, she heard it, the unmistakable cry that could only belong to Zelda. Where was that little devil? Bounding toward her at full speed, Zelda howled and stopped short of Naomi. "Why you little…"

Scooping to grab the fickle feline, Zelda swerved out of

reach and headed back in the direction of her house. There was no rhyme or reason to the recent actions of her crazy cat. Following in Zelda's footsteps, she sighed as she trudged back through the empty cemetery. What was Zelda doing up ahead? Naomi squinted, taking in the bizarre behavior. Zelda was pouncing over a grave, wailing and rubbing her black furry body over the stone. Eeriness crept upon her, this time the sensation even stronger. Chills coursed through her as she jumped at the sound of a squirrel romping through the nearby woods. Clutching her chest, she released a pent-up breath. Upon closer inspection, the cat remained planted on the spot. Naomi bent over, seizing the opportunity to grab her cat, but the name on the headstone caught her eye.

Maggie T. Field. Maggie. She took in the dates of her birth and her death.

The poor thing had only been twenty-six years old. How very sad. Without thinking, she opened her notepad and she scribbled madly. Questions, questions, questions. Zelda brought her here for a darn good reason.

Maggie had a story to tell.

It felt right. With a chill running through her bones once more, at last Naomi knew she had found her muse.

"I CANNOT BELIEVE you went out there without me." Ryan attempted to pout, but then cracked a smile. It seemed he was never in a sour mood.

The comment brought a smile to her face. Ryan was slowly becoming her partner in crime. Since the area was so rich in history, she figured they had plenty of time to investigate together. He seemed to read her mind as she gazed out the window once more. His gaze was directed on the old church with the high tower across the street.

"Next time, we should go over to the church. It's been

19

ages since I've visited. The church dates back to the 1700s. Rumor has it that it was used as a prison and hospital. I believe it was rebuilt sometime in the 1800s. Just like your property, soldiers from the American Revolutionary War are buried there."

Naomi's scalp prickled. He had referred to the cemetery outside her window as *her* property. It gave her the creeps. It wasn't *her* property.

Not technically, anyhow.

Ryan was certainly employed in the correct field. She smiled, unable to imagine him in any other occupation other than teaching.

"I'd like to visit. I'm sure it will be very interesting."

Ryan rubbed his hands together, approaching her. She felt his arms surround her. It felt warm and nice. Very nice.

"I'm sorry. I hope you don't feel like I'm neglecting you."

"No, that's silly."

How do you compete with history in the eyes of a man such as Ryan? Naomi had relished the fact that he had both drive and purpose. It was actually refreshing.

"If it makes you feel any better, I can tell you if you lived in an ordinary apartment building, my focus would be entirely on you."

Somehow that didn't make her feel better. It was okay, though, this preoccupation Ryan had with her house and the surrounding area. Someone to share her interests with was never a bad thing.

"I'm fine. I enjoy your enthusiasm over this kind of stuff. Maybe you could become a writer one day."

Minds such as his were priceless in the writing field. He would surely delve into the research with glee.

"Writing? Nah. I think I'll leave that up to you. Teaching is what I enjoy best. But enough of this for now." His warm lips met hers. With a sigh, she felt herself give in to the sensation of Ryan. He made her feel safe, protected.

"What do you say we head out for dinner?"

Dinner? Yes, they had dinner plans. He never rushed her or pushed her too far. Right now they were just getting to know one another, no pressure for anything heavy. She respected him for that. Not many men that she had known would be satisfied with just a kiss. It was kind of cool how different Ryan was. The more she got to know him, the more he surprised her.

ZELDA HAD BEEN in her dreams. Zelda, Ryan, Nick, and Maggie T. Field. The constant setting for her dreams lately was the dark, windy cemetery. Naomi couldn't grasp the finer details, but the dream had felt important, meaningful somehow.

Trying her best to recall the dream, she let her mind wander. Zelda had been center stage in her dream, acting peculiar, pouncing around the graveyard until she found Maggie's headstone. Nick was yelling at her from across the property, trying to stop Zelda. Ryan was fixated on wandering around, studying the headstones, ignoring Nick's screaming. Naomi stood silently taking it all in, not an active participant, but more of an observer. At one point Zelda had run over to Nick, leaping up and scratching his face. Nick's cries were the last thing to register in her memory. What a dream. It had seemed ominous somehow, as if she were in danger. No, it wasn't quite danger. Perhaps a sense of dread. Quite frankly, she wasn't sure what to make out of it. At moments like these, she wished she had knowledge in dream interpretation.

Naomi was glad the dream was that, just a dream. Maybe living so close to the cemetery wasn't healthy for her mental state. Interesting, yes, but she wasn't sure if the ancient property was conducive to getting a good night's sleep.

After running some errands, Naomi figured she should get home and try to be productive. As she drove home, the dream continued to linger in her mind. Forgotten bits and pieces coming back, but not serving to clarify the whole picture.

Today she would do some writing. She bit down on her lip. Ryan wished to come explore the church across the street today. She had almost forgotten. The church would have to wait. Writing was top priority today. Tonight, she would see if Ryan would like to do something together. Before she changed her mind, Naomi called him and asked if she could come by his place later.

"Oh. But what about the church?" Disappointment touched his voice. He sounded like a child who was being told a trip to the amusement park would have to be postponed.

"The church can wait until another day. Listen, I've never even seen your place. What do you say? I have to work for a bit, but later on we could walk through town, maybe head over to that new steakhouse for dinner?"

"Okay, I guess. But we'll go to the church soon, okay?"

"Yup."

That was a relief. Curiosity took hold of her as she imagined what his apartment would be like. Ryan rented a one-bedroom place on the bottom floor of an old Victorian down by the river. Wasn't that the area where one of the houses was presumed haunted? Local legend claimed the house was officially haunted, however "official" that kind of thing could be. It would probably be best not to mention the fact to Ryan tonight, but chances were he already knew. How could he not? Inquisition was his middle name.

"I'll see you soon then. I'm looking forward to it."

"Bye."

There. That wasn't too bad. They would have a nice walk in town and discussions could revolve around other things, *normal* things. After grabbing a cup of coffee, Naomi walked to her desk.

Research on Maggie T. Field was proving to be challenging. How was it that she had missed the story of Maggie's disappearance? This story dated back several years. Maggie's family had reported her missing after not hearing from her for a few days. Apparently Maggie had been close to her parents and had missed her usual brunch with them. Police had called it a missing person case for months. Nobody knew where she had gone, only that she had been dating someone and then ended the relationship prior to her disappearance. His name was being withheld from the public.

Interesting. It turned out the ex-boyfriend had a solid alibi. An unnamed woman claimed they had spent the night together.

Naomi sighed as she thought about the outcome of Maggie's story. Her body had been found washed up near the river. Awful. What a horrible thing. The location of the body had been a place where people walked along a path by the river. Naomi herself had been close to the crime scene many times, unaware of the traumatic events that had taken place there.

No clues, other than it appeared to be a drowning. Evidence pointed to Maggie going out on a friend's boat, perhaps, and falling overboard. But how? And where was the friend? It didn't make sense. A piece of this puzzle was missing—a rather large piece.

A cold mystery was all that was left of Maggie's story.

Come on, come on. Maggie. Talk to me. Tell me what happened to you. What kind of girl were you?

A sudden screech sounded from the window.

Zelda.

How was she supposed to concentrate on writing when Zelda kept intruding with her unpredictable behavior? Naomi needed to write Maggie's story. It was calling to her.

If she didn't write the story, she wouldn't be able to write anything else.

Cries filled the air. This was ridiculous. Naomi wouldn't even waste her time trying to figure out the cat's problem. "You're a piece of work, you know that?"

Zelda cried out in response. Now the cat had broken her concentration. Naomi needed to get out and clear her mind. She grabbed her notebook and her jacket from the hook in the entrance foyer.

Once she was out of the house and down the narrow path heading into the graveyard, she turned around. It wasn't surprising to see Zelda pacing back and forth on the windowsill. Crazy.

After walking around for a few minutes, she was pulled toward Maggie's grave once more.

"Maggie, tell me your story. I'm listening." Naomi didn't actually expect to hear a response, but she knelt down and listened. She strained to hear the slightest sound, anything at all that would open up this mystery.

Of course, she heard nothing.

Nothing but the faraway sound of cars passing down the one-way street adjacent to the cemetery, then the faint cry of a crow overhead. Lifting her head to the darkening sky above, Naomi could have sworn the crow was staring right at her. Was she in the middle of her own eerie dream? Brushing off the uneasy feeling, Naomi shook her head and sat in the grass.

"Was it your ex? Was it a stranger? Or was your death your own doing?" Naomi's fingers touched the cold stone, running up and down the gravestone. A sharp crackling from behind caused Naomi to spin around. There was nobody there.

Naomi could have sworn she heard someone. Perhaps it had been a darting squirrel or other small animal. Her attention returned to Maggie's grave. Call it a gut feeling, but Naomi was convinced there was foul play at work here. It could be her overactive writer's imagination, but instinctively, she knew Maggie had been killed by someone.

Most likely someone close to her. Wasn't that usually the story?

More determined than ever to solve this crime, Naomi stood up and brushed her pants off. She leaned over and spoke directly to Maggie's headstone.

"I will figure this out, girl. Just give me some time. I'll find out who was responsible for this, and you'll give me my story. How does that sound? Fair?"

The sound came from the woods this time. Whatever was creating the sound remained hidden.

CHAPTER FOUR

Naomi

DREAMS HAD INVADED her sleeping hours once more. This time, she had a new version in which she was a key player in a horrifying game of cat and mouse. The setting had also changed this time; Naomi found herself in the woods, running. Someone was chasing her, but she couldn't see the predator, she could only sense him. Tall trees all around, her vision was limited to the thick woods.

Naomi was at it again, wandering the old cemetery, after hours of writing. Evening hours would be upon her soon. She found herself right back at the exact spot she had discovered the day before.

Chills prickled all the way up her body, right to her scalp. Knowing what she would find if she turned around, she did so anyway. Time seemed to slow down as Naomi willed herself to look at her house in the distance.

Zelda's pacing was manic. She could see the cat's agitation from here. A shadowy form shifted behind Zelda and then disappeared. Naomi shivered as she tried to make sense of what she had just witnessed. There was no denying the fact that some type of otherworldly presence was occupying her house, sharing it with her. She could only hope the spirit had no intentions to cause harm.

Although the figure was now gone, Zelda's activity continued. The cat was attempting to communicate with Naomi. She was sure about it. Instinct told her it had everything to do with Maggie T. Field.

What on Earth was it about this particular grave that hyped up Zelda? Notepad in hand, Naomi scribbled furiously, trying to imagine what Maggie must have looked like, what her occupation had been. A bit more research and she would have her answers.

In this day and age, it was simple enough to search names on the Internet. She now had a plan, and she could feel the words bubbling, boiling over in her head. Jotting down some more notes before she lost her train of thought, Naomi smiled. Darkness began settling in upon the graveyard. Even with the impending nightfall, it didn't seem as scary out here as it had the past few days. Unsettling, yes, but now that she had the beginning of her plot etched out, she didn't focus on the reality of the property surrounding her. The fading light brought an end to her note taking, but no matter.

This cemetery was now the inspiration for her story.

"TELL ME ABOUT your students. What are they like?" Later that evening, Naomi wanted to know everything about Ryan, including his work.

"Oh, well, it's kind of complicated. You see, prior to teaching online, I was in the classroom, I got to see the faces of my students, interact with them. "

"And now?"

Ryan paused, glancing at Naomi for a moment. "Now? It's great but I don't interact as much. I give the assignment and encourage my students to interact with me and with each other through the discussion posts. They do converse quite a bit, but I'm not getting much in the way of personal communication."

Naomi felt sad for him, because she knew he was a

passionate man. He must be amazing in the classroom. "Can you ask to go back to the classroom?"

"Oh, believe me I've tried. I would love nothing better."

"And?"

"For now the answer is no, but I was promised the next position at the college. Still, it could be years. I haven't even been paid for some time. With the challenging economy, I'm waiting it out and volunteering my time. Ah, listen to me, complaining when this is supposed to be a pleasant date."

"Wait. Did you just say that you weren't being paid?"

"Yes, I did. It's fine for now..."

How could that be? What kind of college hired instructors but didn't pay them? Something felt off about this. The college had an excellent reputation. That only made it more peculiar.

"If you don't mind me asking, how do you pay the rent? Your bills?'

"I come from some family money, so it all works out."

If anyone else had mentioned they came from money, it would surely come across as bragging. Not Ryan. He remained humble, modest.

"But seriously, I didn't mean to complain. It's not my style." Ryan gazed down at the sidewalk.

"Don't worry about that, Ryan. I'm enjoying this, walking with you and getting to know you."

"Are you sure? I'm not usually such a whiner, but when I find myself thinking about the fact that I'm dying to get back in the traditional classroom, I get upset."

"Have you ever thought of applying at another school? Even a high school?"

Ryan turned and placed a soft kiss on Naomi's lips. "You're sweet, you know. Yes, I have considered it, but right now I'm biding my time because I do love the college up on the hill."

Wouldn't he love a paycheck? Naomi bit the words back. It wasn't for her to judge.

Funny, he referred to it as the college up on the hill. Naomi supposed it was because of the beautiful view of the river. Why call it by any other name when it was in such as breathtaking location?

She had been about to change the subject when a familiar figure was spotted across the street. Nick. *Oh my God, Nick.* She must have tensed her body because Ryan stopped right there on the sidewalk, gazing at Naomi. He seemed to look right through her.

"Are you okay? What's the matter?"

Naomi gulped, pulling at Ryan. She headed into the first nearby store, the local hardware store. It was no use. Her heart raced as she spied him crossing the street. What if he came in this store? *Please, no.*

"Naomi, answer me. You're worrying me now. What is it?"

Please, just walk past. Please. But Nick headed straight for the hardware store.

He had seen her.

"Is there something you need to buy in here?" Ryan glanced around, down the aisle they were standing in.

"It's *him*; it's Nick. Come on." Naomi kept a firm grip on Ryan's hand and rushed to the back of the store. He had spotted her, she was sure of it. If he hadn't, he surely had a vision problem. Her heart pounded and she sweat through her blouse, although the temperature was far from warm.

"Nick?" Ryan called out.

"Sh!" What the heck was the matter with him?

"I... uh, sorry."

Naomi pressed her body close to Ryan's, squeezing them both against the back shelf that held cans of paint thinner. She could only pray he would move on, think she slipped out the back door or something. If she leaned over carefully, she could just about make out the front counter. Nick was talking to the cashier in the front of the store, but then his gaze was then directed right toward her.

This was worse than she had imagined. She didn't want Nick to see her with another man. What would he do if he found she had moved on already?

"No!" Naomi buried her head in Ryan's shirt. Would he make a scene?

"Can I breathe now?" Ryan whispered in her ear.

Funny, she had forgotten that she was squashing Ryan to the spot behind them. "He saw me. I know he did."

Ryan grabbed hold of her wrist. "Naomi. Are you really that afraid of him?"

Naomi finally released the deep breath she had been holding in. "Yes. I guess I am." Cold sweat dripped down her back. What did she think he would do to her at this point? She supposed her fear was fueled from the fact that she and Nick had ended their relationship without major disaster. Yes, that's what was really bothering her. Fear from the fact that perhaps things weren't over. It worried her to realize that one true fact.

"Listen. I'm not going to let anything happen to you, you hear me?" Ryan kissed her wrist lightly. She breathed again.

"Thank you." But she knew what Nick was capable of, and she also knew how kind-hearted Ryan was. When it came down to it, Ryan was no match for Nick. She only hoped Ryan would never come face to face with her ex-boyfriend.

"Let's get out of here. Then I think it would be best if you and I had a talk about what you're not telling me. I need the truth."

What hadn't she told him? She'd told him the basics, brushing over the nasty details of her life with Nick. She could inform him about every wretched detail of their years together, but she didn't wish to revisit the past. Move forward, that had been her mantra as of late.

"There's not much more to tell." That wasn't entirely true.

After a few moments, Ryan placed his hand in hers, leading her out the door. Nick should be gone by now. Store after store, Naomi glanced in the shop windows, looking for traces of Nick. She couldn't go on this way. Each time she headed into town she would worry. Moving to another area was out of the question. Naomi was in love with her little house and having her friends close by.

Finally they settled on a cafe that was occupied by many young couples. The area was rich with men and women exploring the scenic town of Mystic and all the culture it had to offer. Naomi grabbed a table while Ryan ordered their drinks. Just when she thought she couldn't like the man more than she already did, he brought back two glasses of red wine.

"Wow. You're going to spoil me, you know that?" Taking care of Naomi had never been a priority of Nick's. If anything, Nick had wanted her to take care of him. There was no give-and-take in their relationship.

"Get used to it."

She could do that.

A young waiter came to take their order. As predicted, Ryan ordered enough for two men.

"You don't ever worry about counting calories?" There. She said it.

"Ha. No. Funny thing is, I never used to be able to eat like this. Go figure." His face lit up as he glanced at the food on a nearby table.

'Well." What else was there to say?

If only she had his problem.

Ryan reminded her of her friend Sharon's four-year-old son, Sam. Sam had such zest for life and all it had to offer.

"What's on your mind?"

Naomi took a second to process her thoughts. "You have such a love of life. It's admirable."

"I never really gave it much thought. I just kind of live in the moment."

"I see that. Like I said, it's a great quality to have."

Ryan's grin spread as he reached for Naomi's hand. "Right now I'm enjoying being here with you. I'm glad we met that day."

Warmth spread through Naomi. Thoughts of that day, from weeks earlier, filled her senses. "I'm happy we met, too. Hey. Remember when you commented on my horrible date?"

That earned a chuckle from Ryan. "Of course."

"How did you know how my date was going? What were you doing? Eavesdropping?" She was teasing him, but she was curious, nonetheless.

"Honestly?"

Naomi nodded her head, encouraging him to continue.

"Your face said it all."

"It did?"

Ryan ran his hand over hers, suddenly serious. "You looked miserable."

Naomi pulled back momentarily. "Miserable? I wasn't miserable."

"Okay. How's this? Unhappy. You looked unhappy with your date, possibly more."

What was that supposed to mean? Naomi considered herself to be level-headed and content with her life.

Her shoulders slumped forward. Except for her situation with Nick. Could Ryan possibly be that intuitive?

"I like to think..."

Ryan stopped her with a swipe of his hand. Instinctively, Naomi shrunk back.

"Whoa. What was that?" Concern etched Ryan's brows. "What did I do?"

Heat crept up Naomi's chest, flushing her cheeks.

"Wait. Did he..."

He was that intuitive. "Ryan..."

"My God, he did. He hit you?"

Naomi's eyes darted around the café. "Sh!"

"I'm sorry." Ryan lowered his head as he grabbed her hands from across the table. His voice was a whisper. "Please, tell me. Did he lay a hand on you?"

Tears rimmed Naomi's eyes. Embarrassment yielded to sadness as a memory filtered through her mind. He hadn't raised a hand to her, but when he shoved her against the wall, the force had smacked her head against the wall. And there was the time when he threw a dish across the kitchen, one which she narrowly avoided. Worse than anything was the verbal abuse. The head games he loved to play. Half the time, she hadn't known what he was even talking about. Pressure built up in her head as Naomi removed her hands from Ryan's, placing them on her head.

"What is it? Do you have a headache?"

Stress had a way of giving her splitting headaches.

"Yes. Can we change the subject, please?"

"Sure." Ryan reached for her hands once more, his gaze intense.

"I think you'll feel better, though, if you talk to me about it."

The waiter set their plates before them. It gave Naomi just the break she needed.

"Ryan, I hope you don't take offense to this, but I really don't want to. Not now. I gave you the gist of the situation and for now that's all I want to discuss. It's too painful to rehash everything. He was flawed and had issues that he never sought out help for, and our relationship suffered as a result."

"I have one more question. Are you afraid of him seeing us together?"

"Yes."

"But that's ridiculous. You and him, you're finished. What kind of guy is this?"

Naomi couldn't bear to meet his eyes. She felt a sense of shame at staying in a toxic relationship for as long as she did.

"Okay, sweetheart. It's fine. If and when you're ready, I'm here. I won't push, I won't ask again. But I'm not about to hide how I feel about you."

Fair enough.

And that was what she liked about him. "Thank you."

"How about this salad, huh?" He devoured a forkful.

He was a keeper for sure.

CHAPTER FIVE

Naomi

No more writer's block for her. After some additional research on Maggie, she hadn't come up with much more. Something was holding her back from searching for a photo of poor Maggie. The online articles hadn't provided any and Naomi had decided that she didn't wish to see one. Her own image of Maggie would do just fine for her story.

Imagination often proved to be more exciting than reality. Naomi's story flowed from her head to the paper. Free writing was her first step. Then she would start her chapter outlines and drafting on the computer. *Oh Maggie, Maggie...* She could almost hear the woman's voice, see her at her ex-boyfriend's house. She could envision her having coffee with friends.

More thoughts jumped into her head as her cell rang. Nearly leaping out of her chair, she clutched her chest. This story was getting to her. Touchy nerves proved she was getting emotionally involved with her story.

"Hey, Ryan." She felt the smile form on her face at the sound of his voice.

"What are you up to?"

"Writing. You?"

"Doing my curriculum paperwork. I'd love to hear about your story. What do you have so far?"

Naomi wasn't ready to share yet.

"There's something you need to know about me and my

writing. I don't really share much until I'm deep into the plot. Please don't take it personally."

The pause was audible. "Oh, sure. No problem."

His feelings were hurt. She hadn't intended for that to happen. "I'm sorry, Ryan. What I can tell you is that my main character is based on a person buried in a grave outside."

"Ooh. Which one?"

And he was back. She chuckled loudly. "I don't want to say. It's a woman, though. She's in her twenties." She had expected more questions. "Hello?"

"I'm here." Ryan cleared his throat. "Sorry, it's just sad, so young, you know?"

"I do. It is sad, but I'm going to tell her story, try to make it right."

"Make what right? This woman... how did she die?"

"Well, nobody knows, not really."

"Whoa, back up. What are you talking about?"

Naomi knew she should have been more tight-lipped. "It's a mystery of sorts. It's presumed this woman drowned."

"Wait—what's her name?" His voice picked up a notch.

Naomi figured she might as well spill what she knew. "Maggie. Maggie T. Field."

There was a brief pause. "Maggie Field. Now why does that name sound so familiar?"

"The boating accident. Down by the river." She waited for his immediate reaction.

"That's right. The girl found in the Hudson River. She drowned, Naomi. That's what all the papers said."

Naomi's cheeks flushed. "Yes, I know. But there's more to this story, Ryan. I can feel it."

"That's just ridiculous, Naomi. It's no mystery. Case closed."

Naomi straightened in her chair. She didn't like to hear the negativity in his voice. "But, listen, Ryan. Let's talk about it more when we see each other later." It would be best to have this conversation face-to-face.

"Please just promise me you won't do anything stupid."

What the hell was that supposed to mean?

"Like what, Ryan?" she cried out.

"This Maggie, how are you going to tell her story? She can't exactly tell you now, can she?"

"Oh, come on now, Ryan. I thought you had more imagination than that. My story will be loosely based on fact. Maggie is more of a muse to inspire the story for my novel. Then I take my creativity and run with it. Besides, I can conduct some more research if need be."

"You see, that's what I'm worried about. That's just the kind of talk that will get you in trouble."

"Ah, I see. I'll put myself in danger... something like that?" Why did this annoy her so much? So he was concerned; was that the worst thing? She knew the answer, though. This was why she never shared her writing until she was well into her books. Now this negative energy could potentially ruin her creativity. Another thing that bothered her was that Ryan was full of spunk and adventure. She had expected him to be supportive and excited about her new book. She was surprised by his attitude toward her ideas.

"Well, yes. Something like that. I care about you, Naomi." He paused a moment before continuing. "Hell, Naomi. If you're going to conduct any research just promise me you won't go it alone."

That was more like it. The thought gave her pause.

"You mean like a partner in crime?"

"Exactly." He exhaled. So he was worried and didn't want her to go it alone. It wasn't the worst thing.

Before she hung up the phone, they made plans to go to the church and explore. Ryan would swing by later in the day and they would go off, investigating once more.

How she heard Maggie's story, or any of her characters' stories for that matter, baffled her. Like every other character she had ever written, Maggie's voice rang through Naomi's head. Her Maggie had been a beautiful woman, a kind person and good friend. What kind of job did she do? Knowing that she could easily find out, Naomi decided that she would use her imagination, a little creative license so to speak, for Maggie's career.

Teaching? Yes, just as she could picture Ryan in front of a room filled with eager students, she saw Maggie in the same light. Maggie had dated, probably several young men throughout her years, but she had yet to meet just the right one. *Well, guess what, Maggie? Your luck is about to change.* Love. True love.

Her Maggie would fall in love. Her heroine would get the guy. But who was worthy of such a woman? Her hero would need to be handsome, warm inside, smart, and blessed with the gift of imagination. Giggling softly, Naomi pressed the keyboard, filling up one page after the next.

Time had gotten away from her as it always did while writing. Ryan was due in about a half an hour. Satisfied with her writing for the day, Naomi shut down her computer and then stretched.

It felt good to be productive. It also felt good to give Maggie her story. In her mind she pictured her heroine as fair and blonde. Her hero was dark and handsome, not unlike Ryan.

Ah, was Ryan slowly becoming another muse for this story? That was something she would keep to herself for now, as she didn't want to scare him off. Later, when they hopefully had time to get to know each other better, she could tell him he was her inspiration for Maggie's one true love.

CHAPTER SIX

Maggie

WITH MUCH DELIBERATION, she went on the date with him. Having just broken off her latest relationship, she wasn't in any rush. But he was so adorable, from his sexy grin to his dark brown eyes. When he opened his mouth to speak that first time they met, she nearly clutched her heart. His voice was deep and sincere.

Now he was seated beside Maggie at Patty's Pub. How could a man like that be single? She longed for the answer but was afraid to ask. Something about him was a bit dark; she might even venture to say mysterious.

"I'm so happy you agreed to meet me here tonight, Maggie."

"Me too."

Without warning, he reached for Maggie's hand. Her pulse sped up. What was going on here? It's not like she hadn't been on a date before. This guy was different, though. She just knew that somehow he would be significant in her life.

Maggie could barely finish her dinner. Her stomach was in knots. If she hadn't been out with her friend Christine for coffee the other day, she never would have run into him.

Fate must have intervened.

"I'm probably going to say this a thousand times, but I'm so happy I stopped to grab that cup of coffee the other day." His eyes were intense as he spoke. It was getting difficult to breathe.

"Yes. Yes, me, too," Maggie managed.

There was a moment of hesitation. Although she hated the awkward silences that first dates often included, Maggie figured *this guy was probably worth it. Worth going through the uncomfortable moments that would hopefully pass so that she could get to know him.*

"How is it that someone like you is available? There must be more to your story."

She hadn't even begun to tell him her about her life, and quite frankly, there wasn't much of a story to tell. Some might even consider her life to be a tad boring. Boring wasn't necessarily a bad thing, though. Not when she had snagged an adjunct professor position at one of the many local colleges. It was nerve-wracking to imagine that in the fall, she would actually be a college professor. The school wasn't her first choice, but she figured this was a start.

Maryview College was in the neighboring town, not far from Mystic. The college up on the hill was her first choice, but financial strains prevented her from securing that position. The only spots open were online teaching opportunities. Teaching in a real, live classroom was an absolute priority at this stage in her career.

"My story? Not much to tell. Sorry to disappoint you." *Maggie gazed up at him, fingering strands of her hair.*

"Fine, be secretive. I've always been intrigued by mysterious women." *He chuckled.*

Mysterious? Hardly, but why not let him think so. Couldn't hurt.

"So what about you? Why is it that you're alone?" *She figured she'd turn the tables a bit.*

"Me? Come on, I'm nothing special."

Maggie blew out an exaggerated breath. "Please." *Something told her that this guy had his fair share of attention from the opposite sex.*

"Okay, so I have dated a bit, but it's been awhile since it's been anything serious."

Maggie pondered over his admission. "So you're not rebounding?"

"Rebounding?"

Ouch. Maggie had heard that when someone repeats a question prior to answering, that they might be stalling.

Maggie's brows shot up, waiting for his response.

"No, no. It's been quite some time since my last serious relationship."

Maggie studied him for signs of lying, but she didn't notice anything out of place. No nervous glancing around, no anxious scratching. Then again, she had never been skilled at discovering lies. She supposed she would just have to believe him.

"So where were we?" He reached for Maggie's hand and kissed her fingers tenderly.

All thoughts of dishonesty were gone.

ALMOST EVERYTHING WAS *going well.*

Almost.

It had been several weeks since she had stopped for coffee that morning and met her handsome new boyfriend. There was one nagging voice that reared its head from time to time. Everything with him seemed perfect except for the fact that Maggie hadn't been to her parents' house for her usual Saturday visits. She made a habit out of enjoying breakfast with her mom and dad to catch up each week. Her new man wanted to have breakfast with her each weekend morning and seemed upset whenever she tried to make plans without him. She wasn't ready to bring him along to meet her parents yet, so begrudgingly, she had just cancelled the Saturday visits. It seemed easier.

Also, she hadn't seen one of her good friends in quite a while. She supposed it was due to the fact that this friend was male. Something told her that her boyfriend wouldn't understand. It was nothing that was directly said to her, but more like a feeling. He had mentioned that one of his ex-girlfriends had stayed friends with her guy friends. If nothing was going on, then what was wrong with that? Maggie bit her lip as she had let him continue. He had stated that no man could ever stay friends with a woman, that there was always that undeniable attraction that would leave

41

one, if not both, of the friends wanting more.

Maggie had been on the verge of telling him about R.J.

She and R.J. were friends, on their way to becoming the best of friends. How would Maggie feel about her new boyfriend having a drop-dead gorgeous girl "friend?"

Probably not great.

Maggie had been certain that R.J. was on the verge of asking her for a date, but then nothing had come of it. R.J started dating a woman from out of town, and that had been it. Their friendship had remained, even grown stronger, but any hopes of romance had been extinguished once Jackie materialized.

It wasn't meant to be. Maggie tried to put her feelings of attraction to the side and be genuinely happy for R.J., even when she could see that Jackie was a shallow woman out for herself.

Perhaps her boyfriend did have a point.

Bottom line? Maggie had spared any mention of R.J., and as a result, their friendship had become strained and distant.

The summer season was upon her, and plans of teaching at the college would surely fill her time over the next couple of months. Maggie put those thoughts aside. She had plans to go to the park by the river in just a few minutes. What could be more romantic than a stroll by the water?

Maggie rushed into the bathroom to take a last look at her hair. She had tried her hand at straightening her wavy, blonde hair and was pleased with the outcome. Her locks were smooth and shiny. Nodding at her reflection, Maggie smiled. She glanced at her watch. He was running late, about ten minutes to be exact.

A sharp knock on the door sounded and Maggie sprinted to the door.

"Hey!"

"Hi, beautiful!" He reached for her and kissed her firmly on the lips.

"Whoa. Hello there," Maggie gasped. No shyness there. "Ready to go?" She already had her purse in hand.

He glanced upward toward the living room and cleared his throat. "Sure. Let's go."

Did he want to come inside? The few times they had been at either of their places, it had grown heated. Maggie knew that she liked him, but she wanted to wait for the right moment. Right now she preferred to keep things safely outside of her house until she was sure.

"Do you have plans for later after our walk?"

"What did you have in mind?"

"I don't know... dinner?"

Dinner sounded nice. "Sure."

"I figured we could come back to your place after our walk and maybe order some takeout, watch a movie?" *His eyebrows shot up. He opened the car door to let her in.*

She fanned herself with her hand, feeling a sudden warmth. Maggie sat beside him as they headed for the river. "Oh. I was thinking that we could go to that Italian place in town." *Maggie's chest thumped.*

"I was kind of looking forward to being alone with you."

Maggie swallowed as she contemplated her next words carefully. "Listen..."

"No, Maggie. It's been awhile and I'm trying my best to be patient with you."

Awhile? When was the time considered right? One thing that Maggie knew was that she shouldn't feel pressured.

"Please. I'm just not ready."

"Not ready?" *He stopped mid-sentence, smoothing his hand across his hair.* "Okay, Maggie, okay." *He turned his face forward, eyes on the road.*

"It's not you, it's just that..."

"Maggie. It's fine. I said it's fine, didn't I?"

He did. But the tension in the car said otherwise. Maggie opened her mouth to speak and then decided against it. She wasn't wrong and sometimes words weren't necessary.

"What did you do to your hair?"

"Excuse me?"

"Your hair. It's different."

"Yes, I straightened it. Do you like it?"

43

He glanced over at her and frowned. "I don't know. I think I like it better the other way."

Maggie didn't know why he would have even brought up the subject of her hair unless his intentions were to hurt her feelings. Maybe he just opened his mouth and didn't think before he spoke. Maggie grabbed at her hair, smoothing her locks down.

Moments later, he smiled and rubbed her thigh. It was as if the conversation had never taken place. "I like you, Maggie. I really like you."

They had arrived at the river. Maggie was anxious to get out of the car. She unbuckled her seatbelt and her hand was on the door.

"Wait, Maggie. Wait."

Maggie looked into his warm brown eyes. She saw kindness there. All traces of tension were long gone.

"I said I liked you."

"I like you, too."

"Maggie, this is crazy, but I think I'm falling in love with you."

Oh. It was fast.

So fast.

They had only dated several weeks. "I..."

"Don't. It's okay. Don't feel you have to say it back. Right now I just want you to know how I'm feeling. When you're ready, you tell me. Deal?"

He just assumed it would eventually happen. Before she could respond, he leaned over and kissed her. His kiss was passionate, warming her from inside. He loved her.

CHAPTER SEVEN

Naomi

"WHAT WOULD YOU say to a cozy dinner at my house later tonight?" Naomi was feeling romantic, so she had taken a break from her writing to call Ryan. She and Ryan had been busy exploring the town, the cemetery, and discussing her novel. Quality time was in order. Ryan was definitely the most handsome man she had ever met, as well as the kindest.

"Dinner? Um, sure. We need to talk a bit about your plans for researching Maggie's story."

Be careful what you wish for. Of course Naomi had wanted a partner in crime, but she was also interested in pursuing this relationship on another level. It seemed their dating relationship was being pushed to the side at the moment.

Ever since Ryan had fallen in love with her house and the surrounding property, she felt as if she was second best. How ridiculous it was to be in competition with a house and graveyard, though. He was just so darn curious and clever. Worried that although their friendship was growing stronger, the passionate side of their relationship was waning, she sighed. She figured she would just have to put forth some effort to change that.

As Naomi considered her next words, a book from her shelf came crashing down. She sat back, grabbing at her chest.

She really needed to get used to these strange happenings. Focusing her thoughts, she breathed deeply. Naomi made a mental note to share her ghostly suspicions with Ryan soon. But for now, she craved some normalcy.

Especially after the latest dream she had experienced the night before. High cliffs had touched the sky, seagulls screeched ahead. She had sat planted to the spot on a large boulder in the middle of the woods. A faceless man had shouted at her, the words muffled, but his mood was evident. She was threatened by this man in her dream. She didn't feel safe. Naomi had wanted to run and hide. It was the very same scene, thick, hovering woods, closing in on her. There was something else. An etching. A heart with initials carved inside. M and R.J.

What did it all mean?

Wait—wasn't the setting of last night's dream by the cliffs? That was where Maggie's body had been found. It might mean something. But what? Could it be that with her mind on Maggie's story, her thoughts were just getting jumbled together?

"Ryan, I have a request for the evening." A break was most definitely in order.

"Of course. What is it?"

"How about we put all of the research and talk of history to the side for tonight, huh?"

There was a brief pause. "Oh. Well, what will we talk about then?"

Good question. He had her stumped. The topics she had requested be laid to rest for the evening were essentially the only things they did discuss lately.

"I don't know? Work?" But her writing was off limits, so that left his work. Which he wasn't particularly passionate about at the moment.

"My work? Or yours?" He had her there.

"Yours." She predicted his sigh before she heard it.

"I know what we could talk about. We could talk a bit

more about what really happened with you and Nick."

Was he kidding? No, she already knew the answer to that. He wasn't even being a wiseass. His curiosity ran over to the topic of her past relationship with Nick as well.

"Forget it, Ryan. You win. We can talk about research all you want." It was useless. She knew between the two of them, the topic of her novel was bound to come up somehow.

"I didn't mean…"

"I know you didn't. It's fine."

She would just have to devise another plan to grab his attention. Naomi's mind was already wandering over the possibilities of her outfit for the night. She knew just which dress might do the trick. That little black number she wore to a Christmas party last year. It was perfect.

"I'll pick you up at seven?"

"Sounds great, Ryan. Looking forward to it."

Her mind whirled with thoughts of their date tonight. Naomi grinned as she imagined his reaction to her appearance later. She had the perfect shoes that would pull off the look. A loud knock jolted Naomi from thoughts of seducing Ryan.

Who could that be?

"Coming!" Naomi hustled to the front door. At this rate, she'd never be able to focus on writing for the rest of the day.

Naomi flung the door open, coming face to face with a man and a little girl. Both of whom she'd never laid eyes on before.

"Hi."

"Hi," the man answered back.

"Hi!" the little girl chimed in. The child couldn't have been more than five or six years old.

"Can I help you?"

A rather large hand extended forward. "I wanted to introduce myself and my daughter. We just moved into the old farmhouse."

The old farmhouse?

Naomi didn't even know the historic property had been up for sale. Talk about history. That property was amazing.

"Oh. I had no idea it was for sale. It's nice to meet you." She pumped his hand as she glanced quickly at the little girl before turning her attention back to her new neighbor.

Dark brown eyes met her gaze. His shaggy brown hair partially covered one eye. She took in his flannel shirt and work boots. She cleared her throat and looked away when he smiled.

"It isn't. We're renting the property for now. The owner is an old friend of mine. Holly and I needed a fresh start."

The mention of Holly's name brought Naomi's focus back to the girl. An innocent smile met her. She was adorable. Same dark hair and dimples as her dad.

"Hello, Holly. Welcome to the neighborhood. Are you registered for school?"

"Of course, lady," Holly began sweetly. "I'm a big girl now."

"I can see that." Naomi locked eyes with Holly's father. Those dimples were sure to drive his wife crazy.

"Let me guess... you're in first grade!"

"No, silly. I might be a big girl but I'm not *that* big."

The man chuckled loudly as Naomi covered her mouth with her hand. Her hearty laugh escaped.

"She's in kindergarten." The man gazed down at his daughter with pride in his eyes. He ruffled her long hair a bit before returning his attention to Naomi.

"I'm Naomi. It's nice to meet the both of you."

"I'm Bryce."

"Holly and Bryce, it was great to meet you. Anything you need, please don't hesitate. I'm usually here since I work from home."

"Oh? What is it that you do, if you don't mind me asking?"

"I'm a writer. I write contemporary fiction, mostly."

He smiled widely. "Do you hear that, honey?" He reached for Holly's hand. "Naomi is a writer. We live next door to a famous author."

Holly jumped up and down, squealing in delight. "Goody, goody!"

"Oh, no. I wouldn't say that I'm famous." Her cheeks warmed.

"But you do make a living from it, no?"

"Well, yes. I suppose."

"Then you're a successful author and we're proud to be your neighbor," Bryce gushed.

"Yeah. We're *proud*," Holly added with a toothless grin, exaggerating her last word.

"Okay. Thank you." Naomi felt warmth spread to her cheeks. "What do you do for a living, Bryce?"

"I'm in the electrical union in the city. Pays the bills."

"Great. Well, it's nice to meet the both of you. Can I get you something to drink? Water?" Naomi was raised to be cordial to her neighbors.

"No, thank you. We don't want to take up any more of your time." Bryce began prompting Holly to say good-bye, but she didn't require any assistance.

"Bye, Nomi." The way that Holly pronounced her name made Naomi chuckle. It was very cute.

Before she saw it coming, Holly plowed into Naomi, knocking the breath out of her.

"Wow."

"Yes, she's extremely friendly." Bryce tilted his head and scratched at his cheek.

"I can see that. She's wonderful. I guess I'll see you guys around."

"Don't be a stranger." He held her gaze a bit longer than necessary.

What was that about?

Most likely nothing. He was a friendly man introducing

49

himself and his daughter to a new neighbor.

Naomi stood for a moment, watching them disappear before closing the front door.

"THIS FOOD IS delicious." Ryan closed his eyes with every bite. He was definitely a man who enjoyed his meals, but then again, she already knew that.

"Yes, it is."

Naomi's plan to draw attention from any talk of history or research appeared to be working so far. Ryan's reaction upon seeing her dress when he opened the door earlier was almost enough to get her through the rest of the evening. She just needed to continue her course of action. Mentally reviewing her list of topics she had planned to bring up, she started with the first at hand.

"Do you have dreams to travel?"

"Travel? Now where the heck did that come from?" He almost spit out the piece of bread he had been chewing.

"Yes. I just got to wondering if you had any dreams to travel across the country, maybe Europe even?"

Ryan paused before grabbing another slice of the warm bread. He took his time buttering it before popping it into his mouth. "This is good."

Naomi fidgeted in her seat. She almost had to laugh out loud at his expression while chewing. The loaf was almost gone and Naomi realized she had only taken one piece.

Ryan signaled the waitress, holding up the empty basket with a wide grin. Naomi caught the woman rolling her eyes slightly. Naomi's hand went up to her mouth to contain her smile.

"What? What's so funny?"

"Nothing, Ryan. Back to the question. If you could choose anywhere in the entire world, where would you like to go?"

Naomi imagined that he would respond with a distant location such as Paris or Spain. She shouldn't have been surprised at his answer, but it still served to do just that, surprise her.

"Now why would I want to travel anywhere when we live in the most historically rich area in the world? With New York a stone's throw away and the culture here in this county, my God, why would I waste money looking for a place to rival what's in our own backyard?"

She should have known. "Yes, but…"

Ryan proceeded to share all the sights of the surrounding area. "We've got the river, the mountains, the shops, the historical buildings…"

"Perhaps you missed your true calling. You should have been a travel agent." The words were out of her mouth before she had a chance to think. Luckily her sarcasm was lost on him.

"Not a bad idea. Maybe when I retire from teaching I can be a local tour guide or something. Good thinking, Naomi." The waitress placed a fresh basket of bread before him. His hand reached into the bread instantly. Wow, there was no stopping him.

Naomi twisted her hands together.

On to item number two on her list of distractions. "You know, I don't even know what kind of music you enjoy. What do you listen to?'

"Oh, classic rock, some country, even some classical. How about you?"

"I enjoy all of those genres. My taste in music is actually pretty eclectic…"

"Miss? I think we're ready to order. I'm famished."

What the heck was going on here?

What was happening to the romance? She was slowly losing this battle. With a deep sigh, she placed her hands on her chin.

"What's wrong, Naomi?" He stopped with his bread mid-air.

"I just wanted to talk about some other things tonight. You know, concentrate on us."

"I'm sorry. Sometimes I have a tendency to get carried away. My focus is entirely on you now. What would you like to discuss?" Ryan gazed into her eyes.

That was better. But then her mind went blank. All of the topics she had previously planned on discussing went out the window.

"I don't know, Ryan." Naomi gazed at the floor.

He reached across the table, taking her hands in his. "You look amazing tonight."

She was pleased he had noticed her effort. "Thank you, so do you." She meant it. He was just her type.

For reasons unknown, a flash of her neighbor Bryce and his daughter Holly came to mind.

Naomi shook her head to clear the image.

Now that all of their most favorite topics of conversation were forbidden, they remained silent. The silence was deafening. Awkward silence wouldn't do. Not between them.

To hell with this.

"Okay, Ryan. What's on the agenda for tomorrow? Should we head over to the library or the police station?"

Ryan sat up straight, his smile growing wide. "I thought you'd never ask."

And they were back.

CHAPTER EIGHT

Maggie

SKY HIGH CLIFFS, *the serene Hudson River, and blue skies surrounded them. Seagulls screeched overhead as they made their way up the wide, winding path. Maggie jumped out of the way as a cyclist whizzed past.*

"Oh!"

He grabbed her waist, holding her tight. "You need to watch out for those guys. They can be relentless around here."

Didn't she know it. The local roads were dominated by the cyclists in the warm weather. More than once in the past few weeks, Maggie had to pull over to the side of the road to allow them to pass.

"This is nice." Maggie followed the sound of the gulls' cries overhead. Not a cloud in the sky.

"It is, but then again, anything would be nice with you by my side."

"Thanks." She snuggled her head against his shoulder for a moment as they walked hand in hand further up the path.

Walking in a companionable silence, Maggie was happy. This was nice, being here with him.

"Would you look at that?" He pointed up toward the edge of the cliff. Maggie could just about make out the tiny figures of two people. She swayed slightly. They had to be nuts to get that close to the edge. They had to be nuts period.

"Yeah, well if you ask me, they're crazy."

"Crazy? How do you figure?" His eyes bore into hers.

"Going way up there? They must have a death wish." Maggie nearly shivered even though the temperature was mild.

He stopped her, placing his hands on her shoulders. "You're afraid of heights?"

"No, don't be ridiculous."

"You are, aren't you?" His eyes lit up.

"If I'm not mistaken, it seems as if you're deriving some kind of sick pleasure from this," Maggie mumbled, head down.

"No, honey. No." He wrapped his arms around her as more cyclists scurried by. "I didn't mean to react that way. It's just that in my eyes you're perfect. I didn't imagine you'd have a fear in the world."

If only he knew. She had plenty of fears, but Maggie figured most people did.

"Really? That's nice of you to say. Untrue, but nice."

"Come on. Say, what's your greatest fear? Top fear of all time?"

Strange turn in conversation. "Where are you going with this line of questioning?"

He blew out a hearty chuckle. "Come on, it's all in good fun. I'm just trying to get to know you."

"Okay. Heights. My top fear is heights." She wished to change the subject but wondered what his own fears were now that the topic was on the table.

"What about you? What are you afraid of?"

"I guess it would be drowning." Yes, drowning was also high on her list.

He was uncharacteristically quiet. Now would be a good time to lighten the mood.

"Enough of this macabre talk. Back to the beautiful day before us." Maggie stepped away from him to spread her arms wide. His face remained serious.

"Yes, it would be drowning."

A dark look passed over his brown eyes. He had already mentioned the fact.

"Okay. Can we move on? Maybe talk about something else?"

"Since you're the one who brought it up, I guess so."

"I didn't..." He was the one who had pointed out the hikers up high on the cliff.

"Yes, you actually did. But I suppose that's neither here nor there. I never learned how to swim, did you know that?"

"No, I didn't." Maggie took a step away from his reach. She felt uncomfortable with the vibe he was creating. More than anything, Maggie wished he would just stop talking about his fears, her fears.

"Can you imagine that? Being raised without swimming lessons?"

Maggie could almost taste the hostility that was radiating off him. Someone had unresolved issues from his childhood, it seemed.

Now wasn't the time to inquire about his past, though. Maggie slipped her hands into her light sweatshirt, wondering if it was time they should be heading back.

"It's getting late. What do you say we head back?"

It was as if a switch had been flipped. There was no other way to describe it. As suddenly as his mood had become dark and brooding, he was now light and charming once more.

"What? And miss out on sharing this spectacular day with you?" He leaned over and kissed her. Hard.

It was a bit uncomfortable, standing there in the middle of the path, in plain view, being kissed with such intensity.

"Come." He led her off the path and into the thick of the woods. She had no choice but to follow.

He chuckled as he led her to a large boulder. "Here."

He scooped her up and placed her on top of the large rock. Following suit, he climbed up the slight incline and joined Maggie. Kissing her again, he cupped her head in his hands. Moments later, his hands smoothed over her body.

Maggie stiffened, pulling away. He sat back, eyes wide. "What is it, Maggie? What the hell is the problem now?"

"I'm just not ready."

Placing his head in his hands, he sighed dramatically. "You're not ready." His laugh was sharp.

"Why not? Didn't I just tell you I love you?" His tone rose in agitation.

Was that why he had declared his love for her? Her face must have given away her thoughts.

"Are you kidding me? You think that's why I shared my feelings with you?" He stood and paced on the boulder. "Let's go. Time to go."

What had just happened here? How had everything deteriorated in a matter of mere minutes? And how much of it was her fault?

"No. Don't. Sit down. Please." Her eyes looked up at his height, pleading for him to stay.

"I don't get you, Maggie. I have to be honest here with you. You're kind of driving me crazy. Pushing my limits, you know?" His face flushed red as he paced.

How was she pushing him? "Sit, please just come back and sit beside me." Maggie patted the spot beside her, her lip trembling. She didn't know why he was so upset, only that she wanted things to return to how they were prior to this walk by the river.

"Fine." He plopped himself beside her, leaving at least a foot between them.

Maggie reached over for him, taking his hand in hers. He didn't move closer but didn't pull away either.

"Maggie. You're killing me. I love you. I freaking love you, and I feel you not returning my feelings."

"I..."

"Let me finish. I open up to you, try to show you how much I love you and I'm met with a slam of the door." His hands moved dramatically. Maggie leaned back so that he wouldn't swipe her as he spoke.

"No response from you, telling me that you love me back, and now I can't even show you how I feel." He was upon her, grabbing her face, his eyes intense.

It was true. She hadn't said she loved him back. She hadn't been ready. What she definitely wasn't ready for was showing him. The words slipped out of her mouth before she could think.

56

"I love you, too."

Tears sprang from his eyes as he kissed her face over and over. "Oh Maggie, you have no idea how happy you have made me."

Maggie's shoulders slumped. Uneasiness washed through her. It was almost as if she had been bullied into saying the words. Then again, she had always had the tendency to overanalyze her thoughts and actions. Maggie bit her lip and kissed him.

CHAPTER NINE

Naomi

TURNS OUT THAT searching the Internet is more productive than conducting research at the library and police station combined. The library's information was outdated and the police basically informed Naomi and Ryan that they would do best minding their business and leaving the investigating to the police.

"But that's just it. With all due respect, it seems that you guys just closed the case. No suspects, no leads, nothing."

Ryan grabbed at Naomi's jacket, mumbling under his breath. She brushed herself free from him. "No, Ryan. It's the truth."

"Ma'am, are you telling me that we're not doing our job?" The officer crossed his arms over his puffed-out chest.

Somewhere from the back of Naomi's mind came a memory. A memory of a brief conversation with Nick. He had an uncle on the police force and was telling Naomi that the cops would do anything to protect their hides.

"Okay, let me ask you a question. If Maggie Field was your relative, your daughter, say, would you just close the case?"

Officer Frank fidgeted in his seat and avoided making eye contact. Two sure signs that he was about to fib, in her opinion.

"Yes, in this case I would. You want to know why? Because it's an open and shut case. Maggie Field drowned that day in the river. Yes, it was unfortunate, but it is a fact. Now if you don't mind?" He turned his back to them.

Naomi's mouth opened wide as Ryan suddenly stepped forward. "But what about the fact that nobody knows where the boat is or who owned the boat? Have you guys even inquired as to whether or not she had a friend who had a boat?"

Ryan's words sparked with energy. Officer Frank slowly spun around in his swivel chair and faced them.

"I said: case closed." And he faced his computer, shutting them out once more.

"Okay, now you're being rude. I want to speak with the officer assigned to this case." Naomi stepped forward with her finger jabbing the air.

"The case was mine. I think we're done here."

Naomi opened her mouth to speak but words didn't come. Ryan shook his head in disbelief.

"I don't think we're anywhere close to being finished with this case, Officer Frank," Naomi exclaimed.

Officer Frank spun around one final time, and this time his eyes bore into Naomi's. "I'm going to give you both a piece of advice. Let it go." His words were slow and deliberate.

"And if we don't?" Naomi challenged.

He shrugged and laid cold eyes upon Naomi. "Well then I won't say you haven't been warned. Keep your nose out of other people's business."

His tone was ominous. Naomi was sure he knew something he wasn't sharing.

But what?

"If that's some kind of threat, I have a witness here." Naomi glanced at Ryan, who nodded his head in agreement.

With a smirk set on his thin lips, Officer Frank kept his eyes on Naomi.

"Good day."

"Good day?" Naomi repeated the officer's words, hours later, back at her house. Ryan held his head in his hands.

"I know, Naomi. It looks bad. I agree something is amiss, but Officer Frank might be right about one thing. Maybe we should mind our business."

She couldn't believe her ears. "Are you serious?" Naomi grabbed Ryan's shoulders, shaking him slightly.

"This is our biggest clue yet. The very fact that Officer Frank is being so unhelpful and rude speaks volumes." Her eyes were wide. "There's something up here, I can practically taste it!"

"Maybe. Or perhaps it's just a matter of pride. He could feel as if we don't think he did his job thoroughly enough."

"Because he didn't!" Naomi raked her hands through her messy hair.

"Or, if something is up, if, let's just say, Officer Frank is hiding something? We could be in danger. Either way, I say we drop it."

Where the heck was his sense of adventure? What happened to serving justice for a dead woman?

"I can't believe you're saying this. I thought we were in this together."

"We are. We *were*. Just think about letting it go, Naomi."

"Fine. You want out? Done. But if you think for one moment that I'm dropping this, you don't know me at all."

Ryan stood, then met Naomi's gaze head on. "Don't. Just write your story. What was that phrase you use all the time? Creative license? Use your creative license and let the crime aspect go."

"Creative license?" Naomi practically laughed in his face. "I'm in this until I find answers. Do you see that poor woman's grave out there in the cemetery?" Naomi paused, walking over to the window. She opened the curtains to expose the bleak darkness outside. Maggie's soul was all alone, in the cold night.

Ryan put his head down, defeated.

"Do you see what I see? Feel what I feel?"

Ryan's head came up, eyes pried on the cold darkness. "I see it, dammit. I see it."

"So are you in or out?" Naomi's hands were planted firmly on her hips.

"In or out?"

Ryan's gaze met hers.

He sighed deeply. "I'm in, Naomi. Of course I'm in."

"Ryan. There's something else." It was time.

"What? What is it, Naomi?"

"Do you believe in ghosts?"

Ryan's jaw dropped slightly. "Um. I'm not sure. Why?"

"There's something going on in this house." She gestured toward the window once more. "And out there."

"Wait a minute. What are you talking about?" He drew closer to Naomi. "You're freaking me out here."

"Yeah, welcome to the club. Hang around here a bit more and you'll see what I mean. I see flashes of shadows, books falling off my shelves. Zelda senses it too."

"Come on, Naomi. I think your writer's imagination is getting to you."

"No, I'm sure about this. I feel it in the air."

Ryan's eyes narrowed. He didn't believe her. It didn't matter.

"Naomi…"

She cut him off. "No, Ryan. It's fine. Like I said, stay around here long enough and you'll see for yourself."

"Okay, so humor me then. Who do you think this spirit is? Maggie?"

It was odd, but she had never actually considered the fact that the spirit could very well be Maggie. Or it could be a hundred other people in a state of unrest outside her very window.

"I don't know, Ryan. I just don't know."

Ryan meandered over to the window and parted the curtain. He bit down on his lip as he studied the dark graveyard beyond Naomi's property.

IT SHOULDN'T HAVE been that hard. Ryan was supposed to have just as much passion for solving this mystery as she did. They were kindred spirits, or so she thought. If anyone in the world was up for this task, she was sure it would have been Ryan. Bottom line, he had acquiesced. But it had taken some doing.

And the fact that he wasn't buying into her resident spirit had disappointed her as well. A thought struck her as she recalled his solemn expression when he had peered out into the night. Perhaps he did believe her, did believe in ghosts. It could be that the very thought was too much for him to handle.

Sleep wasn't exactly beckoning her that evening. Glancing at the bedside alarm clock, Naomi sighed. It was no use. She wouldn't be sleeping anytime soon. The faint shadow of Zelda appeared at the bottom of the staircase. The cat spied Naomi and let out a sharp-pitched shriek.

"I can't..." This was becoming ridiculous. Now she could really forget about getting any sleep. Zelda howled relentlessly.

She was spooked. She could admit it to herself. This time felt different.—there was tension in the air.

"Zelda?" Naomi reached the bottom of the steps and searched for the cat's black figure.

"Zelda? Where are you?" She flipped the light switch on, but darkness remained. How odd. "Darn. Zelda? Where are you, you insane cat?"

It wasn't like Zelda to hide, but it appeared she was

doing just that.

"Fine."

Naomi sucked in her breath as she felt her scalp prickle. The flash of a vision appeared so quickly, it was gone before Naomi's mind could register what she had seen.

It appeared once more, and this time the shadow lingered for a few moments longer. Naomi planted her feet firmly on the floor beneath her.

"My God."

The air surrounding her was instantly colder. As she gasped for air, she could see her cold breath before her.

First the electricity and now the heat.

Zelda's screech jolted her from her thoughts. The cat was on the windowsill, prancing and wailing.

What was that? Edging closer to the window, Naomi joined her cat. She could just about make out the figure of the back of a woman with flowing blonde hair. She wore a long, white gown. Naomi's hand went to her chest as she followed the form to the area right near Maggie T. Field's headstone.

The vision disappeared and all that was left was the memory of the ghostly image.

"Did you see that, Zelda?" She whispered.

Judging from the feline's pacing and agitation, it was clear she had also witnessed the very same vision.

CHAPTER TEN

Maggie

I LOVE YOU. Those words held magic. They also held apprehension and fear. It seemed that once those complicated words slipped from one's lips, relationships were never the same.

You couldn't take the words back.

It was a fact. For good or bad.

Since she had spoken those three little words weeks ago, he had become more clingy, possessive even. Maggie was having second thoughts before this relationship even had much of a beginning.

She needed to speak with R.J. Easier said than done. Unfortunately, she had continued to neglect her relationship with R.J. Her worries about how her boyfriend would react to a male friend had been easily confirmed.

"R.J.? Why is it that I never heard his name mentioned before?"

"Please, you'll cause a scene." Maggie spun her head to see if anyone had noticed his raised voice. Nobody was staring at them. That was a relief. It had been a mistake to bring his name up here. Heck it had been a mistake to bring it up at all. Maggie had slipped. It wasn't intentional, and now she regretted her loose tongue.

"Maybe because I was worried that this conversation would happen."

She felt a sharp pinch on her thigh.

"Ouch!"

"Will you be quiet? Look who's causing a scene now." His

hand came back out from under the table. He had pinched her. Pinched her.

"Don't you ever..."

"I asked you a question and I'm waiting for an answer. Now don't be rude. Who is this R.J and why are you still speaking with him?"

How dare he? How dare! "I think we need a break." She was up from her seat. He pulled her hand with force, this time earning stares from customers close by.

Maggie's pulse sped up. She didn't wish to cause a scene. Not here in the town she lived in. Cautiously she lowered herself back to her chair.

"You need to calm down," Maggie managed, glancing around.

"I need to calm down? I need to calm down?" His voice rose. "And where do you get off telling me we need a break? You don't get to do that. There's no break here, honey. Not now."

"What? What does that mean?" He sounded crazy. His irises sparked wide with emotion.

After glancing around, he lowered his voice to a hiss. "You and I are in this together. You said the words. You love me. I don't take those words lightly. You don't tell someone you love them and then take it back."

Maggie didn't know how to respond. Her stomach twisted.

"You hear me? It doesn't work that way. You and I are committed to one another. Couples have disagreements all the time. This is normal."

"No, I don't think so." Maggie didn't have tons of experience with dating, but her gut told her otherwise. This was far from normal. He was becoming more jealous and irrational with each day that passed.

He scared her.

"Don't. You. Tell. Me. I said it's normal. Now what's not normal is the fact that you have this guy R.J. as a friend. Get rid of him."

A burst of courage shone through. She had had enough. Enough of the comments, the glances, the accusations. Their relationship was deteriorating and here was the last straw.

"I won't." Maggie sat back, pushing herself away from the table so that he couldn't pinch her or pull her again.

He looked around and smashed his fist on the table. Maggie cringed.

"I told you I loved you, dammit!" He pounded his fist once more. "Nobody speaks that way to me. Nobody. Tell you what; you get rid of him or I will."

Sweat formed on his upper lip. She barely heard the hushed whispers coming from the other diners.

Maggie's jaw hung open as she watched him walk out of the coffee shop.

"R.J., I NEED to see you." She had no one else she could really talk to. Maggie's relationship with her parents was a close one and that was the very reason she didn't wish to upset them. To worry her parents was unnecessary at this point. If she could avoid the subject altogether with them, even better. Problem was, R.J. wasn't answering her calls. Jackie had probably sunk her teeth into him by this point. But she knew better. R.J. would at least call her back. She would try once more tomorrow and then let it go for now.

Just as she placed her cell phone down, it vibrated.

"R.J."

"Hey, Maggie. What's up?" Cool greeting, but he had at least called back.

"I'm so glad you called."

"Yeah, yeah. Of course. Sorry I couldn't call after your first message, but I was kind of busy last night."

Well.

"No problem. Look, I was wondering if we could meet up for coffee or something."

"Oh? You do realize that I'm in a relationship?" he teased.

She felt her face heat up. "Oh."

"I'm joking. Well, I am in a relationship, but I'm kidding. Forget it."

His nervous laughter put her at ease. That was the way it was between the two of them. Nervous energy.

"Is everything okay?"

How should she respond? *"I hope so."*

That seemed to grab his attention. *"Maggie. What is it? Talk to me."*

"I'm okay. I just need a little advice."

"I'm listening. Where and when?"

She had known he would be there to support her.

"I don't know. Let me think. How about we meet at the bookstore? You know, like we used to?"

"Romance aisle?" She could just imagine his smirk.

"You know it."

The large bookstore had been one of their favorite meeting spots— the very spot they had first met, as a matter of fact.

Maggie would grab a romance book while R.J. usually went for non-fiction. They would sit side by side and read for hours, just enjoying one another's company. The private joke was that the romance aisle or any aisle in the massive bookstore would be the perfect spot for secret lovers to meet. Not that they were secret lovers by any stretch, but one thing Maggie didn't need right now was for her jealous ex-boyfriend to see them together.

Ex-boyfriend. The words brought her relief. She was done with him. His irrational behavior earlier had cemented the fact they were finished. As disappointing as it was to find out that Nick had so many issues, she was glad it was over. The man she had originally met had quickly been replaced with a jealous, controlling stranger. She couldn't even begin to imagine how much worse his behavior would have become if she stayed any longer. She had said those three little words way too quickly. Heck, she hadn't even meant to say them, she just wanted him to stop pressuring her. Saying the words was a lame attempt to buy her time, to stall him.

Maggie was looking forward to seeing R.J. It had been far too long. Stepping into Barney's Books and Café, Maggie breathed *deeply.*

Did books have a smell? She swore they did. Nothing made her happier than relaxing with a good romance or delving into a captivating mystery. Sometimes a break from reality was in order. Making a mental note to pick up a new paperback before she left, Maggie made her way to the romance aisle. He was on time, as usual. R.J. never surprised her, but perhaps that wasn't such a horrible thing.

"Hey." R.J. rushed over to embrace her. He smelled like fresh soap and aftershave. The familiar sent put her at ease as she buried her face in his shoulder.

"Hey, you." She kissed him on the cheek. Stepping back from him, she took in his appearance. He looked good. Quite good.

"I've missed you. It's been too long."

"Yes, R.J., it has and I'm sorry."

R.J. pumped her hand with his, never breaking eye contact. "You can't take all the blame. Some of it is my fault as well."

"True, I suppose. How is Jackie anyhow?"

Maggie swore she saw a flicker of emotion pass in his glance. "She's fine, Maggie."

Maggie cleared her throat and broke free from R.J. Sweat clung to her blouse. "Don't you have your book picked out yet?" She hadn't seen a book in his hands.

"I didn't think this visit was about reading, Maggie. Sit, tell me what's up." He sank down and propped up his knees.

Maggie joined him on the carpeted floor. "I don't know where to begin." Where did she start her complicated tale? At the beginning? Or should she skip to the part where her boyfriend basically threatened R.J?

"Come on, sweetheart. Just relax." He took hold of her hand and Maggie felt her heart race. His touch shouldn't have this effect on her, but damn, it always did.

"I met a guy."

R.J. laughed. "Okay. That's a good start. Now tell me more."

Maggie stared at the specks on the tan carpet.

"Don't tell me you're engaged already?" R.J. lifted her hand,

inspecting for a ring.

Maggie's laughter bubbled out. "First of all, that's the wrong hand and no, I'm not engaged. Hardly."

"Then what's with all the mystery, sweetie? Talk to me." His smooth voice eased her a bit. Maggie opened her mouth and then closed in tightly.

"We're friends, right?"

"Of course, R.J."

"Good friends?"

She met his dark eyes. "The best."

He didn't take his eyes off her face. "The best? I like that."

Maggie liked the sound of it also. It gave her the strength to continue. "I just ended a relationship with a guy that frightens me." There, she said it.

"Frightens you? How?" R.J.'s brows scrunched together.

"He's jealous, possessive." Need she go on?

R.J. shook his head firmly. "That's not good. But you said you ended it, right?"

"Yes, I did. Problem is, he didn't. And to make matters worse, he threatened to hurt you if I continue to see you, talk to you."

"Me? How did that come about?"

"I'm embarrassed to admit that I had started backing away because I was afraid of his reaction to you. I knew he would be jealous and then I mentioned you by mistake and he flipped."

"Geez."

"Tell me about it."

"So you're afraid that he won't let this go. Won't let you go?"

"Exactly."

R.J. hesitated a moment. He squeezed Maggie's hand before continuing. "Tell you what. I think it's a good idea if you watch your surroundings for a while. If you notice anything out of place or if he contacts you in a threatening manner, you have to call the police."

"What will they do? I can only hope he gives up."

"They can issue a restraining order, for one thing. Let's just see how this plays out. Be careful, though."

"Okay. I just wish there was more I could do." Maggie could only hope her ex wouldn't make an issue of their break-up.

"I'm here for you. You know that, don't you?"

Her heart warmed a bit. "I do."

"I'm not going to let anything happen to you, not if I can help it."

"Thank you, that's very sweet." Jackie surely wouldn't appreciate their friendship, either. "What about Jackie?"

"How about you let me worry about Jackie? She's got nothing on us."

His words brought tears to her eyes.

"Maggie?"

She turned to face R.J. and he moved forward, placing the sweetest kiss on her lips. She melted into him, her senses alive.

"R.J." Maggie broke this kiss. She quickly jumped to her feet, steadying herself against the rows of books.

"Maggie…"

"Oh my God. That shouldn't have happened." What had she been thinking? She needed a friend right now, not another man.

"I blame it on the romance aisle." R.J. chuckled as he stood to face Maggie.

Whether it was the high emotions or just being in the company of R.J., she saw the humor of his comment and tried to hold back her laughter. It was no use. Her giggles filled the air until she felt R.J's touch once more.

"I want to see you again."

Her heart skipped. "But…"

"It's different for me. My feelings have always been strong for you, Maggie."

She couldn't deny that she felt the same. The timing was awful, though. It was all wrong. "R.J."

"Don't. Don't say anything. All in good time, Maggie."

She nodded.

He swept her blonde hair from her eyes and then kissed her once more.

"We've got all the time in the world, you and I," he whispered.

CHAPTER ELEVEN

Naomi

"I LOVE YOU! I Dammit, I love you! You can't say those words and take them back!" This time, the words were too close, too close to home. In her dream that night, Naomi had covered her ears, his words filled her head with pain. It was something Nick had said to her before they had broken up. Perhaps not word for word, but it was close enough. Now her dreams were all mixed up with Nick as the leading man. Why hadn't she seen it before?

Maybe these dreams had nothing to do with Maggie but everything to do with her lack of closure with Nick.

Researching Maggie's story was melding with her relationship with Nick. Pieces of her life were coming together, mixing and mixing until she thought she would lose her mind in her dreams. She needed closure with Nick. That must be the message that was trying to come though.

But wouldn't it be better to let him fade away? She shook her head. Fade away? Nick? Doubtful.

Again, Naomi wondered how she could have been caught in his trap. She was still ashamed she had fallen victim to him. What did it say about her that she would get involved with such a troubled man?

Naomi's mom had always said she had a knack for trying to help the wounded, the needy. Even from a young age, she had proven that to be true. Once she had cried with a small, injured bird in her hands. She had attempted to nurse the little guy back to health but it was too late. Just as it had been too late with Nick.

Much too late.

Nick needed counseling in order to heal. She wasn't qualified to help him. Realizing the fact and removing herself was the best she could do.

Then why did she feel guilty for leaving him lately? Was it the recurring dreams, the dreams that were now changing, revealing a deep-rooted fear?

Naomi would wait this one out.

For now.

For now, she would take the time to think through her plan. Should she attempt to speak with him, to give them both closure or should she let it go in hopes of the slight chance he would move on?

She was supposed to be concentrating on her writing. She had a story to write and Maggie was waiting for her. Her head felt like it would burst as her thoughts were tangled in so many directions.

Coincidence had never rung true in her mind, in her experience. The blonde apparition must be Maggie T. Field.

It had to be her.

Naomi couldn't wrap her brain around any other scenario. Amy would never believe her. Ryan would never believe her.

Or maybe he would. Ryan surprised her with his unpredictability. At first he had seemed to have such a zest for investigating, such curiosity. Slowly, he seemed to be backing up, almost as if he were scared of the unknown. His behavior gave Naomi something to think about. She would attempt to put her feelings regarding Ryan on a shelf for now. It was too much to figure out until she got to know him better. Easier said than done.

There was also another concern. His curiosity wasn't the only thing that seemed to be waning. Rarely did they kiss romantically anymore. He was like a best friend. She already had a best friend. She wanted more from him but didn't know how to make him see her, see her for more than the friendship that was taking over. Would another special dress be in order? Hm. It may require more drastic measures.

Her coffee spilled on her sleeve as she heard the knocking on her door. "Shoot."

Ryan should be busy with his online courses. She had no clue who could be at her door at such an early hour. Peeping through the frosted glass on the side of the door, she straightened.

"Bryce. Holly." This was a surprise.

"Hi, Miss Nomi." Nomi. Holly's pronunciation of her name made her laugh once more.

Naomi smiled down at the young girl. Her cheeks were a rosy red from being outside.

"Well, hello there. If it isn't my favorite neighbors from up the street."

Holly rolled her eyes upward. "Silly Nomi. We're your *only* neighbors from up the street." It was true, but she enjoyed watching the little girl smile.

"Hi, Bryce."

"Hi." Their eyes locked for a moment.

Naomi was the first to break the silence. "Come on in, guys. It's chilly out there with that wind this morning."

"Thank you," Bryce said as he hustled Holly through the door. "Say, this place is very nice."

Naomi recalled Ryan saying something similar the first time he came to her house. "Thanks. I bet your place is just as charming."

The old farmhouse looked amazing from the outside. Quaint, historic homes always piqued her interest.

"It is. It's got a very cool, super-secret hidden stairway. Daddy says people used to hide there. A long, long, long, time ago."

Holly's enthusiasm was contagious. "That I'd like to

see."

"Well I'm sure we could arrange for a visit. What do you say, Holly? Maybe our new friend could stop by one day for a cup of hot cocoa and a little exploring."

It sounded amazing. "Oh. I would love to."

"It'll be nice to have a visitor. It's so quiet there with just the two of us." He glanced down and nodded toward Holly.

So there was no wife.

"Well, then it's a date."

"A date? I don't think you're old enough to date, Miss Nomi."

Naomi's flush spread straight to her face. "Oh, I don't think that's what your dad had in mind, honey." Not old enough? Now that was hysterical. She couldn't bring herself to meet Bryce's eyes.

"Um, no."

She dared a glance at Bryce and noticed his own cheeks were a bright shade of pink.

"Daddy says that sometimes men and women date and that since Mommy's not around anymore, it's perfectly ⊓cceptable."

Bryce scratched his neck, which was growing a deeper red by the moment. "First of all, it's *acceptable,* honey."

"Acceptable." Holly confirmed as she struggled with the multi-syllabic word. "Just what I said."

Naomi couldn't contain her laughter. Holly was absolutely adorable. She couldn't help but wonder what had happened to her mother. It would be rude to inquire, so she kept her questions to herself.

'Speaking of hot cocoa, how would you like some right now?" She probably should have asked Bryce first before offering the beverage to Holly. "That is if it's okay with your dad."

"Please, Daddy. Please?" Holly jumped in place, her hands clasped together.

Bryce nodded his agreement. "Of course, that would be

wonderful. As long as I could ask for a cup of that delicious smelling coffee."

"It's a deal. Come, Holly, take a seat."

Naomi grinned, listening to the casual banter of father and daughter as she prepared the drinks. A bang sounded from the living room.

"What was that?" Bryce lifted his gaze toward the sound.

Zelda flew in from living room, jumping smack on top of Holly's lap.

"Zelda!" She was in awe of her cat. Zelda had never done anything like this before. She was acting more unpredictable by the day. Well, not surprising, Naomi figured. Not with a resident ghost roaming the house.

"Kitty!" Holly brought Zelda closer, squeezing her to her chest.

"I hope this is okay with you?" Naomi glanced at Bryce through her laughter.

"What can I say? Holly seems to attract a lot of attention from animals. Cats, dogs, they all love her."

"They do, Daddy. Why can't we get a kitty?"

"Oh, boy. She's been begging me for a kitten for the past year." Bryce ran a hand through his thick brown hair. "The last place we were living in didn't allow pets."

"But our new house does! I asked John!"

Shaking his head, Bryce gazed at Naomi. "Yes. He did say that."

"I'm sorry, I didn't mean for Zelda to cause any trouble."

"She's no trouble at all. No worries. Besides, I love cats, and I was kind of leaning toward getting one soon."

"Daddy!" The words were enough to cause Holly to leap up, Zelda in her arms, and cuddle against her dad. Naomi enjoyed witnessing the sweet interaction between them.

"Well, it's settled then," Bryce announced.

"How about that hot cocoa, Holly?"

Holly returned to her seat and Zelda remained planted

right on her lap, meeting Naomi's gaze directly. That cat never ceased to amaze her.

AN IDEA WAS brewing in Naomi's mind. It could possibly work.

As juvenile as it sounded. Naomi couldn't believe she was being reduced to such tactics.

"Any more ghost sightings?" Ryan munched on an extra thick cheeseburger. Ketchup oozed out onto Ryan's cheek.

"You have a little…" Naomi reached over to try to wipe the smeared ketchup off his face and then retreated as he took yet another giant bite.

"Huh?"

"Nothing. It's nothing." She sat back and watched him chew over and over again. Her own appetite was decreasing as her frustration took hold.

"I have a new neighbor." Here goes. "He's a single father. Quite handsome, actually. "

Ryan popped some fries into his mouth. The ketchup was still smeared across his cheek. "That's nice."

That's nice?

"His daughter, Holly, is adorable. They came to visit today and we had some hot cocoa."

She watched for any signs of jealousy at the mention of Bryce. Nothing. Heck, was she crazy? A jealous man was the last thing she needed after Nick. Who was she kidding? Another idea took hold of her before she had a chance to think it through.

Leaning over across the table, she made the move. First she pulled his head toward hers and then planted a firm kiss on his lips.

"Naomi. What's gotten into you? I was in the middle of chewing." Ryan's eyes were wide with confusion.

Naomi huffed out a forceful breath. It was no use. She grabbed a napkin and wiped off the ketchup that was now on her own face. With her arms crossed around herself, she watched him chew.

CHAPTER TWELVE

Maggie

IT HAD BEEN *eerily silent on the ex- boyfriend front. Maggie was shocked that he hadn't contacted her over the past several weeks. It was like he was just gone. Vanished. She wouldn't have thought it possible. After the threats and promises stating that their relationship wasn't over, how could it have ended so neatly?*

A nagging thought remained.

The hang-ups.

And the text messages.

There had been a few ominous text messages the first week or so after the incident at the coffee shop. He had threatened that he wouldn't let her go. She ignored all of the messages and then he stopped.

Just stopped.

She was on her way to meet up with R.J. Keeping her friend at arm's length had been challenging. Ever since that kiss weeks ago at the bookstore, R.J. was never far from her mind.

But for all she knew he still spoke with Jackie. She wasn't about to steal another woman's man. It wasn't her style. Maggie knew deep down that Jackie wasn't the one for R.J., but he would have to figure that out in his own time. So successfully avoiding any more meetings with R.J had been trying, but necessary.

It didn't mean she couldn't speak with him on the phone, though. They had spoken for hours at a time, about her ex, about their dreams, you name it. He hadn't mentioned Jackie once, so Maggie figured he was still holding on to their relationship.

R.J. had called that morning to tell her he would like to see her, that it was important. After some deliberation, Maggie decided to go. She would hear him out and then keep her distance.

The little Italian restaurant was one of her favorite restaurants in town. She came here often with Christine and had even brought her ex-boyfriend here once or twice. To sit down here and dine with R.J. would be a treat. Upon walking in, she saw R.J., on time as usual, at a table toward the back of the dimly lit dining room.

Nodding at the familiar waiter, she smiled as he approached her. "Hi, Ted." She could have sworn the man blushed. He was sweet.

R.J. straightened his posture and rose to his feet. "Maggie." She leaned forward to kiss him on the cheek.

"You look amazing."

"Thanks, R.J."

Within minutes, they were given menus and had ordered a bottle of red wine. Now that all the formalities were out of the way, conversation was stilted.

"So what's up, R.J.?" She was anxious to hear why he wanted to meet with her.

He fidgeted in his chair and hesitated before speaking. "Yes, about that. Maggie, I've been trying to see you over these past few weeks."

"I don't know what to say. I figured given the fact you're in a relationship, it might not be the best idea." She crossed her arms over her chest.

"First of all, since when has that stopped you and me from being friends before?"

"Well, I think it's fair to say things have changed since that..." She paused.

"Since that kiss at the bookstore." Ryan finished her sentence.

Maggie felt her pulse speed up. "Well, yes." She couldn't bring herself to look him in the eye.

"Maggie, I haven't been able to stop thinking about it since. Hell, you've been on my mind every second of every day." His voice rose as he clenched his fist on the table.

"R.J." She didn't know how to respond to him. If she were to be honest with herself, she'd admit he had also been on her mind.

A lot.

"I wanted to tell you that I broke things off with Jackie. The day after we kissed."

He did? "What?"

"You heard me. It's over."

"Why didn't you just tell me?"

"Heck, Maggie. I don't know. You've got my head all screwed up. I guess I also wanted to give you some breathing room since you just split with what's-his-name."

"Yeah, him." She didn't wish to speak his name out loud either.

He reached across the table and held on to her hands. "Maggie. What I'm trying to say is that I'm crazy about you. I guess I always have been, since that very first day we met. Do you remember?"

Of course she did. Swiping a tear from her eye, she recalled the very first time she had laid eyes on R.J. He was the most handsome man she had ever seen. Still was.

"If I recall, you were in the travel aisle."

She had been. Going to Spain had always been a dream of hers. She figured she'd check out the travel books before heading to the romance section.

"And you said, wait a second, let me quote you," she giggled. "'Why go anywhere else when you're already in the best place in the world?'"

"That sounds like something I would say." His eyes sparkled.

"How did we even end up friends?" Maggie considered the chances for meeting a guy that ended up being just a friend slim to none. But they did it.

Until now, of course.

"I wanted to ask you out, but you were dating that guy, the one with the horses, right?"

"Tim. That's right." She and Tim had only dated for a few weeks before she knew he wasn't the one. By that time, R.J. had already met Jackie. And the rest was history.

"Where does this leave us, Maggie?" R.J. grew serious.

Tough question. "I don't know."

"What do you mean? Do you realize that finally our timing is right? I mean, this is the first time since we met that we're both single."

"I know that, but…"

He sat back in his chair and bit down on his lip. "Wait a minute. Are you still worried about that guy?"

She was. "Yes."

"Has he done anything?"

"Well, no. Not in some time, but something doesn't feel right. Call it intuition, but I have a feeling he's not over everything yet."

"Who cares? What can he do? Maggie, I'm here for you."

"I know. Maybe I'm just being silly."

"Maybe you just need me to take your mind off your troubles." He leaned over and gently kissed her. Her racing heart told her this couldn't be wrong.

As she opened her eyes, she met R.J.'s gaze. It felt right. "Thank you. I think you just succeeded in taking my mind off my worries."

Maggie gazed around the cozy restaurant, taking in twinkling white lights and warm atmosphere. Their waiter caught her eye and quickly glanced away.

A swift movement from outside caught her eye, too, as she turned to the front glass window. A man stood, grounded to the spot.

Maggie gasped aloud.

His eyes locked on hers.

He looked right through her.

CHAPTER THIRTEEN

Naomi

"It's LIKE HE doesn't even see me anymore." Naomi had been complaining to Amy for at least twenty minutes at this point. Amy's own dating life was still going strong. She and Peter, the guy from their double date, seemed to be getting along well. Naomi missed Amy, though. Why did Peter have to occupy Amy's time every single weekend? She could use some girl time.

"I'm surprised. Very surprised. I would have sworn Ryan was a hundred percent into you."

Naomi released the breath she had been holding. "I thought the same thing. I can't figure out what's happening."

"Well, let's think back. When did you first start to notice him pulling away?"

It wasn't quite pulling away. "See, that's just it. He wants to see me, spend time with me…"

"So what's the problem?"

"The problem lies in the fact that we're becoming close friends, but that's it." How could she even begin to explain that everything was fine until Ryan had seen her house and then the cemetery beyond?

"Aha. I see. Maybe he's not interested in women."

"Come on." That was absurd. "That's not it. I'm sure it's not."

"Then what? Maybe Ryan is still in love with an ex-girlfriend."

An ex-girlfriend. Why hadn't she thought of that before? "You know, you just might be on to something there." It made sense.

"Ask him. It couldn't hurt."

"You're right, Amy. Thank you."

"Of course. How's everything else?"

Naomi hesitated. "Good, I suppose."

"You suppose? Come on, I've known you too long, what's the matter?"

She blew out a deep breath. "It's Nick."

"Oh, no. Is he bothering you?"

"No, not in my waking hours at least."

"I'm not even going to ask what that means. Has he contacted you or something?"

"No, but that's just it. It's not like Nick to just let things go so easily."

"You might have a point there. What are you thinking?"

"I don't know. I'm stumped. I'm having these awful dreams in which I feel like he's after me or something. Do you think I need closure?"

"Well, normally I'd say yes, but in your case? I'd let things be."

That's what Naomi had initially thought, too, but these dreams, they were so vivid. "I guess you're right. I just hope the dreams stop. They're like nothing I've experienced before."

"Listen, if you need to talk, I'm here. Don't do anything stupid like contact him or anything, promise?"

"Yeah, yeah."

"I'm not getting off this phone until I hear the words."

"Fine. I promise."

"Good, now I have to go. Talk to you soon, Naomi."

Naomi stood to pace the floor. So for now, she promised she wouldn't contact him. Biting down on her lip, she shook her head. God, she hoped she was making the right decision.

Her mind wandered back to Ryan. The mystery of Ryan

might be unraveled, but if it were true that he was still in love with a past girlfriend, where did that leave Naomi?

One thing at a time.

Right now she had to meet up with Ryan to try to uncover some more facts about how Maggie T. Field had died. She could casually bring up the question of an ex-girlfriend when she saw him.

Rushing to get out of the house on time, she grabbed her keys and jacket. Out of the corner of her eye, she could see one of her kitchen chairs move ever so slightly, then topple over as if someone had pushed it. Zelda howled from the living room, running in to inspect the situation.

"Oh, I don't have time for this now. You guys play nice now, you hear?" It struck her as ridiculous that she was just speaking to a spirit, reprimanding it like a child.

Ryan would lecture her about her lateness again if she didn't get to the coffee shop soon. The traffic on weekends was getting out of hand here. It seemed this area was becoming a popular autumn destination for many.

As she pulled into the parking lot of the café, she spied Ryan's small truck. Figures. She would love to arrive first, just once.

Just once.

He was sitting at a table perusing a newspaper, a determined stare in place.

"Ah. Look who finally decided to grace me with her presence." He looked up from the paper.

"Yeah, yeah. I'm only five minutes late this time."

"Five minutes this time, ten minutes last time," Ryan joked.

He had taken the initiative to grab her a cup of coffee and a bagel with cream cheese. "Wow, I guess this makes up for your rude behavior. It looks delicious. Thank you." She leaned over to kiss him hello.

"*My* rude behavior? Looks who's talking."

Naomi took a sip of her piping hot coffee. "You couldn't

have been here for long. My coffee is still really hot."

"Ah. But I was on time."

"I'm going to get you one of these days, you hear? One day I will arrive on time *and* first."

"Doubtful," he challenged as he sipped at his own coffee.

Naomi bit her lip as she wondered how to broach the subject of a possible ex-girlfriend that may or may not have crushed him.

"This bagel is ridiculously good." He bit into the everything-flavored bagel, proceeding to cover his cheek with globs of cream cheese.

Oh, man. Her mission couldn't contend when food was in the picture."

"I see. Listen, Ryan?"

He chewed and sipped. Chewed and sipped.

Oh, for God's sake. "Ryan!"

He dropped his bagel to his plate and glanced around the café. "What has gotten into you? Why are you yelling?"

"I'm *trying* to talk to you. I have to ask you something."

"Then why don't you just ask?"

She could continue this frustrating conversation or get right to the point. Right. The latter was more appealing.

"Have you ever had your heart broken?"

She had his full attention now. His eyes locked on hers. "Now what the heck kind of question is that?"

"Can you please just answer it?"

"I don't think so."

"You don't *think so?*"

"I don't know where that question even came from. Why do you ask?"

His response wasn't giving her much to go on. "I guess I just wondered about your past."

His eyebrows scrunched in confusion. "Okay. Since you asked me, now how about you? Have you ever had your heart broken?"

Broken? She didn't think so, but Nick had certainly done a number on her. "No, not broken."

"But?"

"But... let's just drop it, huh?" She wasn't prepared to talk about her feelings regarding Nick right now.

"Oh, no. You're the one who brought this up. Is it Nick?"

Ryan could read her mind, she swore he could. Ryan might be able to give her some insight, though. "I guess I'm still worried, you know?"

"I do. If you would just tell me a little more about him, it might just help to ease your mind." He reached over and took hold of her hands.

"He scared me. Nick had a bad childhood. He suffered from lack of attention, a lack of caring. I felt bad for him at first." As she continued to share with Ryan, she felt something deep within her begin to relax. By the time she had finished speaking about Nick, she felt a better.

"Be careful. It sounds like Nick could be a loose cannon. He's probably moved on, but just in case, keep your eyes open. Wide open."

"They always are."

He pondered over her admission. "That's kind of sad, Naomi."

She supposed it was. Honestly, Nick's lack of attention lately was unsettling. She worried that it could be the calm before the storm, so to speak. God, she hoped she was wrong.

"Ryan?"

"Yes?' He gazed at her from behind his coffee cup.

"I never really had closure with Nick, and now I keep having these dreams."

"What kind of dreams, Naomi?" He lifted his head to meet her eyes.

"Bad ones. Dreams where I feel like he's chasing me. I have a feeling it's not over yet between us."

Ryan waved his hand through the air. "Want my honest

opinion?"

"Sure."

"I think you're being silly. Dreams are subconscious thoughts. Anything could pop up, and I never really believed they mean anything more than our minds sorting through all of our memories and experiences while we rest."

Hm. She had kind of pegged Ryan for having more of an imagination on the topic of dreams, but in this case, his viewpoint relaxed her a bit.

"Really? But you heard how unstable Nick can be."

"Yes, Naomi, I have. But think about it, he hasn't contacted you."

"But don't forget, I have gotten hang-ups, calls with dead air."

"Ah." His hand waved through the air once more. "It might not even be him. Could be a wrong number, for all you know."

"You don't think I should go to him, speak to him, to give us both closure?' She fidgeted in her seat.

"Are you kidding? With a guy like that, it's always best to leave it alone." He glanced over at the pastries behind the glass counter.

"You've had enough." She sighed and sat back in her chair. How could his mind still be on food when she was divulging her concerns over Nick?

"Yeah, I guess." He gazed at her once more. "Feel better?"

"I'm glad I spoke with you about him. I do feel a bit better." Now that both Amy and Ryan had given the same advice, she figured she'd leave it alone.

"Good." With his fingers, he traced small circles on the palm of her hand.

She swallowed back her emotions. "Now back to you. No past heartache?"

"Why do you keep asking me that? What gives?"

Naomi gazed up at the ceiling. It was time for the truth.

"Ryan? What's happening with us?"

He sat back abruptly in his seat. "What do you mean?"

"I don't know. Can't you feel this? We're drifting apart."

He cocked his head to the side. "Drifting apart? How so? We're together nearly every day."

"That's not what I mean. What are we to each other? Friends? Are we dating?"

"Oh. Well. Yes, I had assumed we were dating."

"But you don't kiss me anymore. It seems like the friendship part of our relationship is growing, and that's wonderful, don't get me wrong. But in the romance department? Not so much."

"I thought everything was going well." He looked hurt. She hadn't intended to upset him.

"It *is*. But I want more."

"Like what? What is it that I'm not giving you? I'm trying hard to understand."

"Kiss me."

"Now? Right here?"

Her shoulders slumped. "See? That's exactly what I'm talking about. Where is the spontaneity? The spark?"

"I'm not much for public displays of affection, Naomi. Never was. I'm confused right now."

"It's not *about* public displays of affection, Ryan. You're missing the point here. Even when we're at my house it's all about how wonderful my house is, how amazing it is that the cemetery is right on my property."

He chuckled grimly at her comment. "So let me get this straight. You're *jealous* of a *house*? A *cemetery*?"

"No! That's ridiculous."

He shook his head firmly. "You said it."

He wasn't grasping what she was trying to tell him. "You know what? Forget it. Just forget that I ever said anything. Everything is *just fine* between us." Naomi sat back further in her seat.

"So what? You don't want to see me anymore? I thought

we were going to head over to Maggie's parents' house today."

That had been the plan. Naomi wished to ask them a few questions, hoping to gain a better sense of perspective about what kind of woman Maggie had been.

"I do want to continue seeing you. I like you. A lot." She hung her head down, fingering the rim of her coffee cup.

"Is this our first argument?" Ryan's stormy blue eyes met hers.

"No. Yes. Maybe." Although she was still upset, she felt a smile begin to form.

"I'll try harder, Naomi. I will."

But he shouldn't have to try at all. It should just come naturally. "Okay, Ryan. Thank you."

He leaned over and placed a sweet kiss on her lips.

It was a start.

CHAPTER FOURTEEN

Maggie

"IT'S HIM." MAGGIE felt cold. "Oh, my God. He was standing right there. I swear he was."

R.J. peered toward the glass window. "Are you sure? I don't see anyone there, sweetheart."

"But. He was." She struggled to find the words. "I saw him."

"Okay. Try to calm down."

"You don't believe me, do you?"

"Of course I do. Just try to relax."

Maggie's bottom lip quivered. He had seen her, seen the two of them sitting here dining together. My God, he had probably witnessed their kiss. It felt as if someone had just punched her in the gut. She was going to be sick, right here at this table in the quaint Italian restaurant.

"Maggie. Are you okay? Talk to me."

She attempted to swallow back her fear. "I...I'm okay."

"You're shaking. You're far from okay." R.J. steadied her trembling hands. "I won't let him hurt you. Don't you trust me?"

She chose her words carefully. "I believe that you will try to keep me safe. Of course I trust you, R.J."

"But?"

"But—it's him I don't trust. His head isn't screwed on right. Something is wrong with him."

"And thank God you're away from him."

It wasn't that easy. It couldn't be. "You didn't see that look in his eyes." It made her blood run cold, just thinking about the cold, hard stare.

"What would you like to do? Should we go to the police? Tell them he's following you around?"

Right. She would be laughed out of the station. "He hasn't broken the law. There's no law against looking into a restaurant at your ex-girlfriend."

"You have a point there. But there must be something we can do." R.J.'s hand rested on his chin.

"That's the thing. I don't think there's a damn thing we can do. I feel like a sitting duck."

He reached for her hand across the table. Maggie flinched, pulling away from him. "Don't. He could see us."

R.J. sat up straight and placed his cloth napkin on the table. "And what is he going to do, Maggie? This is kind of crazy. I won't hide my feelings for you, run around like we're having a secret affair. We're not doing anything wrong."

He was right. He was so right. But R.J. wasn't there with her when she was alone at her place in the middle of the night when she heard the wind howling outside her door. R.J. couldn't possibly understand how she locked every single door and window, rechecking each night before going to bed.

"I need you to support me here. For now, I want to be careful."

Her gut cried out for caution. She believed strongly in her feelings. Now wasn't the time to turn her back on intuition.

R.J. sat back in his chair, his mouth turned into a frown. "Fine. We do it your way. For now. If anything else happens though, your ex-boyfriend is going to get a visit from me."

Her intuition kicked into full gear once more. It was telling her that now she didn't have only herself to worry about, but also the safety of R.J.

"ARE YOU SURE you don't want me to come in?" They were outside her place and R.J.'s eyes pleaded with her. Maggie just wanted to put an end to this day, wake up with a fresh start. But looking at her handsome friend standing before her, she wavered.

"I don't know. I'm kind of tired." She glanced over her shoulder, searching for any dark figures out there in the night.

"He's not here. I'm with you, right here by your side."

"Okay, R.J."

"How about I come in for just a few minutes, make sure you're settled in safely? This is part of my job, you know. I promised to keep you safe from harm." He drew closer, wiggling his eyebrows.

Maggie felt her resolve start to fade. "Who's going to keep me safe from you?" she giggled.

He leaned closer, kissing her softly. Her heart swelled and then she remembered they were out here in plain sight, for anyone to see.

"Come inside." She unlocked her door and pulled him inside. Before she had a chance to take off her coat or put her purse down, R.J. pressed her against the kitchen wall.

"Is this okay? Nobody can see us now." He kissed her more deeply, stirring feelings in her that had been dormant before meeting him. Where had this guy been her whole life? She was just happy she had found him.

"R.J." She needed to know if he felt the same way.

"What? What's the matter?" He smoothed her face with his hands, his eyes wide with concern.

"Nothing. It's okay. I just want to know if you're feeling this. Are you feeling the same thing?"

"You mean, this… between us?" He kissed her bottom lip, tugging at it with his mouth.

"Yes."

"You'd better believe it." He silenced her with his kiss.

CHAPTER FIFTEEN

Naomi

TODAY WOULD PROVE to be the most difficult part of their research. Ryan had expressed some concern about intruding on Maggie's parents. He worried that their presence and questions would stir up raw feelings.

"I see what you're saying, but just think, if we solve this mystery, they can finally get closure and see justice done."

"But what if her drowning was truly an accident and we're bringing all this to light for no reason? What then?"

"I trust my feelings. Something's off here and I'm rarely wrong. It's a chance we're going to have to take."

"Fine. You win. But I'm staying in the car."

She turned to face him. "Are you serious?" He was starting to piss her off. "Are you or are you not part of this team?"

"I am half of this team, and therefore, I get to make decisions too. We compromise on this one. Question her parents, but I'll sit this one out. It's too painful for me to see her parents, to look at the hurt in their eyes."

"Fine, Ryan. Fine." She pulled her car up to the address written on the Post-it note. This was it. Before she could change her mind, she slammed the car into park and opened the car door without even glancing at Ryan.

His words must have been getting to her, because she felt anxious as she pressed on the doorbell. What if this was the wrong thing to do? What if by rehashing the events of

93

Maggie's death, she only brought more pain?

Justice. She had to remember that the justice would be well worth it.

Taking in a deep breath and then releasing it, she pressed firmly on the doorbell once more. She could feel her heart race steadily.

A sweet-faced brunette opened the door. Upon looking closer, Naomi saw deep frown lines.

"Hi. Can I help you?"

Naomi stumbled on her words. "I... um. My name is Naomi and I'm a local writer."

A tall, balding man came up behind the woman. She could see the dark circles etched under his eyes. She wondered when the two had last gotten a good night's sleep. She doubted they ever would.

"What's this about?"

Naomi met the man's gaze. Perhaps Ryan was correct in feeling this was the wrong thing to do. It was too late now, though.

"It's about your daughter." Naomi could see the grim exchange between the mother and father. The man placed a firm hand in his wife's shoulder.

"What do you want from us?" the woman spoke.

"Can I come in please?" Naomi turned to glance at Ryan sitting in the car. His eyes were averted to the side.

"I don't think this is a good idea," Mr. Field responded quickly.

"Let her come in. Please." Mrs. Field turned to face her husband.

She half expected to be thrown out on her face, but to her surprise, she was invited into their home.

"Come sit down, please." Mrs. Field led the way to a small living area.

"Thank you. Thank you both." She glanced at Mr. Field but he avoided eye contact.

"Can I get you something to drink, dear?"

"No, thank you, Mrs. Field. I promise I won't take up too much of your time." How did one even begin a topic like the one she planned to deliver?

"Like I said, I'm a writer. I live out near the cemetery." This wasn't going to be easy. Maggie's father clutched his wife's hand.

"I don't know how to tell you this. I know it's going to sound crazy but..."

"But, you think there's foul play involved."

"Yes, Mrs. Field. Oh my God, I can't believe you just said that. Do you mind me asking why you feel that way?"

"Honey, this isn't healthy for you. We agreed to let this rest." Mr. Field stood to pace the room.

"I'm sorry, Mr. Field, but if I didn't feel strongly about this, I would never bother you."

"She didn't know anyone with a boat, for one thing."

Naomi nodded, waiting for the woman to continue.

"Another thing? She was a strong swimmer. I'm not buying this story. Pieces of it just don't fit. Do you know what I'm saying?"

"I do. I know exactly what you're saying. That's why I'm here."

"Wait a minute here. First of all, with all due respect, honey, Maggie could have had friends we weren't aware of, we don't know that she wasn't out on a boat. And Naomi, is it?" He turned to face Naomi now. "Why would a writer suddenly develop an interest in a story that's been cold now for years?"

"Mr. Field, if I told you, I'm not sure you'd believe me."

"Try me."

"Okay. I recently moved into the house that borders the cemetery and I walk out there sometimes." Naomi figured she could skip the part where Zelda pranced over Maggie's grave.

"I developed a particular curiosity over Maggie's story. I was drawn to her, if you will."

"Oh, come *on*."

"Let her finish," Mrs. Fields interjected.

"There's more." This would be the difficult part. "I've seen things, heard things."

"Like what?"

"Mr. Field, Mrs. Field? Do you believe in ghosts?"

"Okay, that's it. You've said enough here." Mr. Field walked toward the edge of the living room. "Time to go." He pointed his finger toward the door.

Naomi glanced at Maggie's mother, hoping she would intervene. Her mother's face appeared ashen, still.

"I said, time's up."

It was no use. She had tried and had only succeeded in upsetting these two struggling people.

"Wait," Mrs. Field spoke softly at first and then raised her voice. "Tom, let her stay."

"Virginia, please."

"Let her stay." Virginia Field met her gaze directly. "Sit."

With some hesitation, Mr. Field finally took a seat beside his wife on the couch. Naomi was seated in a chair across from them.

"I believe. I believe in ghosts. I believe you, Naomi. Please tell me, what has she said, done?"

Mr. Field placed his head in his hands.

"Nothing other than moving things around, showing her form at times."

"It's Maggie, isn't it?" Mrs. Field leaped to her feet, grabbing a photograph from above her fireplace. "Here's a picture of her. Is this the woman you saw?"

Naomi's heart broke at the look of hope in the mother's eyes. She glanced down at the picture of Maggie T. Field. She took in the smiling blonde woman with clear blue eyes. Maggie had been a stunning, beautiful woman, just as she had imagined.

"I don't know. I haven't seen her face. I can only assume it is." Naomi's mind went to the image of blonde hair fading into the night near Maggie's headstone. "I'm pretty sure she's trying to tell me something, or maybe she's asking for closure. I haven't quite figured out what she's trying to tell me."

"Why wouldn't she come here? Why not to her own parents?" At least Mr. Field was talking now. "I mean, I'm not saying I believe you, but let's just say I believed in ghosts. Why you?"

"That I'm not sure about. Maybe because I'm a writer? One theory is that she wants me to write her story, therefore giving her closure. Another reason may very well be the close proximity of my house to the cemetery."

"Yes. I could see any of those reasons. What are we going to do?" Mrs. Field gazed at Naomi with hopeful eyes.

"For one, I'm trying to gather facts concerning the accident. That's another reason I'm here. My friend Ryan and I are investigating your daughter's accident, and we came upon a dead end at the police station."

"You had the pleasure of meeting Officer Frank then?"

It was the first time Naomi had seen Mr. Field crack a smile. "Yes, Mr. Field, and let me assure you, it was no pleasure."

That earned a chuckle from him. "Call me Tom."

"Thank you, Tom. Is there any possibility you guys could put some more pressure on Officer Frank? I get the sense that he's not giving up all of the information from that day."

"We could try again, I suppose. But back when the investigation was open, he was very firm in his belief that it was an accident," Mrs. Field offered.

"Yes, I was told the same. Still, I feel like he's hiding something." Naomi bit her lip.

Tom glanced back and forth between Naomi and his wife. "You both feel the same about Officer Frank? Honey, did you get the impression he was keeping something from us?"

"I do now. At the time, I just remember feeling that he was a real ass."

"Virginia!"

Naomi got the sense that Mrs. Field didn't swear often.

"I think it's pretty clear we all feel the same." Naomi chuckled as she watched the exchange between Maggie's parents. These two held such love for their daughter, for one another.

"So let's make a plan. How about we shake up Officer Frank, and if we're still not pleased with his efforts, let's try to get another officer on the case," Tom suggested.

"It's a plan. We'll keep in touch. If anything comes up, anything at all, give me a call."

"Of course, dear. Same with you. If your spirit over there says anything to prove she's Maggie, please let us know," Virginia said.

"Without a doubt." Naomi fumbled through her purse and scribbled her cell number down on a Post-it note that she kept handy. "Here's my number. Don't hesitate to call."

Mr. Field rattled off his home number and both of their cell numbers. She stood to leave, glancing around the house once more. She could almost imagine Maggie playing here as a small child. A home filled with love and warmth.

"Naomi?" Virginia moved toward her and wrapped her in a hug. "Thank you for caring and listening when no one else would."

Tears pooled in Naomi's eyes. She vowed then and there that she wouldn't give up on Maggie.

Not now.

CHAPTER SIXTEEN

Naomi

RYAN WAS QUIET the entire ride back to the parking lot of the coffee shop. She understood why he felt uncomfortable involving Maggie's parents in their investigation, but after she had shared the outcome, he should have felt better.

The parking lot was busier now that it was getting close to lunchtime. Naomi turned to face Ryan.

'What is it?"

"I think it was a mistake to get their hopes up, to bother them. I'm sorry, but this isn't sitting right with me."

"So, what do you suggest? We drop it?"

"All evidence points toward the incident being an accident, Naomi. You're grasping at straws and now you've dredged up painful memories for her parents."

She didn't know how to respond to him. She had to put it out there, had to know if he wanted to bail. "Then go. I'm used to working on my own anyway."

Ryan's eyes shimmered with emotion. "That's it? That's what you want?"

"It's what *you* want. First the romance is gone, now your sense of adventure has all but diminished too." She turned her face so he wouldn't see her tears forming.

"Dammit, Naomi. Dammit!" He slammed his hand against the car door, his emotional reaction startling her. "Don't you see? I'm worried about you. I care for you. A lot."

She faced him once more as he reached over to wipe a tear from her cheek. Leaning toward her, Ryan kissed her mouth. His kiss left her wanting more.

"Thank you, Ryan. That was nice."

"If you're going to continue this crazy crusade, I have no choice but to follow."

This time *she* kissed him.

HER MIND WAS full with the events of the day. Now that Maggie's parents were on board and had similar doubts about their daughter's death, Naomi's drive had increased. This was now a mission of sorts and she wouldn't rest until Maggie was at peace.

Those damn dreams continued. Each time, she ran as if her life was in danger. It was unsettling. Still, Naomi wondered if the dreams would stop if she reached closure with Nick. But was it Nick that was seeking closure, or was it Maggie?

Or was it both?

Movement from the cupboard in the kitchen startled Naomi. Thinking it must be Maggie at play again, she advanced toward the cupboard and opened it. Zelda flew out in a frenzy.

"Zelda! How on Earth did you get in there?"

Naomi hadn't even opened up the cabinet that morning before she left to meet Ryan. You know what? She didn't even want to begin to imagine the circumstances.

"Whatever the two of you have been up to today, leave me out of it. I have enough to deal with." Zelda meowed a quick response to her comment before sprinting upstairs.

This time the noise sounded from across the room, near the kitchen sink. The faucet had been turned on, water flowing freely. "What the…"

Naomi walked over to shut the faucet off, thinking that this spirit had been becoming increasingly active over the past few weeks. Light from outside the window caught her eye. Someone was sitting in a car that was parked across from her house-someone who appeared to be a man. The light could have been coming from a cell phone or something in the man's car. What was he doing, just sitting there? His face lifted and Naomi fell back against the table.

Nick.

Even though she couldn't be sure it was him in the darkness, it hit her that the car was the same model Nick owned.

Naomi walked toward the window near the sink once more, steadying her shaking legs. He was gone. He must have seen her looking at him from the window. What could he possibly want after this amount of time had gone by? If she had attempted to speak with him earlier, would he still be here spying from his car window?

But why show up now? Why had he started lurking around?

Unless.

A sweeping feeling of fear washed over her. Unless he had been doing it all along, and she had been oblivious to it.

Her first instinct was to bolt. Just like she did in her dreams.

Taking a steadying breath, she reached for her cell phone with trembling hands. Ryan. He would know what to do.

Ryan's cell rang as she held her breath. *Come on, pick up.* The sudden knock on the door startled her, causing her cell phone to drop to the floor.

"Shoot." She kept her call connected to Ryan, although it was still ringing. Edging toward the door carefully, she prayed it wasn't Nick. Her heart pounded furiously as she stood before her front door.

"Who is it?" Her voice squeaked.

"It's Bryce."

Oh my God. Relief flowed through her. She allowed her heart rate to slow down a moment before opening the door.

"Wow. Are you okay?"

Naomi smoothed a hand through her hair, certain it was a mess.

"Yes, I am now."

"What happened?"

Realizing that she hadn't invited Bryce in, she took hold of his arm and pulled him inside. "Come in." She noticed that Holly wasn't by his side.

"I can only come in for a second. My buddy John is at my house watching Holly. I had to work late and I came home to Holly being sick. She's running a fever and I'm embarrassed to admit I ran out of medicine."

"Oh."

"Would you mind terribly if I asked you to watch Holly, just for a few minutes, while I run to the pharmacy? John would do it but he's already late for his daughter's chorus performance. He doesn't want to miss it."

He was rambling. He must be worried sick about Holly. "Of course. Let's go." Naomi reached for her jacket, her own worries momentarily forgotten.

She walked beside Bryce, glad to escape the drama of her house for the time being.

"I cannot tell you how much I appreciate your help."

"Anytime." He led her up the pebbled road to his large farmhouse. She wondered if he had rented out just a section of the house or if he and Holly had access to the entire dwelling.

He led her inside as she glanced around.

"Wow. This house is amazing." She took in the old crown molding and dark hardwood floors.

"I agree. I think I must mention it to John nearly every day."

"Do you have plans to buy it one day?" She could only imagine what a home like this would cost.

"Oh, hardly. This place would sell for a fortune, and honestly, it's way too big for just Holly and me." It was a large home.

"I think this just may be my dream home." Naomi couldn't stop staring at the charming seating built into the window, the window frames, the built-in bookcases that adorned the walls.

"Yeah. Me, too." He chuckled.

A blond-haired man appeared from the stairway. "Hey. You must be Naomi." He extended his hand. "I'm John, it's nice to meet you."

"Nice to meet you too, John. I was just admiring your beautiful home."

"Ah, this old thing?" John laughed. "It was left to my wife's family. Although gorgeous, it requires a ton of upkeep, and it's way too big for us. We're just biding our time before we sell."

"Oh, no. You're not selling it any time soon, are you?" Bryce and his daughter had only just moved in. She would hate to see them uprooted so quickly.

"Don't worry, the plan is long term. Besides, Bryce here has already been working hard at getting this place in tip-top shape so when the time does come, the house will be in prime selling condition."

"You're handy around the house?" She directed her question to Bryce.

"I can manage."

"Oh, he's just being humble. Bryce here could make his own home from bottom to top if he put his mind to it."

"If you ever run into any trouble over there, I'd be happy to lend a hand," Bryce offered.

"Thank you, I'll keep that in mind."

"Anyway, I've got to get going. My daughter has a chorus performance." He extended his hand. "It was nice to meet you Naomi."

"Yes, I hope you're not too late getting to the concert."

John smiled widely. "The concert isn't for another hour, so I think I'll be fine."

Glancing at Bryce, she saw his cheeks flush. Naomi's own face felt warm.

Once John had closed the door behind him, Bryce placed his hands in his pockets. "He...he had said earlier that he was running behind."

"No, it's okay, Please don't explain. I'm happy to help." She wasn't sure what to make of his admission. Why had he stated earlier that John was late?

He nodded his head, brown eyes crinkled with his warm smile. "Good. Well, I have to check on Holly quickly, and then I promise I won't be long."

"Okay."

Naomi waited until Bryce returned from upstairs, taking a moment to wander around the cozy living room. Knickknacks filled the narrow shelving on top of the wide fireplace. Someone had decorated this home with love and care. A small wood figurine of a cat caught her eye. Picking it up, she turned the figure over in her hand.

"That's Holly's favorite."

She jumped at the sound of his voice. "Oh. I'm sorry. I was just looking around."

He approached her as she placed the small cat back on the mantle.

"Here." He gave the cat back to her, placing it gently in her hand. His touch startled her. From behind her, his hand remained over hers as he showed her the delicate carvings on the wood figure.

"Look. You can even see the tiny whiskers."

"That's amazing." For reasons unknown, her chest thumped wildly. Time stalled as she felt his strong presence. His chest touched her back and she closed her eyes for a moment.

"Where did you get this from?" She was the first to break the silence.

"I made it."

"You did? This is incredible."

"Thank you. I started making them as a hobby, back when I was in high school. I made a few bucks here and there, but mostly I made the figures for my own pleasure. It's relaxing, you know."

She didn't dare turn to look up at him. She wasn't sure what would happen if she did. "How many did you make?"

"Total? I'd say about a hundred, give or take."

A hundred. She gulped. Placing it back on the shelf, she stepped away from him.

"I think I should be getting that medicine. Holly's sleeping, so she'll be no trouble. Make yourself at home. There's some hot cocoa and some wine in the fridge."

She laughed at that. "What kind of babysitter would I be if I drank wine on duty?"

"Well then you can wait for me to return, and we'll share a glass together." He grabbed his jacket and smiled.

"Sure. That sounds nice."

"Let me get a fire going here before I leave." She watched in silence as Bryce tended to the task. He leaned over to light the fire and grab the poker and then gazed up at her with a lopsided grin. "Feeling warmer in here?"

She swallowed.

What was wrong with her?

"I'll be back before you know it." He closed the door behind him as Naomi tried to make sense of what had just happened between them.

CHAPTER SEVENTEEN

Maggie

WHERE WAS THE *time going? The warm days of summer were slipping by. Maggie wished she could still time, preserve the days of happiness spent by R.J's side. If only her ex would stop calling and hanging up. Although he didn't speak, she knew it was him. Who else could it be? She thought she had seen him once in town, but then when she turned the corner, he was gone.*

R.J. had tried to figure out where the hang-ups were coming from, but the caller had blocked his or her number.

Coincidence or not?

Maggie didn't believe in coincidences. There was no way to prove that her ex was making the calls, so reporting him was not an option. She had to be careful at the mention of these calls around R.J. because it seemed the closer she and R.J. became, the less tolerant he was over these hang-ups. The last thing she needed was for R.J to get into a confrontation with an unstable man. It would only make matters worse.

Even her fear of heights was improving since she had let R.J. into her life. They had walked the breathtaking cliffs overlooking the Hudson River many times together, her courage increasing with each visit to the cliffs. R.J. would encourage her to venture out just a bit further each time. She wasn't foolish enough to ever get dangerously close, but it felt good to be able to peer down the cliff, even if her legs still wobbled.

When R.J. called that day and asked her to go for a late summer walk at the cliffs, she was more than happy to oblige.

Naomi

DURING THE TIME he had been gone to the pharmacy, Naomi had located at least five more wooden figures. There were some more cats, a wolf, and a horse. She wondered where the remaining figures were. She imagined he had given some to friends, family, and then there were the ones he had sold.

Thinking back to her recent interaction with Bryce, Naomi was still stumped. How could he have brought forth such a reaction from her? She was with Ryan. She was happy with Ryan.

Or was she?

Yes, overall, yes.

So what if their relationship had suffered a bit in the romance department lately? Since their discussion, things had been a bit better.

Then what was with the way her heart raced when Bryce had touched her hand? The way she couldn't breathe when he was standing so close behind her. And why had he lied about John being in a rush?

Bottom line: being here alone with him was a bad idea. When Bryce returned, she would make up a reason to return home.

Home. Hm. Returning home to a haunted house with a most-likely-murdered spirit didn't seem so appealing right now, not when this warm living room with a roaring fireplace stood before her. Oh, and don't forget the psycho ex-boyfriend spying on her through her kitchen window.

Staying here was definitely the safer option.

Or was it?

Still deliberating, she paced the hardwood floors. She could remain here but keep her distance. Or maybe she

107

should go home. She had to return home at some point anyway.

"Everything okay?"

"Oh my God. How do you sneak up on me like that without me knowing?" He had twice succeeded in startling her in the course of only a half an hour.

"I'm sorry. Next time I'll shout my presence before sneaking up on you," he laughed as he approached. "How's Holly? Did she wake up?"

"Nope. Everything was fine."

"Good. Now I have medicine for tomorrow. Thank you, Naomi. I really appreciate you coming over and helping me out."

It sounded as if he was going to call it a night. As much as she was looking forward to that glass of wine, this was probably for the best.

"No problem. Have a good night, Bryce." Naomi grabbed her jacket from the table and headed for the door.

"Whoa. Was it something I said? What happened to sharing a glass of wine?"

"Oh. I just figured you must be tired."

"For the record, Naomi. I'm never too tired for a glass of wine. Especially in good company."

She blushed. "Okay." Slowly, she placed her jacket back on the table and followed Bryce to the kitchen.

The room was warm and inviting. She could imagine family dinners, complete with laughter and good conversation, taking place here. It looked like something right out of the house and home magazines.

"You like Pinot Noir?" He held the bottle of wine in the air.

"It's one of my favorites."

"Me, too."

Watching him pour the wine was almost as much fun as looking at him preparing the fire earlier.

"What shall we toast to? New friends?"

"Sounds good to me." Naomi held her glass up and touched it to his. The wine went down smoothly.

"I was thinking about something on the way to the store. I'm sorry, I forgot to ask what had you so startled earlier when I came to your house."

"It's a long story. A very long story."

"Well, we've got the time, and we've got the wine. What do you say we settle in near the fireplace?"

She liked his sense of humor. She'd have to remember that line about time and wine; she would definitely use that one again.

Now Naomi had to decide how much to share with Bryce. It might not be a great idea to spring both the ghost and her ex-boyfriend on him in one sitting. Deciding on the topic of Nick, she sat on the couch beside Bryce, ready to begin.

"I have an ex-boyfriend named Nick." She glanced at Bryce, who nodded for her to continue.

"He has some emotional problems and our relationship became strained. I'm so embarrassed to even admit I fell into his trap." Naomi placed her head down.

"Hey," Bryce said, lifting her head with his hand. "We've all got baggage. Just wait until it's my turn. Guarantee you'll feel much better after hearing about my ex." He lowered his voice when he mentioned his ex. Naomi was pretty sure he was the kind of man who would never bash Holly's mother within hearing distance of the little girl.

"That does make me feel better." Realizing how it sounded, she cringed. "Sorry."

"No worries," Bryce chuckled. "But that story is for another time, another place." He nodded toward the staircase. Naomi understood.

"He was jealous, controlling, manipulative."

"Sounds like a hell of a guy."

"Yeah. Anyway, he's having a difficult time letting go."

Bryce's eyebrows scrunched in concern. "How so?"

"He promised me that no matter what, he wouldn't let me go. At first there were text messages, hang-ups. It got better, for a while."

"But now?"

"Now, I'm worried. Tonight, right before you showed up at my door, he was parked outside me house, just sitting there." She shivered at the memory of his dark form.

"What? But that's crazy. What kind of car does he drive?"

"It's a dark blue sedan, four door."

"I'm going to keep an eye out for him. Tell me more. What does he look like?"

"Brown hair and eyes. Average build."

"That's a pretty average description, but I'll watch for him. Do you think this guy is dangerous?"

She did. "Yes, I'm afraid I do."

"And he hasn't done anything to break the law, right?"

"He's also smart. If I went to the police, they wouldn't do anything. He hasn't broken any laws. The parking area across from my house isn't technically my property."

Bryce leaned over and took hold of Naomi's hand. Her heart sped up. There it was again, that feeling she got whenever he touched her. She pulled back slightly.

"I'm sorry. I wasn't…"

"It's fine. I guess my nerves are just a bit jumpy." Naomi glanced away.

Bryce leaned forward, taking hold of her hand once more. This time she let him hold it.

"I will not let this man hurt you, Naomi. Call me, any time, no matter how late."

"Thank you. That's very kind of you," Naomi managed. She gazed up at him.

Bryce moved closer until his face was inches from hers. "I haven't had much practice at this, not since Genna." He leaned closer still.

Whatever was happening here, she couldn't make sense

of it. Her mind shouted that she was dating Ryan, that this was not appropriate. But her heart screamed for her to kiss him, that nobody, Ryan included, had ever made her feel such emotion.

Bryce was inches from her. He moved closer, his warm eyes locked on hers.

"Stop." She pulled away, wringing her hands together.

Bryce frowned, his cheeks flushed. "I am so sorry. I hadn't planned on that."

"No. No, it's me." She should get out of here, the wine was going to her head.

"My God, I should have asked. Are you involved with someone?" Bryce sat back, staring at her.

"Yes. I think so, that is." Of course she was, but the truth was that she didn't know which direction she and Ryan were heading. Until she figured it out, she needed to stay away from men such as Bryce.

"I had no idea. I feel like a fool."

Naomi recalled him saying that he hadn't had much practice in the dating department. She believed him. Bryce was no player; he was a single dad trying to find his way.

"Don't. I'm the one who feels like a fool. Truth be told, I'm not sure where my current relationship is headed, but until I figure it out, it just feels wrong."

Bryce nodded his head firmly. "You have no idea how happy it makes me to hear you say that."

What had his ex-wife done to him?

"Tell you what. We remain friends. How does that sound? I don't want any awkward feelings between us." He extended his hand toward her. She reached for it and held on a moment too long.

"Friends."

Naomi stood and smoothed her shirt. She walked over to the small table to grab her jacket. "It's been nice. Thank you for the wine."

"And thank you for keeping an ear out for Holly." He

stood to walk her to the door.

Bryce led her outside and walked her halfway to her property. "Everything looks okay. I don't think that Nick fellow is lurking around anywhere."

"Thanks for walking me out. Have a good night, Bryce." She turned to leave, her mind still on the near kiss.

She had walked for a moment or so before she heard his voice calling out to her.

"Naomi?"

She paused, gazing back at him.

"If you weren't dating someone, would you have let me kiss you?"

He stopped her dead in her tracks. Good thing for the darkness, because her face flushed warm. There was no appropriate response. If he was standing any closer, he might have heard her heart pounding in her chest.

"Good night, Bryce."

CHAPTER EIGHTEEN

Naomi

SHE CLOSED THE door gently behind her, taking a moment to stand and think about her evening. It had been one of the best nights she had in a while. If only she and Ryan could capture the passion that was thick in the air back at Bryce's house. Had they ever been able too? Not that long ago Ryan had kissed her with such intensity, but the air still hadn't been charged with so much energy.

"Oh, what am I going to do?"

As if Zelda understood her dilemma, she meandered over, pushing against her legs. Naomi scooped her up, pressing her close. Swaying gently, Naomi closed her eyes. What was that sound? At first she wasn't sure if it was her imagination, but the eerie crying grew louder.

Was it crying or was it singing? Naomi couldn't be sure. She hugged Zelda tighter, feeling her scalp prickle. Zelda squirmed out of her embrace, howling.

What was that?

In a trance, Naomi followed the sound toward the bay window in the next room. There, sitting before her, was the vision of a blonde woman, her face covered by her own long hair. If only she could just make out her face, Naomi could see for sure if it was Maggie.

The melody shifted, growing even more melancholy with each breath. Mesmerized, Naomi watched as this spirit stood, facing her. Naomi still couldn't see her face.

Naomi couldn't have run if even if she had wanted to. She had to be sure. She needed to know right here, right now, if this was her.

"Maggie?"

The figure stopped short, not moving.

She tried again. "Maggie, is that you? Please. Show me your face. I want to help you."

Still no movement from the spirit, but a faint cry could be heard. Naomi attempted to rub her chills away. She had asked for this, encouraged this interaction with the ghostly woman.

"Maggie. It's you, isn't it? What do you want?"

The apparition drew closer, slowly making its way toward Naomi. She could stay or she could bolt. Her legs were glued to the floor, as heavy as lead. An unearthly white met her gaze. The ghost lifted her arm, her fingers spreading out, reaching out to Naomi.

She gasped for breath, tried to steady her pulsing heart. Naomi squeezed her eyes shut as she felt the ghost touch her face, turn it to the side. Naomi cried out, fear pumping through her body. For the first time she wondered if this spirit was capable of violence, capable of harming her.

It was time. She needed to see her face.

Opening her eyes slowly, Naomi gasped. Clear blue eyes met her. Eyes that held so much sorrow it nearly brought Naomi to her knees. She was stunning, even in her ghostly form.

"Maggie," Naomi whispered. "My God, it's you."

Before her eyes, Maggie's face transformed from hauntingly beautiful to an agonized gray. Her sockets were hollow. Sharp cheekbones melted to a skeleton form.

Naomi closed her eyes tightly, hoping to block out the grotesque image before her. She could feel the frigid air. The ghost was still close, crying an earth- shattering howl. Mentally, Naomi counted to ten.

Anything to attempt to take her mind off the horrifying

image before her.

Once the wailing ceased, Naomi breathed. When she couldn't stand waiting it out another moment, Naomi dared a look.

The air was still chilled, but warmer than it had been seconds before. Maggie was gone. She knew exactly where the spirit had gone. She hustled to peek out the window. A white shadowy form floated through the graveyard then disappeared.

One important piece of the puzzle was now confirmed—even though it had been horrifying to uncover the fact.

The ghost was indeed Maggie T. Field.

Now the rest of the investigation could fall into place. Naomi grabbed her cell, but then looked at the time. It was after eleven p.m., too late to call Maggie's parents to inform them of the incident. Her heart still pounded furiously.

It was not too late to call Ryan.

He picked up the call after several rings. "Hey, Naomi."

"Oh, I'm glad I didn't wake you. I figured you might be asleep."

"Nah. Sleep doesn't come easily for me anymore."

She supposed his active mind must have a difficult time shutting down. Honestly, it was a stretch to even imagine him sleeping.

"I have something important to tell you. Very important."

"Well, are you going to tell me or not?"

She waited a moment before continuing. "It's Maggie."

"Excuse me?"

"My ghost. I've confirmed the fact that it's Maggie. I *saw* her, Ryan. *Saw her.* Do you hear what I'm saying?"

"Whoa. Slow down. First of all, I thought you didn't even know what she looked like."

"Yeah, I may have forgotten to tell you that I saw her photograph when I was at her parents' house. I saw the ghost's face tonight and it was Maggie. Without a doubt."

He blew out a breath. "Wow. Are you sure?"

"I just said I was."

"So now what? Did she say anything?"

"No, she didn't. But she was crying, singing a sad melody."

"What were the words to the song? Could you understand anything?"

Naomi thought back to the melancholy voice. "No. It was more like humming, then wailing. Listen, I think we need to put more pressure on the police department. I felt her agony, her sadness. She's trying to tell me something."

"That would have to come from Maggie's parents, though. What we need to do on our end is try to find out who the boyfriend was. Somebody has to know."

That was exactly what they needed to do. Her gut was telling her this had everything to do with the boyfriend.

"Ryan, brilliant idea. Let's jump on that tomorrow." She had an idea. "Let's head back over to the parents' house, ask if we can borrow Maggie's picture and show it around town."

"Good plan. Maggie's parents didn't say anything about the ex-boyfriend when you spoke with them?"

No, they didn't, but she hadn't asked. "No, I just assumed from the news coverage that the parents had never met him. It couldn't hurt to ask though."

"Right. We'll have a full day tomorrow. Have a good night, Naomi. I'll see you in the morning."

"Good night."

Naomi just realized that all of this ghost business and thoughts of Bryce had served the purpose of freeing her mind from worries of Nick.

But now she had another concern.

Her shoulders slumped as she brought her mind back to Ryan.

There had been no talk of missing her, wanting to touch her, kiss her again. Maybe Ryan just wasn't wired in a romantic way for the long run. And if he wasn't, was that okay? After feeling firsthand with Bryce what attraction could do to her, it was an important question.

Were she and Ryan better off being just friends?

CHAPTER NINETEEN

Maggie

PREPARING FOR HER position at the college was both exciting and stressful. There was so much she needed to do to get ready. Books to order, plans to write, aligning her plans to the curriculum. This was an important step in her career. If she aced this experience, perhaps she could get a position at a more prestigious school. Like the one by the river.

When R.J. had called earlier, offering to take her hiking up on the cliffs, she probably should have declined. She had too much to do.. But she and R.J. were growing closer, much closer, and she justified her decision by telling herself it would be good to take a much needed break.

Her ex-boyfriend hadn't let up. Dead air and then the hang up. Public outings with R.J. were still few and far between, as her anxiety was still high. She wouldn't feel comfortable if her ex spotted them together again. That kiss back at the restaurant still played in her mind. She didn't need to give him anything else to fuel his fire.

More than once Maggie had thought to involve her parents, but each time she spoke to them they had seems so happy. She didn't wish to add stress to their lives.

The doorbell sounded. R.J. Shoot, she wasn't even ready yet. Checking the clock on the wall in her tiny office, she sighed. Losing track of time was somewhat of a problem for her lately. R.J. was always punctual; she wondered how he did it.

"R.J." She smiled at the sight of him, standing there in his green T-shirt and jeans.

"Ready to go?"

"Just give me a minute, okay? I kind of lost track of time."

Hurrying to her bedroom, she smiled to herself. R.J. was special. He was what her mother called "a catch." One day soon she would break the news that they were more than just friends. Her parents had met him a handful of times, and she knew they would definitely approve.

Maggie did her best to rush. A day of play and then back to having her head in the books. It seemed like a fair exchange.

"Ready?"

"Wow. You look amazing."

She blushed. "I'm just wearing jeans and an old top."

He grabbed her hand, and they headed to the car. Maggie glanced at R.J. as he drove toward the river. He was uncharacteristically quiet.

"You okay?"

"Yes. Now that I'm with you, I am." His wide smile put her at ease.

They arrived at the cliffs, parking in the upper lot. "Ready to conquer your fear of heights again?"

Maggie laughed. "I thought I had already done that the past few times we were up here."

"I suppose that was a start."

"A start? Are you out of your mind?"

"Come on. Let's go."

Maggie opened the door to get out and took a deep breath. The day was spectacular.

"Hey, what are you up to?" Maggie peered into the window of the car.

Reaching into the backseat, he uncovered a picnic basket and a bottle of wine.

"Just a little snack for us."

"You are unbelievably sweet," She blushed as he moved around the car to meet her.

R.J. tickled her side and then pulled her close. He leaned his *head down, kissing her softly on the mouth.*

Maggie closed her eyes and gave in to the deep sensation of R.J.'s kiss. She barely heard the sound of people approaching from the woods.

"Later." R.J. mussed her hair.

"Hold on, I want to grab my cell. Take some pictures, you know?"

Maggie grabbed her cell and slipped it into her back pocket. The parking lot was now empty, except for the sound of a distant car approaching.

R.J. grabbed Maggie's waist, pulling her in for another kiss. "Hey! There's a car coming."

He released her, wiggling his brows. "You're in trouble later. Lots of trouble."

"Promise?" Her heart swelled. She was falling in love with him. It hit her at that exact moment. She had thought she was in love once before, years earlier, but this was different. She was in love. This was true love.

R.J. gazed down at her, his eyes serious. "You bet." He kissed her with more intensity.

The dark car stopped, parked in a spot far from them, but it still made Maggie uneasy to think that someone could be watching them kiss.

"Come on. Let's go."

Naomi

BRIGHT AND EARLY the next morning, Naomi was at Virginia and Tom's door. Ryan said he would catch up with her later, that he had some essays to grade, which was fine. She had spoken with Maggie's parents alone before, and she could do it again.

"Naomi." Virginia Field pulled her in for a quick hug.

Tom was close behind.

"I hope you don't mind me coming back again so soon."

"Like we told you on the phone earlier, it's fine. We're always up by seven a.m. anyway," Tom commented.

Naomi followed them into the kitchen where they had coffee and bagels waiting on the table.

"Hungry?" Tom asked, pulling out a chair for her.

"Famished. Thank you."

"How do you take your coffee, dear?" Virginia placed a spoon on the napkin beside her.

"Milk and sugar. Thank you."

Again, Naomi felt the warmth from this house, from Virginia and Tom. Maggie was blessed to have had such loving parents.

"Now, Naomi. It's not that we don't love visiting with you, but something tells me you have a reason for your visit," Tom stated.

"I was wondering if I could ask you a favor. Could I please borrow Maggie's photograph? I'd like to show it around town, see if it sparks anything."

"Of course. What are you thinking? That someone may have seen something?"

"I don't know, Virginia. You never know. Another thing I wanted to speak with you about was her dating life."

Tom shook his head. "We didn't know much about the man she had been dating. Of course, she was living on her own, but I would have liked to think she would have told us if she were serious about the man. Besides, from what we know, they had broken it off."

Unless she wasn't ready for some reason. "There's nobody else you could think of, no one at all?"

Virginia shook her head firmly. "Not that we were aware of. It was like we told the police. The only odd thing was that she had missed her usual visits to us leading up to her accident."

This grabbed Naomi's attention. She opened her purse

and grabbed her pen and notepad. "Please, go on."

"She would always stop by on Saturday mornings for breakfast. No exceptions. It was our special time."

Naomi's heart sped up. "And how many weeks had she missed? One? More?"

Tom sipped at his coffee. "Oh, at least three or four in a row. Right, honey?"

"Yes. I suppose it was quite a few times she had missed. We asked her if everything was okay and she sounded fine."

"What reason did she give for cancelling?"

"Oh, once or twice she had work to catch up on. Another time she claimed her stomach wasn't feeling well."

This new information must be relevant, somehow. "But it was out of character."

Both parents spoke at once. "Definitely."

"Okay. So let's think. Maybe this *is* about a guy. A guy she became all consumed with?"

Virginia shook her head. "It wasn't like her to shut her family out."

"Unless she wasn't comfortable telling you about him or bringing him here."

Tom bit his lip. "It doesn't sound like our Maggie. Maybe she was just busy, like she said."

Perhaps.

"Wait a minute," Virginia began.

"What is it?"

"I'm sure it's nothing, but she did have a friend. A very good male friend. Nothing romantic was going on between them, though I always thought they would make a great couple."

Why hadn't she mentioned this earlier?

"You met him?"

"A few times, yes. He was quite striking, actually. Tall, dark, and handsome. I used to say he was a real catch."

Naomi's pulse picked up. "What was his name?"

"R.J."

"R.J., okay. What's his last name?" She scribbled his name down on her notepad.

Virginia turned to face her husband. "I don't think she ever mentioned a last name, did she, dear?"

Tom stood to pace the floor. "No, no she didn't. We should have asked her, dammit."

"Now Tom, I don't think it means anything." She frowned slightly, looking down at the floor.

"What is it, Virginia? What's wrong?"

"I'm sure it's nothing, but I just got to thinking that it was odd."

Naomi leaned forward, her senses on high alert. "What? What was odd?"

"R.J. never showed up at any of the services."

That did seem strange, if they were good friends. "Well, did he call you? Reach out to you in any way?"

"No. Nothing."

"We should have insisted upon a last name!" Tom bellowed from across the room, his hands in tight fists.

"No. It wasn't him, he would never have hurt Maggie, I'm sure of it."

"How well did we even know the guy? He showed up with Maggie a few times for breakfast, that's it."

"Tom, you didn't notice the way she spoke of him, the way he looked at her? They cared for one another. He didn't kill her."

Naomi glanced back and forth at the interaction between Maggie's parents. This R.J. may not have killed her... but then again he may have. Just because Virginia didn't sense any foul intentions, on his part, didn't mean a thing. Plenty of people were talented at hiding their dark sides. Just look at Nick in the beginning of their relationship.

This latest piece of information was crucial. Even if he was innocent, Naomi had to find this R.J., because perhaps he could tell them more about Maggie. A good friend would know if there was a boyfriend and if she knew anyone at all who owned a boat.

"Tell me anything else you can remember about R.J. What did he do for a living, where did he live?"

"We don't know. Damn, we don't know a thing about this friend of Maggie's. What kind of parents does that make us?" Tom's face fell.

Naomi walked over to comfort him. She reached up to hug Tom as he sobbed quietly. "You are two of the warmest people I have ever met. Don't you ever question what wonderful parents you were to Maggie. She was a grown woman, you couldn't possibly have known everything about her life."

"It just hurts so much."

"I'm sorry, Tom." She released him and sat back down in her chair next to Virginia. Maggie's mother had her head in her hands. Naomi reached over, placing her hands on top of Virginia's.

Now to tell Maggie's parents about what she had witnessed the night before. This wouldn't be easy.

"I wanted to share something with you. I'll understand if you think I'm crazy, but I saw her last night. Her spirit, that is."

Virginia sat up straight, clutching her chest. "Are you... sure it was her?"

"Positive."

Naomi dared a glance at Tom. She wouldn't be offended if he told her it was time to leave. Instead, his eyes held fresh tears.

She didn't enjoy this part of the investigation.

It killed her.

But it was necessary.

"I'm sorry."

"What did she say? Please, tell us," Virginia pleaded.

"Nothing. But she exposed herself as Maggie and that's very important. Now we know. For certain." Explaining about the howling cries would not be part of this conversation. There were some things best left unsaid.

"Nothing? Did she seem happy?"

She wouldn't lie to them either. "She looked beautiful." That wasn't a lie exactly. She had appeared stunning, even if it had been for the briefest of moments before the horrifying transformation had taken place.

"I'll grab the photo, Naomi. Can you give us some time alone?" Tom stood, walking over to grab the photo from the living room.

"I'm so sorry, Virginia," Naomi whispered.

Virginia reached over and held on to Naomi's hand. "Just give us some justice for Maggie, will you? For reasons unknown, she has chosen you to communicate with. You have the best chance of solving this."

"We'll do our part, head back to the police station and try to get that ass Frank off the case," Tom added as he handed Naomi the framed photo. She looked at Maggie's image once more. Same eyes, same hair. She only wished she could see the same bright smile.

One day, perhaps she would.

CHAPTER TWENTY

Naomi

TALL, DARK, AND handsome? A real catch?

That could be half the male population. Heck, her own boyfriend matched the description.

More determined than ever to seek closure and justice for Maggie, she headed over to the coffee shop. If she was correct, Ryan should already be there.

Yup. His black truck was right there in his usual spot.

With Maggie's picture in hand, Naomi made her way into the shop. A large cup of coffee was waiting for her at the table.

"Thanks, Ryan. Here, this is our Maggie." She handed him the framed photograph.

He studied it carefully, bringing it closer to his face. She had expected a comment about how beautiful she was.

Something. Anything.

His mouth pinched into a frown.

"What's the matter? Did you know her?"

He continued gazing at the photo, a glazed look in his eyes.

"Ryan? Did you know her?"

At last he looked up. "No. I didn't. She just reminds me of someone, I guess."

Naomi's eyes squinted as she looked at Ryan. "Who?"

"Nobody in particular."

She did have one of those fresh-looking faces, like a

cover girl model. Ryan turned his face toward the window.

"Are you okay?"

"Yeah. It's sad."

The fact that he could now place a face to Maggie must be upsetting him. She could understand that. She also wondered how he would react if he had seen Maggie at her worst, like Naomi had the night before.

Now Maggie was real to them both, not just some news article.

"Finish your coffee. We have a lot of work to do today." She took a large swig of her own coffee and slammed the cup down on the table.

'Yes, ma'am." He followed her out the door.

"You driving?" She turned her head to speak to Ryan. "I need to take some notes."

"Sure. No problem."

Ryan unlocked his truck with his remote keychain. She hopped into the passenger seat and began scribbling away.

Once or twice Ryan glanced at her, but for the most part, he kept his attention on the road.

"Ryan?" She placed her pen and notepad down on her lap.

"What is it?"

"Nick was parked across the street from my house last night, staring into my window."

"Wait—what did you just say?"

"He was there. At my house."

"Last night? Why the hell didn't you say anything?"

For lots of reasons, lots of distractions, she supposed. "I don't know, I guess with seeing Maggie and all, it wasn't forefront on my mind."

"First of all, we're not positive it was Maggie."

There he went again, questioning her, doubting her. "This has got to stop, Ryan. It *was* Maggie, I'm sure of it. I told you last night, it was the same woman from the photograph."

127

"Your mind could have been playing tricks on you. Your head is so filled with Maggie right now."

Her pulse quickened. Was he serious? "Ryan, I'm going to ask you one more time, are you in or out?'

He sighed and returned his focus to the road.

"Answer me. If you're in, you have to be all in."

"Naomi, I'm in, but I feel like you're heading somewhere you just might not want to be."

"What the heck does that even mean, Ryan?" Her voice rose as she felt heat rising to her cheeks. "Speak English!"

"It *means* that you may very well be heading toward danger. What if she was murdered? Have you even stopped to think of the consequences of your behavior?"

"My behavior? Where do you get off telling me about my behavior? I'm the only one besides Maggie's parents that even gives a crap about what happened to her!"

"Calm down, Naomi," Ryan exclaimed as he pulled the car over to the side of the street. "Lower your voice. If you need me to be all in or all out, I think I'm going to choose out."

"What?"

"You put ultimatums on me, Naomi. You can't do that to people. It's always your way or no way. It's just not fair."

"It is not always my way. I don't do that." But maybe she did, just a bit, when it came to her relationship with Ryan. She didn't like the way he focused on her house, on the property surrounding her house. She didn't like the way he ate, the way he was preoccupied with the history of the area. All of it had been fine in the beginning, but he was so intense. So freaking intense about everything.

Except her.

It hit her, hard, that Ryan was backing away. Not just from the investigation, but from her. From what they once had. Even if it was only for a short period of time, it still stung. There was nothing left here in the romance department. She was kidding herself.

She unbuckled her seatbelt, tears stinging her eyes. Placing her notepad and pen in her tote bag, she hugged the bag close to her chest.

"So this is it for us I guess."

He reached over and placed his hand over her arm. "Naomi, what are you saying? Just because I don't want to go hunting down a possible murderer doesn't mean I want to stop seeing you."

A bitter laugh escaped. "You don't even really like me as a girlfriend, Ryan. Just admit it to yourself. You and I are better off as friends. You know it and I know it."

"Friends? What are you talking about? I want you as my girlfriend. I..." He stopped mid-sentence and removed his hand from her. Staring at his lap, he sighed.

"You what? You aren't in love with me and you never will be."

He nodded his head as he bit down on his lip.

"Can you honestly say that you love me or may possibly love me in the near future?"

He met her gaze with strained eyes. "Can you?"

Interesting question. "No, Ryan. I can't."

There was nothing left to say here. She was going to lose a good friend and that was what hurt the most right now.

"Good-bye, Ryan." Naomi's hand was on the door.

"Where are you going? You can't just get out in the middle of town. How will you get home?"

"Don't worry about it. I'll call Amy for a ride when I'm finished here."

"About that. I have a bad feeling, a real bad feeling. Would you please reconsider this crusade you're on?"

She couldn't believe he was still harping on the Maggie thing. "Good-bye, Ryan." Naomi stepped out of his truck, slamming the door tight.

He didn't try to stop her again. Walking ahead, her tears flowed freely down her cheeks. At one point, she dared a glance back at him and noticed he was still sitting there, just watching her leave.

129

CHAPTER TWENTY-ONE

Naomi

"Yeah, I've seen her. She used to come in from time to time and have dinner," the waiter stated. He stared intently at the photograph of Maggie. "She sure was pretty."

"Yes, she was."

It was the third place she had been to and so far she had heard almost the exact same thing. They recognized her, they stated she was pretty and what a shame it was that she was gone.

Let's see if this guy says the same thing about her guy friend. "Was she ever with anyone?"

The waiter nodded. "Yes, she was. First time I noticed her, she was here with an average looking guy."

"Average, you say?" This was a new one. "What color hair? How tall?"

"I don't know, maybe the guy was five eleven, six feet?"

"And his hair?" She scribbled down the description under the heading of "average guy."

"What are you, a reporter or something?"

"Or something. What color hair?"

"Brown, I think. Say, I was kind of waiting for the police to come by and ask around, you know?"

"And? They didn't?"

"No, not here at least. But the funny thing is, my buddy works over at one of her old regular places, and they never went there, either. Kind of odd, if you ask me."

"I guess, but they figured it was an accidental drowning and how would the cops know which places she visited?"

"I would think friends and family would offer that information up. I mean, come on. She went to Johnny's on Main at least two or three times a month for dinner. And this whole case stinks, just for the record."

Jotting down the name of the restaurant, she felt her pulse quicken. "Johnny's, you say? What's the name of your friend who works there?"

"Ted. His name is Ted."

"Thank you, you've been a big help." Naomi rushed to the door, her tote bag swinging from her shoulder.

"Wait! Don't you want to hear about the other guy?" he called out to her. "Funny thing about him was that I haven't seen him since."

"Tall, dark, and handsome?" she cried out.

He nodded in agreement as she turned to leave. It was the same story all over town with the other man: same description, and he had never been seen again.

What did it all mean? The average looking guy must have been too average looking to leave a strong impression, because it seemed that no one recalled if he had returned to any of the establishments. But Maggie and her *friend* had both left quite the impression.

Naomi picked up her pace as she made her way to Johnny's on Main Street. She was there once, years ago. It was an Italian place that attracted lots of local townspeople.

The aroma of sauce and garlic filled the air as she opened the door. Just being in this place made her instantly hungry. Ryan would freak if he ever set foot in the door, she figured. Ugh, Ryan. She was starting to miss his companionship already.

"Well, if it isn't my lovely neighbor."

Spinning her head to the side, Naomi threw her hand to her chest. "Oh."

"Hey, there," Bryce commented.

Sitting beside him was an attractive blonde. Why did the woman's presence annoy her?

"Hi, Bryce." She walked over to greet him properly. Both Bryce and the blonde stood up.

"I'm Gail. It's nice to meet you."

Gail's cool gaze fell upon her. "Same here. I'm Naomi."

Bryce's hands went into his jean pockets. "I, um... we were just having lunch." His face flushed a light pink.

"Oh. Well, tell Holly I said hello."

"I will, and she'll be sorry she missed seeing you," Bryce offered.

"Who's Holly?" the blonde questioned.

"She's my daughter, I was just telling you about her."

Blondie shrugged and took a seat at the table. Bryce stood for a moment longer and gazed at Naomi before returning to his own seat.

"I'll see you."

It bothered her to see him sitting with the blonde woman. There. She admitted it. So they were having lunch; what was the big deal? She stole a glance behind her and noted that Bryce's eyes had followed her across the room.

"Can I help you?" A middle-aged man approached her from behind the counter.

"Yes. I hope so. Is Ted here today?" She watched as a man in his twenties hustled by, carrying two plates of pasta.

He called out, "I'm Ted. What can I do for you?"

Naomi held her finger up in the air and stood as he whizzed by. Well, then she would follow him. Ted made his way to Bryce's table. Wonderful.

Following in Ted's footsteps, Naomi avoided eye contact with Blondie and Bryce.

"What can I do for you?" Ted dropped the plates of pasta on the table as Naomi took a step back.

"Is everything okay?" Bryce stood up, glancing at Naomi.

"Yes, it's fine, Bryce. Thank you."

"Are you sure?"

Blondie huffed from her seat. "She said everything is fine."

Bryce ignored his date's comment but sat back down, watching Naomi carefully.

"I have a photo I'd like you to take a look at, please." Naomi grabbed the framed photo from her bag and held it up for Ted to see.

"I know her, that's Maggie."

"Yes, your friend back at Jelly's Café said you did. Please, tell me anything you can."

"Hold on a sec. Can I get you anything else?" Ted asked Bryce and Blondie. Blondie's arms crossed over her chest, her icy glare focused on Naomi.

"No, we're good, thanks," Bryce answered.

"Come over here for a sec. Let's talk." Ted steered Naomi over to a table for two in the back of the room. "Are you a cop or something?"

Taking a seat across from Ted, Naomi took out her notepad and pen. "No, I'm an author. Let's just say I've developed a fascination with Maggie's story."

The sound of a text going off interrupted her train of thought. Reaching down to see who it was, she smiled at the words in the message. It was Ryan, stating that he wanted to speak. She wanted to talk to him, too. They had unfinished business.

"Sorry about that. Tell me what you know about her. Anything and everything, please."

"I thought that finally the police would come to ask some questions, you know? This was one of her favorite restaurants. How could they have missed coming here? I mean, what kind of detectives do they have around here, anyway?"

Tell me about it, she wanted to exclaim. "It's because they think it was an accident." She wrote a reminder to ask Maggie's parents if they had ever shared the name of the restaurant with Officer Frank.

"But obviously you don't." It wasn't a question.

"No, Ted, I don't." She frowned.

"I'm so happy to hear someone say that. I thought everyone had given up on her. I even went to the police when she disappeared. That damn officer assigned to the case wouldn't even hear me out."

"Officer Frank."

"That's the one."

This Officer Frank was proving to be a royal pain. But there was more to his resistance, she was sure of it.

"So tell me, who did she come here with?"

"Well, she had some friends she would come here with. I can't remember their names or anything, but then there was the boyfriend."

"The boyfriend?"

"At least I thought it was. He didn't last long."

"Ted, what did he look like?"

"Brown hair, kind of..."

"Average?" Naomi finished his sentence, sure of his response.

"Yeah, I would say he was average looking."

"Anyone else?" She waited for the next predictable answer to come.

"Yes, this one I'm not sure about. I think he started as a friend but then became more to her."

Interesting. "Ted, if you don't mind me saying, you seem to remember a lot about Maggie."

He blushed. "I... Maggie was a beautiful woman."

Ah, so Ted here had a crush on Maggie. She supposed many men probably had felt the same.

"Yes, yes, she was. What did this man look like?"

"If I were to say the first one was average, this guy was quite the opposite. Maggie and her friend made a striking couple. He was tall, dark and..."

"Handsome," Naomi mumbled.

"Yes, that's right."

"What makes you say they were more than friends?"

Ted fidgeted in his seat and blushed deeply once more. Leaning over, he whispered. "If you had seen the way he kissed her that night, you'd know what I mean."

She placed her pen down and looked Ted squarely in the eye. "When was this?"

"Oh, I'd say not too long before she was killed. They came in a few times after that, but didn't show any major public displays of affection. You could tell, though, that they were still a couple."

"How so?" Naomi scribbled down some notes.

"Well, for starters, the way they looked at each other. I can always tell when a couple is in love. I've seen lots of couples dining here, I should know."

Was this guy just extra perceptive or was there more to him? Studying Ted's face, Naomi couldn't be sure. He had a lot of interest in Maggie, but he could very well be a concerned citizen. She wrote Ted's name on her notepad once more and placed a large question mark beside it.

Stalkers could do crazy things... not saying that Ted was a stalker, but she wasn't ruling anything out at this point.

"Anything else? Could you have possibly overheard anything?"

"Well..." Ted began.

"Ted, please. It's very important."

"Maggie seemed more jumpy, nervous, if you will, the past few times she had been in."

"Tell me what you mean by that. Did she appear to be afraid of Tall, Dark, and Handsome?"

He shook his head firmly. "I don't think so. She was always looking over her shoulder, so to speak. That night they kissed? I overheard her saying that someone was staring at her from the storefront window."

The words couldn't come fast enough from Naomi's head to the paper. Her heart raced as she wrote them down.

This was the first real lead she had gotten.

"What did she say?"

From the way Ted squirmed in his seat, she could tell he was embarrassed to have overheard—or rather eavesdropped—on Maggie's conversation that evening.

"Ted. I get it. You liked her. It's okay. In fact, you have the chance to help her right now. Tell me what she said."

Despite his increased flushing, Ted continued. "I can't recall exactly what she said, but something about a man seeing her, staring at them. The good-looking guy seemed annoyed, like he didn't want to hide his affections for Maggie."

"She was afraid of the other man."

"Yes, it seemed that way."

Nick surfaced to her mind. She had felt the very same way when she and Ryan had started seeing each other. That day in the hardware store, she had been petrified of Nick spotting her with Ryan. She could certainly understand how poor Maggie had felt.

'Thank you, Ted. You've been a big help. If there's anything you remember, even a small detail, please give me a call." She wrote her cell number down on a napkin.

"Thank you. Thank you for helping Maggie," Ted said.

Either Ted was a real good guy, or he was monster. She had yet to determine where he stood in her mind. She liked to believe in the best when it came to people, so she could only hope Ted was playing it straight with her.

Bryce and Blondie were still eating their lunch as Naomi walked out of the restaurant. Giving a quick wave in his direction, Naomi opened the door to the late autumn wind.

CHAPTER TWENTY-TWO

Naomi

WHY WAS BRYCE on her mind when she was in the middle of trying to write Maggie's story, solve Maggie's probable crime, and deal with her break-up with Ryan?

Bryce should be the last thing on her mind right now, but just picturing him on his date, right now with Blondie, irked her.

Darn, she needed to concentrate, not worry about what Bryce was up to. First thing she needed to do was to call Ryan and talk to him. Really hash out what had transpired between them, from start to finish.

It wasn't often that she read people wrong, and she could have sworn she and Ryan were going strong back in the beginning of their relationship.

He stumped her.

"Oh, hell." Reaching into her bag for her cell, she sighed deeply.

"Naomi!"

"Hi, Ryan."

"We need to talk. Can you meet me somewhere?"

Coffee sounded amazing right now. "Let's meet for coffee."

"The usual spot?"

"You got it. Heading over there now."

Feelings were being tossed around in her head, in her heart. When she was around Ryan lately, she felt as close to him as she did with Amy. He was one of her very best friends. But the emotions that she experienced when she was around Bryce had her heart pounding.

What did she want from Ryan? It wasn't fair to lead him on. She would come clean and explain her complicated feelings. It was only right.

One thing for sure, she didn't want to lose Ryan's friendship. Her life would be hollow without him. Could she have her cake and eat it, too? Never being one to like cliché's, Naomi shook her head firmly. She only hoped Ryan would still want to be in her life.

Luckily, the café was only a short walk away from Johnny's. She might even make it there before Ryan for once. With a wide grin on her face, Naomi quickened her pace.

His truck was there, right in the same darned spot. Oh, he was aggravating at times. Make that most of the time, lately.

"Hey." Ryan rose from his spot to give Naomi a quick kiss on the cheek.

Two cups of piping hot coffee were waiting on the table.

"How do you do that?" She pointed a finger at the coffee. "How did you even get here before me?"

"Well, I did have a car." He was so smug, she wanted to knock that grin right off his face.

"Yeah, well, I didn't have that luxury."

"True. We need to talk," Ryan stated. "Have a seat."

"Yes, we do." Naomi removed her jacket and took the seat across from Ryan.

"I don't want to lose you."

"I don't want to lose you, either, but where does that leave us? I think it's becoming abundantly clear that we're losing the fight in the romance department."

"Is that what you think?" His eyes widened.

How could he be surprised? Was he that inexperienced when it came to love?

"Yes, Ryan, I do. Come on, can't you feel it? In the beginning, we had a spark." Naomi thought about the day they had first met at the restaurant and then their first kiss. Shortly afterward, the attraction deteriorated between them.

Ryan shook his head and turned away. He knew exactly what she was talking about. "I guess you have a point."

"Ryan, what is it? I need to know. Is it an old girlfriend? Do you just not feel attracted to me?"

"I don't know. God, Naomi, I don't know."

"Don't be afraid to hurt me. I feel the same way. At first, the spark seemed strong, but then I grew to love you, just not in that way."

"You mean like a friend?"

"Yes, Ryan. Does that bother you?"

"No, Naomi. It makes sense to me because I've been feeling the same. I'm confused lately, and I can't even tell you why." He rubbed his hands through his thick, dark hair.

"Are you in love with someone else?"

His eyes glazed over as Naomi waited for him to speak.

"I...I don't think so." He gazed down at the floor, his fists clenched together. Just then, the waitress arrived with some pastries. Ryan lifted his head and covered his mouth.

"Are you okay?"

He looked awfully pale. As a matter of fact, he looked like he might be sick.

"Ryan?"

He took another look at the food before him and pushed his chair back. Naomi's jaw dropped as she watched him rush to the men's room. My God, if Ryan wasn't interested in eating, he must be feeling horrid.

It was after she had mentioned another woman that the green look had come over him. She would give him another minute before checking up on him. What was taking so long?

Just one more minute.

At least five more minutes had passed, and still he

hadn't returned. Damn, she didn't look forward to going into the men's bathroom, but he was leaving her little choice. Standing up, Naomi pulled her shoulders back and marched toward the bathroom. A sudden movement from the corner of her eye caught her attention. There, in plain sight, was Ryan, peeling out of the parking lot. *What the?* He must have snuck out the back entrance.

What the heck had gotten into him?

Immediately, Naomi sprinted to the table and grabbed her coffee. Shoot, he had run out before paying the bill. She scooped some pastries into her napkin; why not? Heading for the counter, she mumbled profanities about Ryan under her breath.

"How much do I owe you, miss?" A thought popped into her head as she waited for the waitress to write up their bill.

"Hold on one second. I'll be right back."

Naomi grabbed her tote bag from the small table where she and Ryan had been sitting only moments before. Grabbing for the framed photo of Maggie, she wondered why they had never inquired as to whether anyone here had known her.

"Have you ever seen this woman?"

The waitress slowly placed the check down and moved closer. Squinting at the photograph, she nodded her head.

"That's the woman who drowned, right?"

"Yes. Her name was Maggie. Did she ever come in here?"

"Yes, as a matter of fact, she did. Not that I knew her or anything, but she would come in from time to time."

"What can you tell me about her?"

"Hm. I'm trying to remember. She was quiet, kind of kept to herself. Most of the time, I think she just grabbed a coffee or a bagel to go."

"That's good. Go on."

"That's it. There's really nothing else I can recall."

"Did she ever come in with anyone else?"

"I think so. I... Oh, I'm not sure."

"What? What is it?" Naomi could see the confusion etched upon the woman's face.

"I thought he looked familiar. I just figured he was a regular, and that's how I knew him."

"Who?" She felt as if could leap over the counter and grab the waitress by the collar. "Who are you talking about?"

"That guy. Tall, dark, handsome."

Naomi's shoulders slumped.

Same story, nothing new. "Oh, yes. Well, thank you." She placed ten dollars on the counter and turned to leave.

"Have you asked him about it?"

Naomi stopped and glanced at the woman. "Who?"

"Your boyfriend."

Black spots came into view, and Naomi felt her legs wobble. She breathed in.

"My who?"

"You know, the guy who just left. Tall, dark, and handsome."

Naomi's head throbbed as she tried to make sense of the words.

"Are you okay? You don't look so good." The waitress came out from behind the counter and grabbed hold of Naomi's arm. Naomi allowed her to lead her to a nearby booth. She couldn't get enough air.

"Do you want me to call someone?"

"Are... you sure?" Naomi managed.

"Yes, I'm positive. That man was Maggie's boyfriend."

Naomi doubled over as if she had been punched in the gut.

"ANSWER THE PHONE! Dammit, Ryan, answer!" Naomi must

have called him twenty times, and he still wouldn't pick up. How could she even begin to make sense of this?

Ryan was the only person alive who held the answers to her questions. Maggie's spirit wasn't much for conversation.

Sitting in her driveway, Naomi pounded the steering wheel hard. Bits and pieces of her investigation with Ryan started to come back to her. The times he refused to see Maggie's parents. Shoot, they could identify Ryan—they had met him several times.

Something told her Ryan wouldn't agree to meet Maggie's parents for the purpose of identifying him. But wait! She had a picture of him on her cell phone. That ridiculous photo of the two of them from the graveyard back when they first started dating.

With shaking fingers, Naomi fumbled with her cell until she found the picture. His piercing blue eyes gazed at her from the photo.

"Got you!" Naomi shut her cell off and started the ignition of her car. As she prepared to put her car in reverse, a dark figure came out of nowhere.

"Nick!" She instinctively went for the door lock button. Her shaking hands gripped the steering wheel. As her heart pounded wildly, Nick lunged for her door. Although her car window was closed, she could hear his words perfectly.

"Get back here! I just want to talk!" He leaned in toward the car window. "Open the freaking door!"

Nick's face was red and dripping with sweat, even in this chilly temperature. He was a madman.

"Get out of here. Leave me alone," Naomi spoke the words aloud as she peeled out of her driveway, leaving an enraged Nick behind.

Heart still racing, she pulled to the side of the road once he was a safe distance behind. *What the hell had just happened back there?*

Nick was far from finished with her. She should have known it was just the proverbial calm before the storm. This was something she definitely did not need right now, not with everything else going on.

She actually lifted her cell phone to call Ryan to tell him about Nick, but remembered that Ryan was no longer who she had thought him to be. No longer one of her best friends. And let's face it, he wasn't picking up the phone anyway.

Damn you, Ryan!

After waiting out her pounding heart for a few minutes, Naomi finally steered her car toward Mr. and Mrs. Field's home.

Determined to get a positive identification on Ryan, she pulled into their driveway and then marched to the front door.

"Come in, Naomi. My goodness, what's wrong?" Virginia escorted her into the kitchen. "Would you like some coffee?"

"I could use something much stronger than that," Naomi muttered.

"Excuse me?"

"It's nothing. Is Tom here?"

"No, he's out running some errands. Please, sit and tell me what's going on."

"That obvious, huh?"

"Yes, Naomi. What is it?"

Her cell phone was already out of her bag. "Here, look. Is this Maggie's tall, dark, and handsome friend?"

Virginia drew her hands to her mouth. "Oh, well how?"

"Is it him?" But she already knew the answer.

"How do you know R.J.?" Virginia's words came out in a whisper.

"It's Ryan. My ex-boyfriend as of now."

"What? I don't understand."

"That makes two of us. Are you sure it's him?"

"Positive. I couldn't forget a face like that. But he always went by R.J., for Ryan James, Maggie told us. Hey, you don't think he has anything to do with this, do you?"

143

As of now, he was Maggie's prime suspect. Couple the lies with the sketchy exit at the café, and he had guilt written all over him. It was her number one priority to find Ryan.

A chill spread through her body as she wondered if she was in danger. If Ryan had anything to do with Maggie's death, of course she was in danger. She had been in danger all along.

No wonder he had been backing away, discouraging her from trying to solve the crime. He had also told her she was ridiculous for believing in Maggie's spirit.

"I don't know, Virginia. But it stinks. He stinks. He's been lying to me all along. What am I supposed to make of all this?"

"You're right. Something isn't right here. I think it's time to pay Officer Frank another visit."

"Tell you what, why don't you and Tom go down to the police station, like we said, and ask for another officer to be assigned to the case? Scratch that, don't ask. Demand."

"Got it. What are you going to do?" She stood to grab her landline phone.

"I'm going to try to find Ryan and lure him into a public place."

"Oh my God, Naomi. Maybe you should just let the police handle this. He's a dangerous man."

"Don't worry, I'll be careful. I just need to see him, look him in the eye."

Was he a dangerous man? Up until this morning, she would have laughed at the concept of Ryan being dangerous.

"Oh, please call me if you find him, and be careful. Tom and I have really grown to like you, and I couldn't bear to see anything happen to you."

Naomi pulled Mrs. Field into an embrace. "I promise you I'll be careful. Keep me posted."

Naomi headed out to her car and shot off a text message to Ryan, stating that she needed to speak with him regardless of his part in Maggie's death. She also threw in some information pertaining to Nick's little visit. That might get him to call her back. Then again, had he ever cared for her, or was it all just an elaborate scheme?

Her cell sounded almost immediately. "Ryan!"

"What did he do to you?"

The plan worked even better than she had anticipated. "Ryan, where are you?"

"No, answer me, Naomi. Are you okay?"

He certainly didn't sound like a murderer right now.

"I'm fine. Please, I need to see you."

"Naomi, I'm so confused. My head is splitting. I need you to know that I didn't hurt her. I couldn't have ever harmed her."

"Ryan, why on earth didn't you tell me you dated Maggie?"

"Dated her? I was in love with her."

Again, she felt a punch to her gut. "Ryan, you're scaring me."

"I was in love with her. I still am. Finally, I know why you and I could never make it. Pieces are starting to fit together."

He was rambling, dammit. "Stop, Ryan. The more you say, the more scared I am."

There was silence on the line.

"Scared of me or for me?" His tone was ominous.

Shaking off the chills that prickled her scalp, Naomi steadied her shaking hands.

"I… I don't know. Perhaps a little of both," Naomi whispered.

"Don't be afraid of me, Naomi. I would never hurt you. Just like I never could have hurt our Maggie."

Our Maggie?" Again, chills coursed through her body. "I want to believe you so much, Ryan, I do. But this doesn't look good for you."

"I know it doesn't. I can't explain what happened. I didn't lie. I never lied to you."

145

"Oh, for heaven's sake, Ryan! All you did was lie!"

"No, I didn't. I need to see you, but you have to promise me you won't call the police. Just give me a chance to look you in the eye, and you'll see I'm not lying."

"I need to see you too. No police. For now. But we meet in a public place and no funny business like last time."

"Promise. But wouldn't it be easier to meet you at your place? Or mine?"

"No way. A public place. Make it the diner on Main, in, say… ten minutes?"

"I'm on my way. Be there in a few."

Naomi sighed heavily. "Could you just let me beat you there this one time?"

"What was that?"

"Nothing, Ryan. It was nothing."

CHAPTER TWENTY-THREE

Naomi

OF COURSE HE was sitting there, coffee in hand. Frustrating, even as a potential murderer.

"Ryan."

He stood to kiss her hello, but Naomi backed away, shaking her head. "Sit down, Ryan."

Pain reflected in his eyes as he looked at her. "Naomi."

"Sit."

He sighed, but followed her direction.

Gazing at the man before her, she had a difficult time picturing him harming Maggie.

But she couldn't forget the lies and the deceit.

He took hold of her hands from across the table. "I need you to look me in the eyes. I did not murder Maggie."

Lifting her head, she gazed into his blue eyes. Kindness, caring, and sadness met her.

Damn him. She believed him. But it didn't make any sense. Why did he lie about knowing her, loving her?

"Why didn't you tell me you knew her? Loved her?"

He looked away from her for a moment and then returned his gaze to her face. "I know you're not going to believe me, but I didn't remember. Not until that moment you asked me if I was still in love with someone else."

"How—how could that be?"

"I don't know Naomi. Dammit, I don't know. You have to believe me. It was as if I had blocked out the entire relationship."

"That's impossible, Ryan. Unless you hit your head or something, it doesn't make sense. I'm not going to sit here and listen to this nonsense." She turned away, hugging her arms across her chest.

"It's crazy, I know it is."

"Okay, so let's say I was going to buy into this amnesia story, and that's a big 'if.' Why did you try to dissuade me from the investigation? It was like you sensed I was getting too close."

"That's just it, Naomi. The closer we got, physically and emotionally, to the case and to each other, the stranger it all felt to me."

"That I believe," Naomi huffed. "You certainly changed your attitude. Three hundred sixty degrees."

"I'm sorry. I really do like you."

"I know you do. I like you too, but you're asking me to believe this ridiculous tale you're spinning, and quite honestly, I'm afraid of you right now."

"Don't be afraid of me." He ran his hands through his hair. "What am I saying? I'm afraid of myself."

Her heart tugged as she saw his pain. "Ryan," she began.

"I need help. There's so much I don't remember." He placed his head in his hands.

"That's probably a good idea."

"You think?" His tortured eyes met hers. "But what if, God forbid, I was responsible in some way?"

"But you just said…"

His fist hit the table. "I know what I said!"

"Ryan," she whispered as she glanced at customers nearby. "Relax, you're causing a scene."

He looked up at her, his face stained with tears. Either he was the best actor around, or he was the most manipulative liar she had laid eyes on. Either way, he was screwed.

"Help me, Naomi. Take me to a doctor. If I am responsible, then I want to be punished. I miss her so much, so much."

He wept openly now, and it literally brought her to tears. If he were an awful, horrible man, then would he be willing to go to jail? Unless the guilt became too much for him to bear.

It was all circumstantial evidence at this point. Nobody knew the truth, not even Ryan, apparently.

"I think I need to take myself into the police station."

"Really?"

"Yes, really. My gut is telling me that Maggie's death wasn't an accident. Let's go. Now."

He pulled at her arm as she attempted to rise from her seat. "But…"

Ryan threw a twenty dollar bill down on the table and steered Naomi to the door.

"Twenty dollars for two cups of coffee? Now I know you're not feeling well."

"This is no time for jokes, Naomi. I might be in serious trouble here."

True. "Sorry. Are you sure you want to do this?"

"I'll meet you there," he stated solemnly. "Hey, wait a minute. What happened with Nick?"

"Oh, that. Nick was in my driveway, waiting for me earlier. I locked the doors to the car, and he just kept yelling at me."

"My God, Naomi. You need to tell the police when we're there. I'm not going to let anything happen to you."

Unless he spent the night — or several — in jail.

Truth be told, she was pleased she wasn't sharing a car ride with him over to the police station. She didn't trust him yet. Hopefully, they could get past all of the difficulties facing them, but for now she was leery.

"I'll come by your house after we finish with the police. I can even spend the night, on the couch, of course."

Oh, hell no.

"Ryan? Please don't take offense to this, but I don't want to be alone with you. Not yet."

149

He turned away. She had hurt him, but what other choice did he give her right now? Heck, most people she knew wouldn't even be speaking to him if they were in her situation.

Maybe she was being stupid, naïve, but given their past, she felt she owed it to him to at least accompany him to the police station.

"Sorry."

"I wouldn't want to be alone with me, either."

"Listen, there's still the theory of the ex-boyfriend, right?" She had a fleeting thought that the waiter, Ted, was most likely cleared in her mind.

"I guess. I can't remember if she even had one."

"That's so strange. I bet something happened. You must have hit your head or something."

"Who knows? Maybe I'm just slowly losing my mind."

"We'll figure this out, Ryan."

He leaned over to hug her, but still she backed away. "I need some space, Ryan."

"See you over there." He headed toward his car. Watching him walk away, her heart ached.

God, she hoped he was innocent, with every ounce of her being.

"We're still waiting."

"Are you kidding me? It's been over an hour since I left your place."

Virginia shook her head as Tom paced the room. The cold, stark office held little warmth for this mission of theirs.

"I see you've become reacquainted with Ryan, here."

Ryan sat with his head in his hands, not speaking.

"Yes, um, we have." Virginia's eyes rolled to the ceiling. "Have you explained that you want another officer assigned to the case?" Naomi took the seat in between Virginia and Ryan.

"We've tried, but so far, no answers. Right now we're playing the waiting game."

"This is ridiculous."

"Ma'am, is there a problem?"

"Yes, there is, as a matter of fact." Naomi approached the desk as a middle-aged man rose to his feet. "Mr. and Mrs. Field are requesting another officer be assigned to their daughter's case."

"I'm very well aware of their request, miss. Who are you, by the way?"

"I'm a family friend."

"Well, family friend, I'm pretty sure this doesn't concern you. We will deal with the parents here."

"Then deal with them. Don't make them sit here. Haven't they been through enough?"

Mr. Field stepped forward. "I want answers. Now. Are we or are we not getting a new officer for Maggie's case?'

"Sir, as I told you before, in order for your daughter's case to be assigned to another officer, it has to be reopened. I'm afraid there doesn't seem to be evidence of foul play here. Maggie drowned, and I'm sorry about that. I truly am, but dredging up the past isn't going to help her."

From behind Naomi, she heard his voice. "I may have had a part in her death."

"Excuse me? Now who is this?" The officer barked.

"I'm her boyfriend. Rather, I was her boyfriend."

"Now you need to open the case. Did you hear that? He may have been involved with her death." Naomi knew why Ryan had chosen his words. He knew the officer would now have to investigate and therefore open up the case.

"I don't know what's going on here, but I still need to go through Officer Hamlin, and then we'll determine whether or not the case will be reassigned."

Naomi's blood ran cold at the mention of the officer's

name. She took hold of the counter before her to stop herself from falling.

Squeezing her eyes shut, she practiced controlled breathing.

"Now wait just a minute here..." Tom's voice rose as he leaned in toward the desk.

"We do not want Officer Frank on the case any longer!" Virginia spoke up from across the room.

"Are you listening to me? I may have killed the woman I love!" Ryan's voice boomed out.

The room spun around her. "Stop it, all of you, just stop it!" Naomi cried out. She had succeeded in silencing everyone. A bit of calm had been restored.

Every eye was on her. Choosing her words carefully, Naomi spoke softly now. "Can you please repeat Officer Frank's name?"

"What's gotten into you?" Ryan asked.

"What's his name?" she repeated, louder this time.

"Officer Frank Hamlin. What's the problem?"

"Oh my God. Oh my God. Ryan, that's Nick's last name." Her mind swam with possibilities. "Does he have a nephew named Nick?"

The officer squinted his eyes. "I have no clue."

"It has to be his uncle. Ryan, I remember Nick saying his uncle was a cop. God, why didn't I think of this before?"

"What are you getting at here?"

Mr. Tall, Dark, and Handsome and Mr. Average.

Average. It couldn't be Nick, could it?

"Nick is attractive, but I suppose he could be described as average looking."

"Huh?" Ryan scratched at his face.

"It's Nick. I think she dated Nick before you." And if that was the case, there were so many possible scenarios for this crime.

"I want to see Officer Frank immediately," Naomi commanded.

"Miss, it doesn't work that way," the officer explained.

"Well it damn well better work that way this time. Get him here, now, or I'll ask to speak with your superior."

"Oh lady, you're killing me." He picked up the phone.

"The best I can do is call his partner in. Officer Marty will be here in a while."

His partner? How had she forgotten? Of course he would have a partner, and Naomi was pretty sure his partner wouldn't harbor a possible murder suspect for a nephew.

"Great. We have all night," Naomi stated as she walked back to her seat and made herself comfortable.

Minutes passed as they waited silently. Naomi could only imagine the conflicted feelings Maggie's parents must be dealing with, having Ryan sitting here so close beside them. As far as they were concerned, Ryan could very well be the murderer of their daughter.

She sensed it wasn't true, but she had been wrong before.

The door to the outside opened as a stunning blonde-haired woman walked into the room.

"Officer Miriam Marty here. What can I do for you, folks?"

Ryan's mouth hung open as he watched Miriam walk up to the front desk.

"Close your mouth, Ryan, before you catch flies." Men.

CHAPTER TWENTY-FOUR

Maggie

"R.J., THIS IS *so beautiful.*" *Maggie spread her arms wide and her head toward the warmth of the sunlight.*

"*You are beautiful.*" *He grabbed hold of her waist and led her down to the blanket.*

She stumbled slightly and giggled.

"*If I didn't know any better, I'd say that someone had too much wine.*"

"*Yes, well, then you shouldn't be trying to get me tipsy.*" *But she felt wonderful, and the slight buzz wasn't hurting.*

She reached for her glass.

"*Ah, I think you've had enough. I want you clearheaded for this.*"

"*Huh? For what?*" *She popped a ripe grape into his mouth.*

"*Hey,*" *he mumbled.*

He was quiet then.

Maggie noticed that he had turned serious. "*What is it?*"

"*Maggie. I know that we haven't been dating long, but I feel like we've grown so close.*"

She swallowed.

"*And you mean so much to me. I...*"

"*Honey, what is it?*"

"*I'm falling in love with you.*"

Oh God. This is where it had all gone wrong last time. Panic rose in her chest.

Those three little words had turned her world around. And

not in a good way.

"Oh, R.J." She didn't want to ruin this with those game-changing words.

"I love you, Maggie. I'm not afraid to say it." His voice rose with passion.

"R.J.!" She glanced around.

"What are you afraid of? I'll shout it out as loud as I can. Maggie, I love you!"

It was ridiculous of her to think her ex could possibly hear R.J., but after being so careful in town, she felt funny hearing R.J. shout his words of love.

He reached for her and rolled her around on the picnic blanket. Placing his lips on her mouth, he kissed her. She melted into his kiss. She loved this.

She loved him.

She just admitted it to herself, but she had known for some time now. Telling R.J. was a different matter. But then, he wasn't anything like her ex. They were worlds apart.

She broke free from his kiss, just for one small moment, and smiled. She could do this.

Maggie pointed at her heart. "I love you, too."

Her mouth met his in a hungry kiss. His hands roamed over her back. This elated feeling was brand new. She gave in to her admission: she loved this man.

She loved him.

A sharp sound coming from the edge of the woods caught her attention. "What was that?" Pulling away from him, she sat up straight.

"Come on, Maggie, get back here," R.J. pleaded as he tugged on her arm.

What is that? Maggie leaned over, squinting her eyes in the bright sunlight. The sound of crunching leaves could have been made by a deer. She thought she spied movement. Leaning closer still, Maggie gasped.

"Oh no, R.J.!"

"Stay perfectly still, Maggie. Don't move, I'm right here,"

R.J. whispered as he clutched her hand in his.
    She closed her eyes tightly, silently praying.

CHAPTER TWENTY-FIVE

Naomi

"DON'T YOU SEE now why we're so concerned?" Mrs. Field pleaded after they had spent the past hour sharing everything they felt about Maggie's case.

Officer Marty shook her head firmly. "Let me see if I got this straight. Ryan, you think you might be responsible for your girlfriend's death?"

"No, that's not what he said at all," Naomi cried out. Instinctively, she wished to protect him.

"Isn't it, though?" Officer Marty turned to look at Ryan. "Well?"

"I'm not sure. I believe I'm suffering from some type of amnesia. I can't remember anything about the circumstances of her death."

A bitter laugh came from the officer. "Sir, with all due respect, your story has an awful lot of holes in it."

"An awful lot," Mr. Field chimed in, glaring at Ryan.

'I'm sorry, Virginia and Tom, for what I did or didn't do," Ryan exclaimed.

"Okay, Ryan. I think one thing is pretty clear here. You need some help. Oh, and don't leave town. You'll be my first interview bright and early tomorrow morning. " Ryan nodded in agreement to the officer's statement.

"Another thing is also clear. It seems that Maggie's case should, indeed, be reopened. Officer Frank and I will both be working on the case. I'm sorry, that's just the way it works."

"But, didn't you hear what I said before?" Naomi had told the officer all about her suspicions that Nick and Officer Frank were related.

"Of course I heard you, but even if they are related, it doesn't mean that Nick knew Maggie, and it certainly doesn't mean that Nick killed her."

"But, don't you see…"

"Naomi, just because you're writing a story doesn't mean you have any rights here. Besides, I will do my job thoroughly. You can count on that."

"It's not just a story to me." Naomi pouted.

"Okay, let me rephrase it then, if you will. Just because Maggie's ghost is living with you, doesn't give you any legal say here."

Officer Marty was mocking her, and it pissed her off. "You don't have to take that tone, Officer Marty. I'm trying to help Mr. and Mrs. Field and Maggie here."

"She's the only one who has cared about what has happened to our daughter since this whole thing happened," Mrs. Field interjected.

Throwing her head down, Officer Marty sighed. "You're right, I'm sorry."

"Thank you." At least she seemed to have a heart, unlike Officer Frank.

"Look, this can't be easy for anyone here, and I feel awful that your daughter has died. I will make it a priority to find out the truth."

"Thank you. I actually think I believe you, Officer Marty." Mr. Field extended his hand to her.

"Please try to do whatever is in your power to keep Officer Frank away from your research. I have a very bad feeling about him," Mrs. Field shared.

"I'll do what I can, but I can't make any promises." The officer threw her hands up in the air. "I have some research to attend to, if you'll excuse me." She nodded at Naomi.

"Thank you." Naomi glanced at the disheveled Ryan and expelled a breath. "Ryan? We need to get you to a doctor."

"You're not afraid to come with me?" He looked up at her from his seat.

"No, for some reason I'm not. Let's go. I'll give you a ride and drop you back off at your car later."

She hugged Maggie's parents. "I'll have my cell on me. Talk to you soon."

"Thank you, Naomi, for everything," Mr. Field exclaimed.

His wife nodded through tears. "After all this time, I feel like we're finally going to get some answers."

Naomi's own tears fell as she embraced the woman once more. Her heart was breaking for the Fields, and she hoped closure was close for the couple.

She had to give Ryan credit. He stood and attempted to speak with Maggie's parents.

"For what it's worth, I'm sorry."

"Just go, Ryan, and get some help." Mr. Field rejected Ryan's handshake, then led his wife to the door.

IT WAS LATE. It had been an exhausting day, for sure. No way around the fact that being with Ryan today was taking an emotional toll on her. He was up; he was down; he was sad; but most of all, he was just plain Ryan.

Try as she might, she couldn't picture him harming anyone. They had decided to head straight to the emergency room instead of going to a doctor's office. Any head trauma could be ruled out through X-rays and MRIs. Problem was, each time the doctors had attempted any type of testing, the electrical system went haywire and tests couldn't be conducted. Figures there would be a problem with the equipment. It was just their luck that they'd have more hurdles thrown in their way.

They were keeping Ryan overnight for observation and would try to get the testing done in the morning. Officer Marty just might have to make a trip to the hospital to interview Ryan. The fact that Ryan wasn't locked up in the county jail overnight confirmed her suspicions that Miriam Marty didn't truly consider Ryan a threat at this point.

She stood alone in her house. Nothing would feel better than a warm shower right now.

Zelda rubbed her warm body across her calves as Naomi headed for the staircase. A creaking sound from the top of the stairs stopped Naomi in her tracks. A faint white form stood at the top of the stairs, moaning as if in pain.

She was suffering.

"Maggie, talk to me. Tell me what I can do," Naomi cried.

Anguished humming rose higher and higher in pitch until Naomi felt she couldn't stand it another second. She held her pounding head.

"Stop, Maggie! Stop!" She covered her ears, tears streaming down her face.

Maggie stopped.

"Maggie. What is it?" It was as if she was trying to tell Naomi something. She almost appeared to be pointing.

Naomi spun around, but it was too late. Seeing a dark figure standing there, she cried out.

He advanced upon her, grabbing her wrist and bending it backward.

"No, help! Help!" Naomi screamed. The only hope she had was if someone heard her. "Maggie!"

Maggie stood, her hand covering her mouth. She bellowed out an unearthly, ear-splitting sound but remained firmly planted at the top of the stairs.

He released Naomi's wrist slowly, his jaw dropping. "What the hell is that?"

Naomi broke free, making a run for it.

"Maggie?" She heard him cry out. His shouting ceased as she heard him pick up speed behind her.

Don't look back.

She sucked the air in as she sprinted for the door. He was closing in on her. She could feel movement behind her.

"Naomi! You're not getting away. Not this time."

She lunged for the door, grasping hold of the doorknob. It didn't matter. He had closed the space between them. His body slammed against her.

"Help!" She cried out as loud as she could manage. Maggie's cries echoed her own. Glancing to her right, she saw Maggie's form sobbing.

He held her from behind, shoving her back up against him.

"Nick. Please don't..." she sobbed.

"Listen to me," he spat through his foul breath, making her want to vomit. Her trembling body was squashed tight against him. "You couldn't let it go, could you?"

"What...what are you talking about?" Naomi's jaw shook with each word.

"Look what you're making me do. It's all your fault." His spittle hit her cheek as she closed her eyes.

"What are you going to do, Nick?"

"You leave me no choice." He leaned closer still and placed his lips on her cheek. Fear spread through her body, her flight reaction in full gear.

Grabbing her by the hair, he pulled her head back. "Don't be mad at me. Be mad at yourself. As usual, your nosy ways have gotten you into a world of trouble. It was bad enough you broke my heart, but then you had to play detective and bother my uncle. I'm not having it, Naomi." He tugged her hair tighter, making her cry out from the pain.

"Please, Nick..."

"I'm not having it!" Nick screamed, shoving his mouth into her ear. Reaching for her throat, he squeezed.

Gasping for air, her arms met his as she tried to pry his hands from her neck. His strength overpowered her.

"It's your fault!"

A piercing scream met his own as Maggie watched. Her scream rose to an unnatural pitch. Shattering glass sounded all around. Naomi struggled to breathe, darkness closing in. Ryan's tortured face came to mind. He was innocent. My God, she should have known it all along.

Her world became black. She didn't have the breath or the energy to resist.

"You didn't love me. You didn't love me back. Just like the others!"

She hit the floor as she heard voices. Nick's hands left her throat, and she sucked in precious air, opening her eyes wide. Before her, she witnessed Bryce tackle Nick to the floor, pinning his head down.

"Bryce!" She attempted to speak, but her voice was a mere whisper. Her throat ached from the fight.

"Call the police!"

Of course. Where was the phone? Glancing around the kitchen, her shaking hands found her landline phone. She pressed 911 and waited for the police to pick up.

"There's been an intruder. Send help. Tell Officer Marty that it's Naomi Morrison," she stated numbly.

Naomi slowly placed her phone down and searched the kitchen. Maggie had saved her life. Naomi was sure of it.

"I'm sorry, I didn't plan to hurt her. I just came here to talk, and I lost it. I'm sorry!" Nick's muffled shouts filled the air.

"What are you looking for?" Bryce followed her movement around the kitchen. Maggie was no longer there.

"Bryce, she saved me. Maggie saved me."

"Sweetheart, I think you need to sit down. You're not making any sense."

He wouldn't understand. Nobody else would ever understand the bond she and Maggie had formed.

162

CHAPTER TWENTY-SIX

Naomi

"PLEASE TELL OFFICER Marty I need her," Naomi repeated once more. They weren't paying attention to her, and she wanted to rip her hair out from frustration.

"Naomi. Just relax. They want to make sure you're okay." Bryce sat by her side, holding onto her hand.

"I'm fine. I'm just a bit shaken up is all."

"I bet." The examining doctor felt up and down her neck. "It looks like you'll be okay, but I'd feel better if you stayed here overnight just so we can keep an eye on you. Standard procedure. Promise." The young doctor winked.

"Oh, fine. Not that anyone would listen to me anyway. I want to see Officer Marty, though."

The doctor glanced at the nurse, nodding his approval. The nurse scurried off, heading out the door.

"We'll call the police station. Haven't you already spoken with the police though? I'm sure they questioned you at your house."

"Yes, they did. But they promised I could speak with Officer Marty. I need to speak with her, only her."

"Then she'll be here as soon as she can, I suppose. Right now, you need to calm down and rest," Bryce added.

"Okay, I guess you're right." She acquiesced, lying back on the hospital bed. As soon as she sat back, she sprang back up, grabbing hold of Bryce's arm.

"I have to see my friend. He's here in this hospital. Get

the nurse."

"Your friend? Who?"

"Please, Bryce. His Name is Ryan. He's here, on this floor." What was his room number? She had asked earlier, and she struggled to remember it.

"Room 76. Ryan, room 76."

Naomi pressed the bedside button, paging the nurse herself.

What was taking so long? Patience was not an area of strength for her right now. She needed to apologize to him for doubting him. How could she have even considered it for a minute? The poor guy even doubted himself.

"Naomi. There's something I've been meaning to say to you." Bryce leaned over so that he was closer to her.

"Bryce. How did you happen to be at my door? What were you doing there?" She hadn't thought it through before. Her only thought was that she was grateful for his impeccable timing.

"Well, that's why I was there. I wanted to speak with you about the other day, you know, when I was at Johnny's. But then I heard a scream, at the time I didn't know what was making that sound."

Maggie.

"Uh. Yeah." Naomi twirled her hair.

"It was chilling. How did you scream so high? I mean, the pitch of that scream..." Bryce shook his head as his eyes glazed over.

"I don't know. There's so much more to this story than what you know, but I'm too exhausted to get into it all right now. Later, okay?"

"Sure, but you've officially piqued my curiosity. However, back to that day at Johnny's."

Seeing him with Blondie hadn't been the highlight of that day, but with so much going on right now, it had slipped her mind.

"Yes." She recalled the cold stares she had received from

the blonde-haired woman.

"She and I, we're nothing." He blushed deeply.

It was her turn to blush. "Oh, Bryce. It's none of my business. You don't have to tell me this."

"No, but you see, it does concern you."

She thought carefully before speaking. "How so?" She hoped she had guessed the answer to his question.

"Naomi," he began softly, reaching for her hand.

"What's the problem, miss?" One of the nurses walked briskly into the room at that moment.

Bryce cleared his throat and sat back.

"I need to see a man named Ryan. He's here in room 76."

"The good-looking one?"

The nurse's comment earned a raised eyebrow from Bryce.

Oh, so Ryan had been charming the nurses already. She laughed out loud, picturing Ryan chatting it up with them.

"That's the one."

"Nice guy. I'll see what I can do," the nurse stated.

"Thank you."

Bryce waited a moment before the nurse left to speak. "Is this Ryan guy your boyfriend?"

"Um, no. But he used to be. It's kind of complicated."

"I see." He glanced away.

"Bryce, what were you saying before?"

"I…" Bryce began as Ryan walked through the door, looking fresh-faced and, well – tall, dark, and handsome.

"Ryan!" Naomi leaped to her feet to meet him.

"It was nothing." She heard Bryce mumble as Ryan wrapped his arms around Naomi.

Bryce stood and excused himself. "I'm going to head out now. John is watching Holly and I said I'd be back soon. I'll check in on you tomorrow?"

"Yes, hopefully I'll be home by then. Oh, I'm sorry. This is Ryan. Ryan, Bryce."

Ryan reached for Bryce's hand and pumped it. "Great to meet a friend of Naomi's. Take care."

"Yes, you too." Bryce kissed Naomi gently on the cheek and left her alone with Ryan.

"What are you doing here? Are you okay?" Ryan smoothed Naomi's hair, studying her face.

"I have so much to tell you, Ryan. Sit down, please."

Ryan took his spot beside Naomi on the hospital bed. "Look at us, a bunch of fools, sitting here in the hospital." He chuckled as he held on to Naomi's hand. She looked into his sparkling blue eyes and squeezed his hand.

At that moment, she realized she loved him. Loved him as a friend. Their relationship would survive this and become even stronger.

"Tell me everything."

"I'm so sorry that I didn't have faith in you. I should have known you couldn't have harmed her. I'm sorry, Ryan."

"Sh. Slow down. What happened?"

"It was Nick. He went nuts. He didn't want us investigating Maggie's death. She was his ex-girlfriend, and he killed her!"

Ryan let go of her hand. "Are you sure?"

"Hell, yes. Why else would he tell me to back off? Why would he try to kill me?"

"Kill you? Where is he?" Ryan's blue eyes sparked with anger.

"He was arrested. It's fine. Thanks to Bryce and his perfect timing, I lived to tell the truth."

Ryan's arms found her, squeezing her tight. "I shouldn't have let you out of my sight, honey. I'm sorry."

"You didn't exactly have a choice. You are in the hospital, in case you haven't realized." Naomi giggled as she rubbed the top of his head.

"Does any of this ring a bell? Do you remember a crazy ex-boyfriend named Nick?"

Ryan bit his lip, his mouth turned down in a frown. "I can't remember."

"It's okay, Ryan. It's fine." She didn't wish to stress him out any more than he already was. But, secretly, she was losing her mind, waiting for him to recall anything that would help put this case to rest.

"Are you okay?" He held Naomi's face in his hands and studied her.

"I am. How about you? Did you remember anything else? Were the doctors able to give you an X-ray?"

"No, it's so strange. Seems the electrical problem is still continuing. I'm out of here soon, though. Maybe I'll talk to a therapist instead. I feel that something awful must have happened, otherwise why would I block out this whole period of my life?"

Naomi winced as she heard his words. She herself had been given an X-ray, and there were no problems. It was as if fate was out to get him. A far as his theory about his memory loss went, she wasn't sure, but his words made sense. Whatever had transpired with Maggie must have been so awful. As long as he wasn't a suspect for murder, she knew they could move past whatever it was that was holding him back.

"I don't know what happened to you, Ryan, but I'm here for you, and between the two of us we're going to figure it out. Promise."

"I hope so, Naomi. I certainly hope so."

RYAN WAS RELEASED the next morning as well. There was nothing else the doctors could do for Ryan except tell him to try to come back for testing. One day, they figured, all of his memories would come flooding back as if a door had opened.

New theories surfaced in Naomi's mind as to why Ryan would block out such an important person and time in his life. He must have witnessed her death. The more she thought about it, the stronger her theory became.

It was the only reasonable explanation.

Now the hardest part came: waiting Ryan out. The doctors had said not to push him, that his past would come back to him when he was ready to face whatever it was that was holding him back. She would have to practice patience on her part.

"Maggie." Naomi held her hands up in the air, calling out. "Give me some kind of hint, some clue."

Maggie held the key here. A strange sensation washed over Naomi as she came to terms with the fact that she had dated two of the same men Maggie had. Look where it had landed Maggie.

"Maggie, this connection we share is amazing. Just tell me, somehow, what happened to you. What did Ryan see? What did Nick do to you?"

She heard her presence before she saw her appear. From the harsh slamming, she sensed Maggie's mood immediately. Smashing cabinet doors gave way to Maggie's unearthly features.

"Maggie," Naomi whispered.

Naomi winced as she covered her ears. The sorrowful weeping filled her head. It hurt to connect with Maggie in this way. It hurt so much.

The spirit took a step toward her. Naomi didn't so much as flinch. Maggie stepped closer, still, her hand reaching out for Naomi. Naomi maintained eye contact, despite her pounding heart.

A sharp rapping sound stopped the ghost in her tracks.

"No, Maggie. Don't go!" Naomi cursed the person on the other side of the door. Naomi had been so close to touching her. What would she have done next? What would Naomi have discovered?

"Dammit!" She clenched her fists, stomping to the door.

"I'm so happy you're home." Bryce smiled brightly as Naomi opened the door.

"Bryce." She unclenched her fists. How could she be upset with him? "Come in, please."

"What's wrong? You look upset."

If only he knew. "It's complicated."

"I'm a good listener."

Naomi was sure he was. Everything about Bryce was likable. So likable, in fact, that he was finding his way into her head more and more these days.

"Can I get you anything? Water, coffee?" She led the way into the kitchen.

"Naomi, stop."

His words gave her pause. Turning to face him, she saw the raw emotion in his eyes. Sucking her breath in, she waited for him to speak.

"Naomi. I have been trying to tell you since I met you…"

"Tell me what?" she managed.

He stepped closer to her, reaching out.

She didn't move. She didn't dare.

"I like you. I like you a lot, Naomi."

He moved in, clasping his hands over hers. She closed her eyes and gave herself over to his kiss. His hands broke free from hers and roamed over her face. Her heart soared with feelings; time stopped until it was just the two of them. This spell she was under—she never wanted it to end.

"What is that?" Bryce released her. The faucet ran full force as Naomi shook her head. She made a mental note to tell Maggie later that her timing was awful.

Of all times for Maggie to announce her presence.

"I don't know that you'd believe me if I told you." She sighed as she prepared herself for the impending conversation.

"Um, try me. I just witnessed your faucet turning on all by itself. First the unbelievable screaming, now this? What is going on in this house?"

"If I were you, I would sit for this one, Bryce." A small chuckle escaped her lips as she attempted to formulate her words. The last thing she wanted was for him not to believe her, to think she had lost her mind.

"What is it?" He found a seat at the kitchen table.

Naomi joined him, sitting in the chair beside him. Talk about ruining a mood, Maggie. Nice going.

She would have to just say it. "Bryce, do you believe in ghosts?"

Waiting a moment before he responded, Bryce shook his head firmly. "I didn't before today. Are you telling me you think you have a ghost here, in this house?"

"No, I don't *think* I have a ghost here, I *know* I have a ghost. Her name is Maggie."

"Maggie? But how do you know?"

There was no better way to tell him than to show him. "Come on, let's take a walk." Reaching for his hand, she offered him a half smile. He just may think she's crazy before the day was through, but there was the water gushing out of the faucet by itself, so maybe not.

"Where are we going?"

"You'll see. Promise me you'll keep an open mind?"

"Sure. I'll try." He shrugged and then grabbed hold of Naomi's hand.

"Are you going to tell me what this is all about?" He struggled to keep up with Naomi's pace now that they were outside in the nipping air. Naomi was focused on reaching Maggie's grave and chose to ignore him until they reached the headstone.

"Here." Naomi stood, wind whipping through her hair as she faced Maggie's grave.

"Okay. I repeat, what's this all about?"

"This is Maggie Field," Naomi stated. Bending down, she removed some dried leaves from the stone.

"I see that. Did you know her?"

"No, I didn't. I mean… Oh, hell, I don't know."

"Relax, honey. Tell me about Maggie." He reached for her hand. His warm eyes gave her the courage to continue.

"It's her ghost. She's been coming to communicate with me back at the house." Seeing that Bryce's jaw dropped and he stood speechless, she continued. "I'm attempting to write a story, loosely based on her life, but the mishandled crime against her has been getting in the way."

It was then that she realized how little she had actually been writing the past week or so. It seemed that her priority had become to solve the case and then write her story. With her tangled emotions, it would be impossible to concentrate.

"Fill me in. I'm not familiar with her. What happened to Maggie?"

"Well, the police closed the case several years back. Claimed it was an accidental drowning in the river. Her parents and I had reason to suspect her death was no accident. There were too many things that didn't sit right with me. My gut feelings are usually spot -on. After many frustrating attempts, we finally got the police to take us seriously and reopen the case."

"I don't know what to say." He ran his hands through his thick hair. "You've been very busy, Naomi. I had no idea."

"There's not much to say. I'm not going to rest until she's at peace." Naomi stepped forward, before Maggie's headstone, her arms crossed across her chest. Coming from behind her, Bryce wrapped his arms around her and kissed the back of her head.

"What can I do to help?"

"Say you believe me. That's all I need to hear."

Bryce kissed her once more and leaned closer. "I believe you," he whispered into her ear.

"Thank you." Just hearing his words made Naomi feel better. She moved to face him.

"So that was Maggie back there in the kitchen, turning on the sink?" he asked, eyes wide.

"Yup. Seems she doesn't spend too much time out here. She prefers haunting my house." Naomi laughed, although it wasn't really very funny at all.

Oh, Maggie. She glanced at her headstone once more, a frown forming on her face.

"How close are the police to solving the crime?"

She chose her words carefully. "The police aren't close to solving anything. We are. Me, Ryan, and Maggie's parents." Was she being fair to Officer Marty in leaving her name off the list? Too early to tell.

"Seems Maggie and I have a lot in common." If Bryce didn't run after hearing this, she would be impressed. "We dated two of the same men. One who I wrongfully suspected of killing her and one who actually did."

"Wait—what?" Bryce took Naomi by the shoulders, his eyes intense.

"Exactly what I said. The guy who tried to kill me last night? It was him. I'm sure of it. Now all I have to do is prove it."

"Wow, Naomi. Let's say you're right about everything. That leaves you in a lot of danger."

"Nick is locked up."

"Yeah, for now. If there's no evidence, they'll never hold him.'"

"Oh, no? What about the fact that he nearly killed me with his own hands?"

"I get it, I'm not the enemy here. You know what he told the police."

"Yes, of course I know." Nick had claimed that he had only wanted to talk, that seeing her and feeling the sting of her rejection made him temporarily lose his mind.

She couldn't get wrapped up in the drama of Nick right now. "I'm not particularly concerned about that right now. I have bigger plans, ones that involve setting a dead woman's spirit free. She's been trying to tell me something, and I haven't been listening very well. It's time I did."

She went trudging back to the house with Bryce calling out from behind. "Naomi. Hold up, I'm coming."

If she had to get into Maggie's face and scream out her name, she would. Somehow she must open herself up to Maggie and hear what she was saying. With a smug grin on her face, Naomi felt better knowing Bryce was by her side.

CHAPTER TWENTY-SEVEN

Naomi

"I'M HERE! MAGGIE, come to me."

It had been at least a half an hour of shouting and Maggie had yet to materialize.

"I'm no expert here, but I don't think this is the way it works. I think she comes to you on her own terms."

Naomi shot Bryce a filthy look.

"Just saying."

"Maybe it's you."

"Me?"

"Yes," Naomi began. "I think you should go back home for a while. This is personal and she may not feel comfortable with you around." It was a guess, but she could be right.

"Okay, fine." Bryce threw his hands in the air. "Doubtful, but I'm game. Call me if anything happens. And, Naomi, please be careful." He ran his hand through his hair.

"Yes, sir." Naomi raised her hand to salute him. She leaned over and kissed him good-bye.

"I meant what I said before. About liking you." Bryce pulled her closer.

He smelled of aftershave and the outdoors. "Mm. I like you too, Bryce." This time he met her halfway. Once his lips touched hers, she was lost. Feeling Bryce's hands come up to smooth her back, she sucked in a breath.

The refrigerator door opened, spilling the condiments out on the hardwood floor.

"Go!" Naomi felt chills run up her arms. Either Maggie was pleased about Naomi and Bryce getting together, or it pissed her off to no end. Right now, all Naomi cared about was being alone with Maggie.

"I'll call you later," she whispered as she motioned for him to leave the house.

Naomi turned her attention back to the ketchup and mustard scattered on the floor. Kneeling down, she scooped the items up and placed them back in the door of the fridge.

"Talk to me, Maggie. Talk to me, girl," she called out into the empty room. Intent on listening, Naomi stood silently and closed her eyes.

It had been at least five minutes and still, no Maggie. Naomi breathed evenly, telling herself that she would give it a minute more. That was it.

She felt the push and struggled to keep her balance.

Zelda.

"Zelda, what is the matter with you?"

The cat screeched, slamming her furry body into the cabinets before running up the stairs. Another sound was heard from the top of the stairs, and it wasn't Zelda.

"Maggie."

As soon as she appeared, she was gone.

Now the sound came from the kitchen table. It was her purse. Maggie threw Naomi's bag to the floor. Sprinting over to grab her purse from the floor, Naomi noticed her cell phone spilled out.

A prickle slowly spread out across her scalp. Ryan's contact information was on the screen.

"I'm listening, Maggie. I'm listening."

This was a message. She was sure of it.

Still kneeling on the floor, Naomi peeked up, taking in the ghostly form. She couldn't move. Maggie's arm pointed to the cell phone and cried out. Was it fear or sadness causing the reaction?

"Maggie, I don't understand. Yes, it's Ryan, I get that.

What about him?"

The pitch of her cry climbed higher and higher until Naomi was forced to cover her ears.

"Tell me!" Naomi attempted to scream above the deafening sound. "Maggie, for the love of God!"

Silence. Naomi's ears throbbed, even in dead silence.

Next, Maggie did something quite peculiar. Transfixed, Naomi watched as the spirit wrapped her arms around herself. Maggie then pointed to her heart and cried out. She then dropped and her hands rose high into the air, and then Maggie fell to the floor dramatically.

"I... Maggie." What was she doing? Her heart, the floor. It was a message.

Then she was gone.

"Naomi."

"Oh my God, Bryce."

"I'm sorry, but I heard the screams again. This time I know who they're coming from at least."

Naomi sat back on the floor, covering her head in her hands. Only when she felt Bryce's arms wrap around her did she cry out and hold him tightly. He rocked her gently, holding her until she wasn't sure how much time had even passed.

"WHAT DO YOU mean? How could you have done that?" Naomi shouted into her phone. This was crazy. She had prepared for this, but didn't expect it to happen so soon.

"I'm sorry, Naomi. I truly am, but we have nothing to hold him on right now."

"Are you kidding me? Officer Marty, he tried to kill me. If you're going to hide your head in the sand about Maggie, then focus on what he did to me." Her voice shook as she struggled to speak.

"Okay, calm down. He didn't kill you, and he certainly didn't plan on going to your house to kill you."

"Are you listening to yourself? I mean, do you even hear what you're saying? He tried to *kill* me."

"Naomi, I agree it wasn't a good thing, and if you'd like to file a restraining order, I'm sure you have grounds, but his intention was not to murder you. He lost control, he admits it."

Swallowing hard, Naomi bit back her tears. "I…I can't believe you're saying this. I thought you were on my side."

"I *am* on your side, Naomi. I promise. Listen, we will thoroughly investigate Nick. He said things… about you minding your business and leaving Maggie's case alone. We take these things seriously."

A creeping headache forced its way into her head. Lifting her feet, she rocked herself in the kitchen chair. It made sense.

"It's because he's Officer Frank's nephew. Oh my God, that's why you guys let him go. That's it." She should have pieced it together sooner. Not only was Officer Frank covering up for Nick, but now Officer Marty was doing the same.

"With all due respect, Officer, I think the fact that Nick is your partner's nephew is skewing the playing field here."

"I'm going to pretend I didn't hear you say that, Naomi. I am beyond insulted but understand why you're so jaded when it comes to the subject of Nick."

"Jaded? He killed Maggie, and he tried to kill me as well. Wake *up*."

"If that is indeed the case, then we will serve justice accordingly. Believe it or not, I'm not the enemy here."

"That's yet to be determined," Naomi muttered.

"I have work to do. I'll be in touch."

The nerve of that woman! Naomi let out a deep breath. At least dealing with her was a tad better than dealing with Nick's uncle Frank.

Now that Nick was on the loose again, Naomi admitted to herself that she was frightened. It wouldn't be a bad idea to alert Bryce to the latest course of events. Besides, it was an excuse to stop by for a quick visit.

Although it was still daylight outside, Naomi felt the prickle of fear as she headed down the gravel lot toward Bryce's house. And this time, it wasn't due to ghosts. Nick was responsible for her apprehension today. Breathing a sigh of relief at the sight, she focused on Bryce's large farmhouse ahead of her.

Her breathing slowed down as she stepped up to the front door. Before she had a chance to knock on the door, it flung open, and Naomi heard Holly's delightful shrieks.

"Nomi!" Holly wrapped her arms around Naomi's waist and held on tightly.

Scratching his head, Bryce chuckled as he watched his daughter's smiling face. "She saw you coming up the walkway."

The past few times Naomi and Bryce had seen each other, Holly was either at school or with John. It was nice to see her again.

"Hi there, Holly. How's school going?"

"It's okay, I guess. I get to meet other kids, make friends, you know?"

Holly spoke like a little adult. Sharp as a tack, Holly would be giving her father many years of laughs, Naomi figured. Headaches, too, she imagined. That's usually how it went with intelligent children. Naomi's mom had often joked that she should have been a lawyer because even as a child, her inquisitive nature had been apparent.

Bryce kissed Naomi on the cheek and led her inside to the living room. It wasn't difficult to notice that Holly couldn't pry her eyes from both her father and Naomi.

"I see. I think Daddy has a new girlfriend."

Heat spread quickly to Naomi's cheeks. "I…"

"Where would you get an idea like that from, Holly?"

Bryce asked, leaning over to touch his daughter's head.

"Don't all the princesses get kissed by their princes? A kiss means love."

My goodness. Even Bryce remained speechless for a moment.

"Well? Doesn't it?"

"Holly, Naomi and I are good friends." Bryce's own cheeks flamed a deep red.

"You're not in love?"

Talk about an awkward question. Naomi would let Dad respond to this one. Part of her enjoyed watching him squirm while the other part felt his pain.

"I like Naomi a lot. As a friend, Holly. She's our neighbor."

Crossing her tiny arms across her chest, Holly stood her ground. "John is your friend and I don't think you kiss him." She waited a beat. "Hm?"

"Well," Naomi began. It seemed Bryce needed to be rescued here. "Holly, we're friends, and sometimes friends and dads kiss to say hello that way."

The child's eyes squinted as she peered at her father and then Naomi. "Okay. If you say so. I like you, so I'm okay if you want to be in love."

Bryce ran his hands through his hair and blushed deeper, if that was even possible. "My goodness, Holly."

"My goodness yourself," Holly exclaimed before running up the stairs.

"She's a little precocious, that one, huh?" Naomi laughed once Holly was out of sight.

"You think?" Bryce chuckled himself. "I'm so sorry." His eyes peeked at her.

"No need to apologize. She's adorable. I think you're going to have your hands full with her, though."

"So I've been told. Can I get you anything?"

"Water would be great." She followed him into the kitchen and waited until he had poured two glasses of water before she spoke.

"I came here to tell you about something."

He placed his glass of water down on the counter. "What is it? Is this about what happened before, between us?"

"No, no. Nothing like that. It's Nick. He's been released from the police station."

His arms went around her. "No. How could that be? He tried to kill you."

"Apparently he didn't."

"But that's insane. He did."

"Yes, but he's saying that it wasn't planned, that he just lost control when he saw me. The police are going to continue to investigate, and well, I'm just going to have to wait this out."

He paced the floor, a grim line set on his mouth. "Wait a minute. So you're telling me the police don't care that he told you to mind your business and leave the Maggie case alone?"

Naomi threw her hands up. "Looks that way. It doesn't help that Nick is Officer Frank's nephew."

"I agree. It stinks. Another thing: you can't stay at your house alone."

She smiled wide. "Technically, I'm not alone."

"Yeah, yeah. You have Zelda and you have Maggie. Somehow that doesn't make me feel much better."

Maggie. At the mention of her name, Naomi realized something. "You know, Bryce, Maggie saved me from him. She alerted me twice, as a matter of fact. That night when he was outside in his car, and her piercing scream when he was close to killing me."

"Yes, that's true."

"It's like she knew he was dangerous that night when he was spying on me from the parking lot. It has to be him, Bryce; otherwise, why would she have turned on the water by the sink?"

"She sure likes to play her little tricks, doesn't she?"

"Yes, she does." Naomi thought of Zelda, the way Maggie liked to rile the cat up, the way she directed Naomi's attention to her grave through Zelda. Maggie had purpose. There was a reason behind almost everything she did.

Almost everything.

Naomi grinned as she recalled Maggie's play with Zelda. It seemed Zelda and Maggie enjoyed each other's company and that was just fine with Naomi.

The one thing Maggie didn't seem capable of was communicating directly with Naomi, or anyone else for that matter. She could move, she could appear, she could hum, moan, and scream. Words, however, proved to be beyond her capabilities.

Maggie was trapped in a world of silence when it came to using words. No wonder she was so frustrated.

It all came back to listening. There it was again, the idea that Naomi needed to *hear* what the ghost was trying to communicate.

"I think you should stay here with us for a while. Just until we're sure Nick can't harm you. I have plenty of spare rooms here."

She shook her head firmly. "No way. I will not put you and Holly in harm's way," Naomi whispered as she looked over her shoulder. Luckily, Holly was still upstairs.

"I can handle Nick, but you're right. I can't chance it."

"Good, at least that's settled."

"You need somewhere else to stay for now."

"Absolutely not. Not when I'm so close to communicating with Maggie. I'm almost there, Bryce, I can feel it."

He rubbed his chin. "I don't like the idea of you over there alone. There's got to be another way."

There was another way, but she was pretty sure Bryce wouldn't like it. She wouldn't put Amy in harm's way, and there was only one other person she could think of that would protect her at any cost. Someone who was every bit as invested in solving Maggie's crime.

Ryan.

"There is. Now before you get the wrong idea, there's some things you must know."

Bryce held his hands against the counter, his eyes focused on Naomi. "What are you talking about?"

"Ryan. My friend, Ryan. He's the one you met at the hospital."

"I know who Ryan is. How could I forget?" He turned his gaze from Naomi.

"There's nothing between us, I swear. Just the fact that he was in love with Maggie makes this plan even better. Maybe she can communicate better with him. He's the perfect choice."

"I like you, Naomi, I barely know you. I can't tell you what to do. I can only support your decisions." He hesitated. "But that doesn't mean I have to like them."

"You're an amazing man, and I'm true to my word. You'll see." She stepped over and wrapped her arms around him.

"I have no hold over you." He turned his eyes away.

Naomi placed her hand on his chin, directing his gaze back to her. "That's where you're wrong. You do have a hold over me." Standing on her tiptoes, she kissed him. He placed his hands on her waist and kissed her back.

"Holly, she might come down," Naomi wiped her face and spun around.

"I'm not going to let you go so easily next time, you know." He kissed the top of her head.

"And I'm not going to let you." Naomi couldn't tear her eyes from his face. She lifted her hand to touch his cheek.

"Daddy, Nomi!"

The whirlwind of energy was back, rushing over to show them her stuffed bear. "Look, Nomi. His name is Bernard. I call him Bernie for short."

Leaning over to kiss Holly on the top of her head, Bryce caught Naomi's eye, and she knew then that she was a goner.

CHAPTER TWENTY-EIGHT

Naomi

LATER THAT NIGHT, she and Ryan were settled in with a bottle of wine. True to her word, Naomi's heart was wrapped around one person right now, and that was Bryce. Knowing that she was falling for him, she enjoyed the many emotions she felt but reminded herself to keep things slow for now.

"So if you like this guy, then why the caution I'm sensing?" Ryan gulped back his wine. His voracious appetite for all things was returning.

"Maybe it's because of the fact that I really like him. I want to do this right, you know? And he has a vulnerable daughter. I don't want to see her hurt."

"Is this weird for you?" He swirled the wine from his long-stemmed glass. "You know, me and you, sitting here, talking about other people?"

It actually wasn't. Strange enough.

"No, it's kind of nice. I think you and I are better like this."

"I agree," Ryan mumbled as he popped a piece of cheddar cheese into his mouth.

It made her sad, though, to think that Ryan's heart was still so attached to Maggie. He deserved to find happiness and love again, but how could he when Maggie's memory wouldn't allow it?

Maybe with time, he could open up and find love.

"Ryan? Can you see yourself down the road, ever loving

anyone else?"

He scrunched his brows and guzzled back some more wine. "I don't think so."

"But Ryan, you have so much to offer." She sat forward, placing her wine glass down.

"I don't see it." He munched on a cracker, crumbs falling onto his chin.

Oh, Ryan. Hopefully he would change his mind if the right woman came along.

"You should have some of this cheese, it's delicious." He placed a slice on to another cracker and finished it off in one mouthful.

"Wow, Ryan." His one-track mind was certainly back, though she was kind of pleased to see his appetite return.

Picking up her wine glass, she studied Ryan. She ran her hands up and down the stem of her glass as she considered how to broach the topic of Maggie.

"I'm glad you're here with me, Ryan."

"Of course. I'm not going to let that loser within a hundred feet of you. I blame myself for what happened last time, you know."

"That's ridiculous, and you know it. It wasn't anyone's fault except Nick's. You couldn't have known, and they would have never released you from the hospital. Enough of that, though. I wanted to talk to you about Maggie."

"What about her?" He put his cracker down and waited.

"She's here, with us in this house. Heck, she's probably watching us right now, biding her time before her next grand entrance." Naomi looked over her shoulder.

"I want to see her." He stared straight ahead.

Taking hold of his hand, Naomi waited a moment before continuing. "I know you do."

"Where is she?"

"Ryan, it doesn't quite work that way. She comes when she's ready."

Zelda took that moment to leap onto Ryan's lap. "Hi,

sweetie." He stroked Zelda's fur, a frown on his face.

"Hold on a second. I'll be right back." Naomi had an idea. With Ryan's help, they would go through all the events that had taken place up until now. She sprinted to her desk, grabbing hold of two pens and a pack of Post-it notes.

"Here," Naomi said, throwing some of the paper in Ryan's direction. The pen came next.

"Start thinking. And write down every single thought that comes to mind. There's nothing too little to consider here."

Naomi scribbled furiously, writing down anything that came to mind. She would sort through all of the notes later.

There. That's was a start at least. Satisfied with her notes, she placed her pen down and stretched.

"What do you have there, Ryan?" She peeked over at his notes. Or make that note.

One blank note.

"What's the matter with you? I asked you to write down anything you can remember. You've got nothing!"

"I don't remember," he mumbled, head down. "I don't remember anything."

"Sure you do. You know that you loved her, you know she loved you."

He threw his pad down and stood. "Oh, what's the use? Nothing is going to bring her back."

"You're right, nothing will bring her back, but we just might be able to bring her peace. That's what she's crying out for. It's what she wants."

"Is it?" Ryan turned to face her. "Is it? Did she tell you that?"

Her mind whirled with all of the events which had taken place.

"I think so, Ryan. What else could she possibly want from me?"

"I don't know and neither do you."

His words gave her pause. From the start, Naomi had

assumed that Maggie had been seeking closure, looking for justice.

What if, just what if, she was asking for something else? But what?

Bending over, Naomi grabbed all of her Post-it notes and ran over to the kitchen table. A grim-faced Ryan came around and helped her spread the notes around the table.

"Look. Each and every attempt has been to either warn me about something, like Nick's presence, or to make me aware of her sorrow."

"I highly doubt her intention was to just make you aware of her pain and sorrow. Maggie wasn't like that. She is trying to tell you something, I'm sure of it."

"I believe that she is trying to reach out and tell me something as well. We just have to piece together her clues."

Ryan grabbed a pink Post-it and studied it carefully. After a moment, he dropped the note, his hand trembling.

"What is it? What?"

"This one." He picked up the note once more. "What do you remember about her behavior that day?"

Naomi scanned the note she had written minutes before. "It's just as I wrote. She pointed toward her heart and then fell to the ground, in a very dramatic way."

"What else?"

She tried to recall every detail. "Like I said, it was dramatic. The entire time she was falling, her arms went up as if she were trying to hang on to something."

"Or stop herself from falling," Ryan ventured.

"It could have been that. It was very hard to tell."

"She pointed to her heart, you say?"

"Yes, Ryan, I'm sure she did."

"I remember something about her. I remember." His eyes were wide. He smiled at Naomi.

"Oh my God, Ryan, what is it?" She reached over to clasp her hands in his.

"Her heart. She told me she loved me by pointing to her

heart. Maybe it doesn't mean anything, but it might."

"It does. I just know it. It has to mean something." Her mind raced back to what had happened moments before Maggie had dropped to the floor. Ryan. His number had come up on her contact list.

"She wanted me to tell you that she loves you!" Naomi jumped out of her seat. That was it! "Your name, it was on my phone, and suddenly she was pointing to her heart. It was you! She was trying to tell me she loved you!"

He gasped and then sank back down into his chair. It wasn't typical for Ryan to be speechless, but he was exactly that as he sat, staring into the empty space before him.

"Are you okay?" She was by his side, holding him.

"She loves me," he wept.

"Oh, honey. Of course she loves you." She must have always loved him, from the moment they had met. It was so clear. Their story was the stuff romance novels were made of. What a tragedy that now, her love was out of reach.

"I can't do this anymore. I can't make it without her." Ryan sobbed onto Naomi's shoulder while she held him. Held him until his body stopped shaking, and then she continued to hold him.

"You can do it. I'm here for you, and you will make it. I love you, and I need you."

"I love you, too, Naomi. You know I do." Ryan lifted his head to look at her. Her heart broke seeing the sadness in his eyes.

Just then, all hell broke loose.

First, she saw his face, spying at her from the dark window.

Next, she heard the cries, Maggie's earsplitting wails. This time, it came on full volume, not working its way up to the head splitting pitch. All at once, she was bombarded.

Every sense was on high alert. She cleared her thoughts, coming out of the blackness to focus.

"It's him." Nick was out there, watching them.

"What's that noise?" Ryan screamed out, trying to be heard over the sound of a heartbroken ghost.

"It's her. It's your Maggie."

"Oh my God, it is her. Maggie…" Ryan drifted over to the ghostly form, reaching out.

Another sound now forced her attention to the window. Nick pounded over and over.

"Stop, Nick. Stop!" She held her hands over her ears. Ryan was held in Maggie's trance, so she was on her own.

Through all the noise, she couldn't make sense of what Nick was saying, and she didn't care enough to try to read his lips. All she wanted was for him to leave. All she needed was for him to leave her alone for good.

Turning around, she saw Maggie meet Ryan halfway, and then she did the most amazing thing. She pointed to her heart and then placed her hand over Ryan's chest.

Whether it was the strength she gathered from witnessing Ryan and Maggie or the sheer amount of hostility she held for Nick, Naomi drew her fists into tight balls and stomped out the front door.

On second thought, she went back into the mudroom and quickly grabbed hold of a heavy umbrella before heading back outside.

"Nick!" she cried out, walking into the darkness. "Where the hell are you?" Waving her umbrella in the air, she was intent on using it to hit Nick if need be.

He appeared from behind the bush he had been standing near and approached her. "We need to talk. It's not me you should be afraid of. I'm not the one who killed Maggie."

"Oh, shut the hell up. I'm so tired of your lies." She closed the space between them, holding her weapon of choice in the air. If ever in her life she wished to punch someone in the face, it was now, and it was Nick who had it coming to him.

"Stop! I'm sorry about the other night. I lost it, but I wouldn't have killed you." His hands went in front of his face.

"You were out of control. Seconds away from strangling me. Why should I believe you?"

"You're in danger,' Naomi, and it's a lot closer than you think," Nick shouted. "Take a long, hard look at Ryan."

"What the hell are you saying? You're the killer here. It was you and your precious uncle Frank who tried to stop the investigation."

"I'll admit it didn't look good, and if I could go back and change things I would. All I can do is try to help you now."

"Help *me?*" Naomi spat out the words. "Oh, Nick. You're a hell of a lot crazier than I thought. Now get out of here, and don't ever come near me again!"

Her voice shook as her body quivered in sync. She kept her gaze on his every move.

Feeling someone grab her from behind, she lifted her umbrella, without thinking.

"It's me. Calm down. I've got you."

Sinking into the man behind her, she let her body relax. "Bryce, thank God."

"You heard the lady. Get lost, or your uncle won't be able to fix the damage I do to you with my own bare hands."

Nick's eyes darted from Naomi to Bryce. "Who the hell is that?"

"None of your business, get out of here, now!" Naomi yelled as Bryce steadied her.

"Fine, have it your way, but don't turn your back on him." Nick pointed to her house. Nick had to be nuts if he thought Naomi would believe his story over Ryan's.

But just as Naomi had convinced herself that Nick was only out to cause trouble and save his own skin, she remembered that Ryan didn't have a story when it came to the end of Maggie's life.

Oh, no, she reconciled in her head; he *did* indeed have a story, but it wasn't one that he could remember.

CHAPTER TWENTY-NINE

Maggie

MAGGIE PRAYED OVER *and over, saying the words aloud. When R.J.'s arm was removed from hers, she gasped and opened her eyes.*

"No, where are you going?"

"There's nothing here. What is it that you thought you saw?"

"He was there. Right in the very spot you're standing in. He was right there," Maggie cried out.

"Who, your ex?"

"Yes, it was him. I'm sure of it."

R.J. approached her from the woods and then sat back down beside her. "No offense or anything, Maggie, but haven't you admitted that you thought you saw him before, and then there was nothing there?"

It had happened. Several times. Maybe he had been there the other times as well. Who knew? The guy was stealthy, that was for sure.

Stealthy and dangerous.

Maggie shivered. "I want to go home now."

"Home? But we only just got here. We still have to enjoy our picnic and then take a hike through the woods. You deserve a day off, and I'm going to give you a day to remember."

"But… With all that's happened, I'm not really in the mood." Feeling a slight headache, she rubbed her forehead.

He laughed, running his hands through the air. "All that's happened? Maggie, nothing happened. Except for the fact that I told you I loved you, and you told me you loved me." He leaned in to smooth her hair." What was that cute little thing you did before, when you pointed to your heart?"

Maggie released a deep sigh. "This?" She repeated the gesture, pointing to her heart and biting back a grin.

"That's it. You're adorable, you know."

"I am?"

"You are, and that's one of the endless reasons why I love you." Placing his hands on her head, he pulled her close and kissed her. She responded heartily, forgetting about her ex for the moment. The pounding in her head decreased. His hungry kisses devoured her lips. She only felt R.J.

"Okay," R.J. whispered. "Maybe we should take that walk soon."

"But why did you stop?" She had been enjoying the sweet sensation of his kisses, and it had taken her mind from her troubles. Now her ex was back in her head.

"I don't want to get carried away, Maggie. You and I have all the time in the world. I want to savor you, like a fine wine."

"Speaking of fine wine," Maggie giggled. "How about we have another glass?"

"Great idea, and then we'll walk for a bit. I think the wine is exactly what you need to relax."

He poured the dark red liquid as she held on to the glass and studied his deep blue eyes. Maybe the stress of her teaching position and all the nonsense relating to her ex was getting to her. With each sip of the smooth wine, her worries eased a bit more. It was most likely just a deer in the woods, taking the shape of a man in her anxious mind.

"Oh, this is good." Maggie sipped more of the wine.

"Hey, hey. I think you've had enough." R.J. reached for the glass and placed it down beside him. "I wouldn't want you to get tired and fall asleep on me."

"You're right. How about we go for that walk now?"

"Sounds good. Let's hike up the mountain a bit and see if we can find a new spot to look out over the cliffs."

Progress had been made facing her fear of heights, but the

mention of the cliffs still caused a tightening sensation in her gut.

"I'm game," she managed.

"You sure? We'll play it safe, as always. We'll get just close enough to see the beautiful view of the Hudson River. How does that sound?"

"I'm in. Sounds amazing." She forced a smile.

R.J. reached for her hand as they left their picnic area behind. "Should we take the stuff with us?"

"Nah. We'll be back this way. Nobody will bother with it." R.J.'s smile lit up his face. "Ready?"

Maggie breathed in to steady her nerves.

"Ready."

Naomi

"What do you suppose he meant by warning me about Ryan?" she asked. Bryce poured some herbal decaf tea for the both of them. Holly was fast asleep upstairs. Sleeping the dreams of innocent children, no doubt.

What she would give to have some of the world's innocence. Life had been so much easier even, before Nick, Maggie, and Ryan had entered her life.

Ryan. It worried her that Nick's words still lingered in her mind. She should automatically discount anything Nick had to say. Nick was trying to save his own ass. Case closed.

But what if there was the slightest chance he wasn't? What if she had misinterpreted Maggie's message about loving Nick?

Too many what ifs, that was the problem.

"I wish I knew, Bryce. The only thing I can figure is that Nick is attempting to shift the blame. It does make sense I suppose. Oh, I should just forget I ever heard the spiteful words." Naomi bit down on her fingernails, a habit she had kicked long ago.

'That is a great idea. I don't know much about this Ryan fellow, but if you trust him, that's good enough for me. Hey, what do you think is going on over there?" Bryce nodded in the direction of her house.

"I couldn't even venture to guess. Either they're getting along swimmingly, or she's trying to kill him."

He laughed, despite the seriousness of the situation.

"Sorry. That was kind of morbid, huh?"

"Given the circumstances, I would say the joke was completely appropriate." He rubbed the back of her head, helping to ease away the tension.

"Either way, I suppose I should be heading back. He might need me."

She looked up at Bryce and found she didn't want to leave his side. He was becoming very important in her life. Both he and Holly were on her mind constantly. What it all meant, she would have to sort through at a later time.

"Stay for just a minute more?" He lifted her chin toward him.

Closing her eyes, she felt his lips meet hers. His kiss lingered, and she hungrily reached around his neck and pulled him closer.

"Ah, we should probably stop." Bryce broke the kiss, leaving Naomi wanting so much more from him.

"Yes, that's a good idea." She cleared her throat.

"Naomi. Can I tell you something?" His husky voice only made her want to reach out and grab him again. She nodded, holding eye contact.

"I don't remember feeling like this before. Ever. I don't want to frighten you, but I think I'm falling for you."

Her heart melted as he spoke the words she echoed in her own heart. "Oh, Bryce."

"I'm sorry. It's too soon." Turning away, he looked down.

"No, it's just that I think I feel the same."

"Really?"

"Really. Now get over here, and give me one more kiss to get me through the night," she said, grabbing hold of the collar of his flannel shirt. She kissed him good night.

"Oh, man. You're going to be on my mind all night long. Call me before you go to bed, and fill me in on what happened with Ryan and Maggie, will you?"

"You bet. See you later." She blew him a kiss as she headed out the door to see what kind of commotion was waiting for her at home.

Naomi knew he would be watching to see if she made it home without any major drama. Sure enough, he stood at his door and waved as she entered her house.

"Ryan?" Naomi called out into the dark house. "Ryan? Where are you?" Why was the house dark?

Zelda pranced around, weaving in and out of her legs. "Maggie?" Was she out of her mind, calling to Maggie as if she were a living, breathing being?

"Come on. Ryan, you're scaring me now. Where are you?" Picking up her pace, she walked into her office. "Zelda!" She tripped over Zelda, the cat screeching her disapproval.

No signs of Ryan downstairs. Could he possibly be sleeping? After all he had been through? Quite honestly, nothing would surprise her when it came to Ryan.

"Ryan? Maggie?" Naomi cried out as she climbed the stairs. She flipped on every light switch she came across.

Flip, flip, flip.

Nothing.

"Where the heck are you, Ryan?" she wondered aloud as she saw that his overnight bag was still on the bed in the guest bedroom. So he hadn't gone back home. Did he suddenly get hungry and run to the store? The idea gave her some comfort. Most definitely he would go out at this late hour if it meant eating.

She hurried down the stairs and headed back into the

kitchen. It was simple; she would just call him. Naomi grabbed her bag and reached for her cell. She had his number programmed on speed dial.

It rang, but then she heard the echo of ringing coming from somewhere downstairs. Following the sound, she spied his phone on the couch.

Okay, he left without his phone. He would be back. She could wait him out. It wasn't like she would be getting any sleep tonight anyway.

Settling in with a blanket on the couch, she grabbed her remote and turned on the television. Her mind couldn't focus on any of the programs, so finally she shut the TV off. Somewhere in the back of her mind, she remembered that she had promised to call Bryce before she fell asleep for the night.

Staring into the darkness with her blanket around her and Zelda at her feet, she waited for Ryan to come back.

CHAPTER THIRTY

Naomi

FUNNY, SHE HAD forgotten all about the dreams. Not long ago, her sleep had been taken over by these visions of herself running through the woods.

Running, running, running.

Through the woods with someone or something on her tail.

The dreams had returned. She ran, like before, but this time it was Ryan behind her. Chasing her.

Ryan.

"Ryan!" Naomi sat up straight, gasping for air. Oh my God, had he come home? His absence came crashing back.

She called his name as she raced up and down the stairs. It appeared that he had never come home. What did this mean? Was he in danger?

Could Maggie have hurt him?

Zelda cried out for her morning treat, becoming increasingly vocal. "Oh, for heaven's sake, Zelda. Give it a rest." Zelda became more persistent, rubbing against her as she walked into the kitchen. "What happened here last night, do you know?"

Gazing up at her with her clear green eyes, Zelda wailed her disapproval. "Yeah, yeah. Don't worry, I didn't forget you."

Naomi reached into the cabinet and grabbed the cat treats. Sprinkling a few on the floor in front of Zelda, she watched the cat bite into each morsel.

His car. Why hadn't she thought to look earlier? Moving closer to the kitchen window, her heart sank at the sight of Ryan's small truck across the lot. A sinking sensation took hold as Naomi fell down on the kitchen floor.

It couldn't be good. Whatever had happened to him was bad. She felt it. "Oh, Ryan. Don't leave me here alone to sort out this mess."

Nick's words played over and over in her head. *I'm not the one who killed Maggie. You're in danger, Naomi and it's a lot closer than you think. Take a long, hard look at Ryan.*

No, Ryan. You wouldn't do that to Maggie, would you? You wouldn't do that to me. Or would he? Would he up and leave if he sensed he was going to be caught? Make it look as if something horrible had happened to him by leaving his belongings behind.

Maggie.

Would the ghost make him pay if he was truly responsible for her death? Was Maggie seeking revenge?

What had she done by asking Ryan to come here and keep her company?

Not only was Ryan gone, but it seemed that Maggie was unnaturally silent. Not a good combination. in her opinion.

THREE DAYS LATER, there was still no word from Ryan, and Maggie was still absent from her home. Naomi had gone out to the graveyard, attempting to communicate with the spirit out there.

Maggie wasn't playing and she wasn't talking.

Bryce had urged Naomi to call the police and then the hospital to see if anyone fitting Ryan's description had come in. Officer Marty reported that nothing was amiss. She hit a dead end every way she turned.

She had even considered paying Nick a visit before dismissing the idea. How could she believe a word that came out of his mouth? It wasn't even worth her time.

Above all, she missed Ryan. It felt as if her heart had been torn from her. Friends didn't just up and disappear from each other's lives. It wasn't fair. Another thing that wasn't fair was the fact that he may very well be a conniving criminal of the worst kind, and she had trusted him with her whole being at one point.

Wringing her hands together, Naomi couldn't think of anything past Ryan or Maggie. The duo was all-consuming. Even Bryce couldn't compete for her focus and attention right now.

Bryce. He was upset with her. She hadn't called him the other night before bed and hadn't gone to see him at all the next day. When he had finally taken it upon himself to stop by her house, Naomi hadn't meant to come across as distant. She just couldn't sum up the energy or the will to pretend.

It wasn't that she didn't care. Quite the contrary, as a matter of fact. Naomi found it difficult to pursue her own happiness when Ryan was missing and Maggie was mute.

Relationships were so challenging. They were fragile. In the beginning, middle, and end. Love required a constant sense of attention and nurturing. Without that care, it could wither away and die.

Damn, she didn't want to say good-bye to Bryce, not after coming to care for him so much. She had admitted to herself and Bryce that she was falling for him. Hopefully, she wouldn't fall so hard she hurt herself.

Tomorrow.

Tomorrow she would make Bryce her priority. Even as she said the words in her mind, part of her knew that tomorrow, if Ryan didn't materialize, she would feel stuck.

In the past, Naomi always had her writing to fall back on. The funny thing was, the very reason she had begun to investigate Maggie's death was to tell a good story.

One to bring Maggie some peace and closure.

Laughing bitterly to herself now, Naomi didn't envy Maggie. Now she, too, knew the torture of seeking closure. Without knowing what had become of Ryan and Maggie, a piece of her would forever be exposed and raw.

Naomi walked to her computer and sat. Going through the motions of writing, she pounded the keyboard and made mistake after mistake. After rereading the one paragraph she had managed to get down, she slapped down the cover of her laptop. Her words didn't make any sense at all. It was useless to attempt to create her story right now.

Sobbing openly into her hands, her body was wracked with emotion. Come back, Ryan, come back. She needed to hear the words from his own mouth. Murderer or not, she wouldn't rest until he surfaced.

It could have been minutes or hours that had passed. Zelda licked her nose, waking Naomi from a fitful sleep. Naomi lifted her head from her closed laptop. Someone was knocking on the door. Whoever it was could go away. She would deal with them later.

Resting her head on her desk, Naomi's eyes closed. She found Ryan in her sleep.

Running, running, running, Naomi turned back as she ran through the familiar woods, the woods of her nightmares. She spied Ryan close behind, opened her mouth, and screamed.

CHAPTER THIRTY-ONE

Naomi

INTRUSIVE BANGING WOKE her from her slumber. Who was that knocking on her door? And at such an early hour? For all Naomi knew, it could be noon; she had fallen asleep last night, and the only thing that registered was bright sunlight streaming through her window.

Groaning, she lifted her head. Beeping sounded from her cell. Where was her phone? Turning her head, she saw her cell had been left on the small loveseat near the window.

"Hold on, hold on!" Naomi exclaimed, rising from her spot at her writing desk. Holding her back, she winced. Her body ached from sleeping on a hard chair. Working out the kinks, she walked to the door to see who was responsible for waking her. The person who had left her a message would have to just wait.

She rubbed the sleep from her eyes and winced at the startling sunlight coming through the kitchen window.

As her hand grabbed hold of the doorknob, Naomi realized that given the current state of affairs in her life, she probably should have peeked out the window to see whose car was in the driveway.

"Oh, like it really matters anymore," Naomi mumbled as she pulled the door open.

"Where have you been? We've been trying to get in touch with you all morning," Officer Marty said.

"You're looking at it, and who's *we*?" Naomi craned her

neck to see the familiar looking sedan pull in the driveway.

Her stomach dropped. If Virginia, Tom, and Officer Marty were all here together, that only meant one thing: trouble.

"Where is he? Have you heard from him?" Naomi's pulse quickened as she waited for the officer to answer.

"I have no idea who you're talking about, but can only guess that by *he*, you mean Nick."

Nick? "No, not Nick. Where's Ryan?"

"Not my turn to watch him, but I would hope he's getting some help for his recent slip of the mind."

Naomi felt her sarcastic side come out, ready to match the officer's own nasty wit, but then saw the expression on Mr. and Mrs. Field's faces. Her heart sank in her throat.

"Oh no, what's happened?"

Mrs. Field sank into her arms the moment she arrived on the doorstep. Wrapping her tighter, Naomi cried along with her. She didn't know what had transpired over the past few hours, but the stress from the past few days had taken their toll.

Even Miriam Marty stood speechless, giving Naomi time with Maggie's parents.

"Naomi. I don't want you to think that any of this is your doing. Please, know we mean that," Mr. Field choked through the words.

"What? I don't understand." Her eyes scanned the faces before her.

"It's because of you that we're finally getting our answers. Answers we may not want to hear, but need to hear…" Virginia's words trailed off into more sobs.

"Oh my God, what is it?"

"It's Nick. At least, we think it's Nick," Officer Marty announced, moving forward now.

"Nick? He was involved after all, wasn't he?"

"We have reason to believe so but still lack the precise evidence. Something tells me that this will all fall into place very shortly, though."

Miriam Marty glanced at Virginia and Tom. They nodded for her to continue.

"So as you know, we reopened the case, and part of that meant conducting a proper autopsy."

Naomi turned her head away. She had been so consumed with Maggie's spirit in this house and the aftermath of Ryan's absence that she had failed to notice what was going in her own backyard.

"Pathology reports are consistent with the fact that Maggie did not drown."

"She didn't drown?" Naomi turned Officer Marty's statement into a question. "But how could that be?"

"Mr. and Mrs. Field, would you rather Naomi and I have this conversation in private? You've been through this already," Officer Marty asked.

Although Virginia and Tom couldn't possibly have wanted to hear the gory details pertaining to Maggie's death, they moved closer to Naomi. "We'll stay."

"I don't understand. How could you have figured this out? Especially after all this time?" Naomi couldn't begin to imagine what this evidence meant.

"Autopsies can be conducted decades after a person dies, so three or so years really isn't that long at all to still find evidence."

Naomi watched Tom take hold of Virginia's arm to steady her. Somebody would have to pay for the torture they had put these two people through. Words couldn't begin to describe their unimaginable pain.

"Are you sure you don't wish to go inside? I can put the television on for you, make you a cup of coffee?" Naomi asked, hoping they might change their minds.

Virginia took hold of Naomi's hand and squeezed it lightly. "We're all in this together. Go ahead, Officer Marty."

"I told you both to please call me Miriam." Miriam's gaze fell on Naomi's face. "That goes for you, too. I'm so sorry for the way this case has been handled, from the very start."

"And I think I speak for everyone when I say that we're grateful you came along and took over." Nodding at the officer, Naomi urged her to continue. "Please. I'm ready to hear what you have to say."

"Look, there's no other way to say this…" the officer began.

"Her body, it was smashed. It wasn't conducive to a drowning incident," Tom finished.

"Smashed? No." Naomi's focus bounced back and forth from Maggie's parents to Miriam Marty.

"I'm afraid so. And even after all this time, it was clear that her lungs were never filled with water," Miriam Marty stated.

Her lungs were clear. What did all of this point to? Why would the police have shared that she drowned? None of this sounded right at all, but then again, when it came to Nick and his uncle being involved, nothing surprised her. Not anymore.

"It's a lot to digest. For all of us," Virginia said.

"But the medical examiner? How could drowning have been declared the cause of death?"

"Naomi, I'm embarrassed to admit that the pathologist in charge was Officer Frank's friend. His *close* friend. I'm sorry. We all missed this."

Her mind raced with the enormous amount of information she had been given. Officer Frank, Nick, the pathologist. How could the police have missed the damning evidence that was right in their faces?

Nick. Strange, since Ryan had disappeared, she had barely thought of him. She didn't even fear his presence, not now. Now she was consumed with anger. Anger for the cruel injustice he had taken part in.

Surely this must mean that Ryan was innocent, though. "Ryan's name is cleared then?"

"I would assume so, but of course, he most likely witnessed something pretty awful and therefore holds answers to some burning questions."

If he were here, then that would certainly be a place to start. "Yeah, well. About that. Ryan has disappeared."

"Excuse me?" Officer Marty's gaze narrowed in on Naomi.

"He's gone. I'm not sure where he's gone. He was here to protect me from Nick and then Maggie showed…"

"Oh my God, Maggie. How could I have forgotten to ask? Where is she? Is she here now? Can I speak with her?" Virginia moved around the kitchen, then peeked her head into the living room.

"I'm afraid she's gone, too."

"Wait a minute, Naomi. Back up. Tell me everything." Miriam Marty approached Naomi.

"Nick is crazy, he's gone off the deep end, warning me about Ryan. Saying to take a good, hard look at him. I didn't believe him. Maggie appeared and then I wanted to give her and Ryan some alone time." Nearly chuckling at the thought of some quality alone time with a ghost, she continued. "When I came back, he had disappeared, along with Maggie."

"Are you kidding me? You expect me to believe that?"

"If I hadn't witnessed Maggie and Ryan together with my very eyes, I wouldn't either. I don't expect you to believe me, Officer Marty, but that's the truth."

Miriam Marty closed in on Naomi. "Right now I couldn't care less about ghosts. What's the matter with you? Can't you see what's happened?"

No. She had no idea what was going on. "I…I don't know what you're talking about."

"If it had teeth, it would bite you in the face. Naomi, wake up! Nick and Ryan have got to be in this together."

"No, that couldn't be. Ryan didn't know Nick."

"Well, he certainly wouldn't admit to knowing a

murderer, now would he? Especially one that was your ex-boyfriend. Nick was warning you all right. About the both of them."

"Hey, lighten up with her, will you? Naomi is very upset, as are we. This theory that Nick and Ryan are working together is preposterous."

"Mr. Field, with all due respect, how well do you even know Naomi?"

"Are you freaking kidding me?" Naomi lost it. "Now *I'm* a suspect, too?"

"Suspect, accomplice? Who knows? You're either the most naïve person I've ever met or in cahoots with Ryan and Nick."

If Miriam Marty weren't a police officer, Naomi just might have smacked her striking face. "How dare you speak to me like that! Why don't you get off your high horse, and look at what the hell has been going on with your own partner." Naomi pointed her finger in the officer's face. From the start, her smug attitude had pissed Naomi off.

But to accuse Ryan? Or her?

"You'd better step back, young lady, or I'll haul you in and lock your butt up."

"Enough! I've heard about enough of this crap!"

All eyes were on Virginia as she shouted. Silence followed her cries. "What is the matter with you? Our daughter was killed, and this woman, this amazing woman was the *only* one who cared. Naomi has been like a daughter to both Tom and me, and I am *not* going to sit back and listen to your accusations!"

Officer Marty cleared her throat and looked down at the floor. Naomi shook as the officer reached out and took hold of Virginia's hands.

"I'm sorry. You're probably right about Naomi, but in my line of work, you learn to question everything. Something very odd is up with this case and I need to find out what it is."

"Officer Marty, I get that you have a job to do, and believe me, we all appreciate the fact that you've reopened this case. However, if you don't mind me saying, your bedside manner could use some work," Naomi stated, maintaining direct eye contact with the officer, challenging her.

"Naomi, I'm going to pretend that I didn't hear what you just said. Mr. and Mrs. Field, I have work to do." She nodded.

"Yes, we'll talk soon," Mr. Field said.

"What are you waiting for?" Miriam Marty directed her question to Naomi. "Let's go."

Naomi sighed. She was somehow hoping to avoid the impending inquisition down at the police station.

CHAPTER THIRTY-TWO

Naomi

HAVING BEEN TOLD that she was too trusting many times in her life, Naomi added her latest experiences with Nick and Ryan to her growing list of evidence compounding the fact. She had trusted Nick in the beginning, and she had believed every word Ryan had spoken.

It wasn't looking good for her friend. Even the fact that she still called him her friend was a bit disconcerting. Ryan's recent disappearance pointed to his guilt, plain and simple. Where was the connection between Nick and Ryan, other than the fact they had both dated Maggie?

Had they planned her demise from the start? Why? What was the motive?

Head games. Both Nick and Ryan had been playing sick head games with Maggie, and Naomi was most definitely included as well.

Chills crept through her body as she recalled her most recent nightmare, the one in which Ryan was chasing her through the ominous stretch of woods.

Would Naomi have been next in their plans? *Oh my God.*

Nick's warnings to stay away from Ryan had just been part of their twisted, manipulative, psychological games.

Ryan's face came to mind. His kind, striking blue eyes. How could those eyes have lied to her? He wasn't the first charming cold-blooded killer, and surely he wouldn't be the last. "I still can't wrap my head around the theory that

Nick and Ryan are in this together. We could be missing something."

"You're being naïve again, Naomi. You're too close to this. Take a step back, and think about anything you may have forgotten to tell me."

Naomi raked her hands through her dark hair. "I've told you everything." There was nothing else to say. "Wait a minute. Can I speak with Nick?"

Officer Marty looked up from her paperwork. "Really? Why on Earth would you want to speak with him?"

"I want to look him in the eye when I ask if he knew Ryan. I have to see him."

"Forget it. His lawyer would never allow it, and besides, neither would I. I hope you come away with a lesson learned here. I would choose my men a bit more carefully next time around if I were you."

"Wow. Do you ever stop?"

"Stop?" Miriam chewed on the cap of her pen.

"Being such a miserable witch?"

"I'm going to ignore that, Naomi."

"Yeah, yeah." It never ended. Miriam had no reason to dislike her except for the fact that she didn't trust her completely. When the truth came out about Maggie's death and Ryan's disappearance, the officer would owe her an apology about her recent attitude.

"Can I go now?"

"No, I'm not quite finished."

"You're kidding, right?" Naomi reached in her bag to check the time on her cell phone. "I've been answering your repetitive questions for the past hour and a half."

"I can tell time and like I said, I'm not finished."

"Can I at least have a cup of coffee?" She would fall asleep right here at the table if she didn't get some caffeine soon.

"I think I can arrange for a cup of coffee." Miriam offered her a smug grin.

DESPITE TWO CUPS of coffee, she was exhausted. Every part of her body ached, including her head. This house was lonely without Maggie's presence. Even Zelda showed her displeasure by sulking around.

Aspirin and a shower; that was what she needed. Half expecting to see cabinets flinging open, she shook her head at the silence around her.

"I miss you."

Her words caught Zelda's attention. She meowed and meandered over to her. Forgetting about the aspirin for the moment, she sat down beside Zelda and scooped the cat in her arms.

"You miss her, too, don't you?"

"Naomi?" A soft knock sounded on the door. She could hear Bryce's voice coming from the other side.

Naomi listened to his incessant knocking. Eventually he would go away. She was in no mood to talk.

"Naomi?" She peered up to see him standing there in the kitchen, a few feet away from her.

"The door was unlocked."

"Wonderful. Apparently I am as stupid as Miriam Marty said."

"Excuse me?"

"It's nothing."

Bryce walked over and sat beside her on the floor. "What's going on, Naomi?"

"Oh, Bryce. I'm drowning."

He tilted her chin, holding onto her. "Then let me save you."

Naomi gave up the fight. She melted into his arms and let him comfort her. Sitting there, with Bryce's arms wrapped around her, she sobbed into his shoulder.

Officer Marty's accusations about her choice of men

may have been spot on, but what she found in Bryce felt better, stronger.

"Talk to me."

"I wouldn't even know where to begin," Naomi managed.

"Well, how about starting with a few days ago, when you decided you'd shut me out. What happened, Naomi? Did I do something wrong? Was I moving too fast?"

"God, no. This whole Maggie thing, it's coming to a head and now Ryan's taken off somewhere."

"I see." Bryce hung his head.

"No, you don't. Ryan has disappeared, and the police think that he and Nick may have been in this together."

"Really? I can't picture Ryan being involved in something like this. I mean, you care for him a great deal. I trust your sense of judgment."

"Well, it seems you're the only one," Naomi muttered.

"He just up and left? No note?"

"No clues whatsoever. He left all his belongings, including his car, which the police have taken in to look for evidence. You know the really strange thing about all of this?"

Bryce held onto her hand, encouraging her to continue. "What, sweetheart?"

"Maggie has disappeared, too. She's not with me at all anymore. I can actually feel her absence, and it's breaking my heart."

"But don't you see? It can't be a coincidence. This has to mean something."

The world of spirits left her baffled. Could a ghost seeking revenge kill a living, breathing person? Could she make him vanish without a trace?

"I agree, but what?"

Bryce lifted himself to a standing position and guided Naomi up. "Put on a pot of coffee. We've got some work to do."

210

More coffee. Something told Naomi that she wouldn't be getting much sleep at all tonight.

"Where do you keep your paper and pens?"

"Everything is in my office. It's in the small room off the living room. How do you take your coffee?"

"Just milk, thank you."

Naomi busied herself with the task of making coffee while Bryce cleared off the kitchen table and spread out some paper. Naomi couldn't imagine that she had missed anything, but as the old saying goes, two heads are better than one.

"I told you everything I know, from the shady cop to the immoral medical examiner." The only thing that gave her any satisfaction was that both men would be losing their jobs for the elaborate cover-up.

Naomi was stumped by the blank sheets of paper before them.

"Write it down. Everything, from the very beginning. We'll create a timeline and see if anything jumps out at us."

"I've done this all before." She sighed, her head in her hands.

"Just trust me. Do it, please."

Naomi set to work on the course of events. It was just like she had said. There was nothing else to add to it.

Sighing heavily, Naomi threw her pen down. "There. That's all I have. I'm going to bed."

Perusing the timeline, Bryce spoke to himself, reviewing every minute detail of the document. "No, you're missing something. I just know it. Is there anything at all you may have forgotten to tell me?"

"No. I swear, Bryce, every waking thought has been on Maggie and now Ryan. Hell, I can't even get any peace when I sleep."

"What do you mean?" He lifted his gaze.

"It's these dreams. They're silly, but when I'm dreaming, they seem so real."

"Dreams? Heck, why didn't you mention them before? Why aren't they on the timeline?" He picked up the paper and shook it.

"I don't know. They're just dreams."

"*Just dreams*? You're the writer here. Use your imagination."

"What do you mean?"

"Bear with me for a minute, Naomi. If you were writing a story about a ghost who had difficulty communicating with the woman who lived in this house, and let's just say the woman was having these elaborate dreams, what would you write next?"

He had her thinking outside of the box, something she normally did on her own while writing. That was the problem. She did her best creative thinking while writing, but now she had reached a dead end in the real world.

"That's it, Bryce. That's it!" Naomi reached up and wrapped her arms around his neck.

"I like the way this is going. Tell me, Naomi. What are you thinking?"

Naomi felt her creative juices begin to flow. "Okay, so I've been approaching this all wrong. I needed to treat it like a story. That way I can open my mind to the unknown, imagine all the distinct possibilities and variables here." She paced the floor as her mind opened wider.

"The dreams. That's it. It's all about the dreams. Bryce, don't you see? Maggie very well may be communicating with me in my dreams."

"Can ghosts do that? Control your dreams?"

"How the heck should I know? In a world of spirits walking around and opening cabinets, playing with Zelda and warning me about Nick, I would have to consider the fact that anything is possible. It's all we have left. The dreams are all we have to go on now."

"Now you're thinking. Tell me what happens in these dreams."

"At first, I was being chased in the woods, by an unknown presence, assuming after a while that if Nick were the predator, it was him I was running from. But then it became clear that Ryan was chasing me down."

"Are you sure?"

"Yes and that would support the theory that Ryan and Nick were indeed together in this."

"I'm sorry to say this, but it is starting to appear that way. Do you recognize the woods? Is there any frame of reference?"

"Not really… but wait! I have seen things. In one dream there was a boulder, another, the cliffs by the river. At the time, I remembered considering that it meant something, but damn, I didn't see what was right in front of my face."

"We'll have to go there. If Maggie is indeed giving you clues in your dreams, then maybe there will be an answer somewhere in the woods. If we could figure out the spot you were running from in your dreams, we could possibly figure this whole thing out."

"Wait! I almost forgot! M and R.J., it was in my dream. An etching of a heart with their initials. Oh my God, she was trying to tell me all along."

"Slow down. Where was this heart?"

"I don't know, it looked as if it was carved into a tree, but that could be anywhere." The mystery felt so close. This felt right. In her heart, she was sure she was heading in the right direction.

"Do you still have these dreams?"

"Yes, just last night."

"Tomorrow morning we'll go to the woods by the river, first thing." Bryce pulled her close and kissed the top of her head.

"Thank you, Bryce."

"For what?"

"For helping me to open my mind."

"Sweetheart, you're the writer. You did that all by

yourself." He kissed her mouth lightly. "Maybe with just a little push," he added.

"It was all I needed."

"Get some rest, I think we're going to have a busy day tomorrow. I have a sitter at the house, and I need to get back."

"Bryce?"

His arms were on her hips. "Yes, Naomi?"

"I think I'm falling for you, too."

"You *think* you are? That's what you said last time." He gently lifted her face so he could look into her eyes.

"I *know* I am."

Bryce's lips met hers as her heart soared.

CHAPTER THIRTY-THREE

Maggie

"COME ON. IT'S *just a little bit further.*"

Glancing back in the direction from which they had come, Maggie cringed. "How about we call it quits for now? This looks like a nice spot."

"Here? But there's no view. Come on, don't you trust me?"

Crunching leaves again. "Did you hear that? This time I'm sure, R.J. What was that?"

"Oh, come on now. If I didn't know any better, I'd say you're just trying to get out of this."

He knew her very well, indeed. But she had heard something. Maybe the wine was going to her head.

There it was again. "No, R.J. I'm serious." She tugged on his hand, slowing him down.

"Fine." He lifted his hand to his eyes, scanning the area. "Just like I thought. Nothing." He grabbed her hand.

"You barely looked." But the sound had stopped. A large animal would have been easy to spot, so it could have been a smaller animal, she told herself. Even as she considered the idea, she immediately dismissed it.

"I'm concerned. Whoever or whatever made the noise, it has to be big. A chipmunk does not move around like that."

"Maggie. What do you want me to do? I listened. I looked. Do you want to go back? Is that what you want?"

"Well," Maggie began. Disappointment etched his face. He had gone through so much trouble to plan the day out. She spun

around to gaze at the woods once more. He was right; whatever had been lurking around appeared to be gone.

"No, it's okay."

He yanked her arm, leading her up the rocky dirt path. "Good, we're almost there."

Worrisome thoughts about the noises in the woods were pushed to the side momentarily. They were quickly replaced by concerns of the high cliffs they were approaching.

"R.J., that's close enough." She came to a stop on the path.

"Maggie, do you see that tree up ahead?" He pointed to a large oak tree.

She squinted her eyes at its close proximity to the edge of the cliff. "Yeah, I see it."

"That's as far as we'll go. I promise."

"Oh, that would be a definitive no."

He spread his arms wide. "Oh, come on. Do you think I would let anything happen to you?"

She chose her words carefully. "How should I put this?" She bit her lip. "I don't think you would purposely allow anything to happen to me, but accidents do happen, R.J."

R.J. sighed heavily, throwing his hands down by his side. "Sure, accidents do happen, but not with me."

"Famous last words," Maggie muttered, standing her ground.

"Pretty please?" R.J.'s blue eyes bore into her. His lower lip jutted out.

"Are you pouting?" Maggie's eyes went wide.

He continued his charade. "Maybe just a little?"

Shaking her head, Maggie crossed her arms over her chest. She peeked over toward the direction of the cliff.

"R.J., I've been a good sport, coming up here with you, and I've gotten close enough the past few times I've been here with you."

"Do you remember when I told you I love you?" He stepped forward, clasping her small hands in his.

"Yes, of course I remember."

"I only want to help. I love you, and I want you to conquer

your fears, honey."

"But what if I don't have the desire to overcome my fears? What if I'm perfectly content being afraid of heights?"

"Do you want to know what I think?" R.J. kept hold of her hands. "I believe that you, Maggie, are overthinking this whole thing. All I want to do is enjoy the beautiful view with you and make a memory."

Make a memory. It did sound romantic and maybe she was acting a bit like a baby. It wasn't like R.J. wouldn't be there with her, to hold her, kiss her.

Stepping forward, she blew out a breath. "You're right, R.J."

He kissed her. "It's right up here." He led her forward, hiking up the rest of the short, winding path.

Her heart raced, but she kept her focus and allowed him to guide her up to the very top of the path, to a grassy clearing right by the edge of the cliff.

"Just a step closer, right near the tree."

Keeping her eyes straight ahead, her knees shook as she reached out and hugged the large oak tree before her.

"Oh my God, I did it." She closed her eyes and swore under her breath. R.J. closed his arms around her. Taking in his smiling face, she figured it was worth it. This euphoric feeling of being up here with the man she loved was all-consuming.

"Yes, you sure did," he whispered, pulling her closer until her mouth was inches from his. She gave in to his kiss.

When R.J. released her, he took her hand and gently led her forward. "You didn't really look. Come see, it's an amazing view. I've got you."

She could do this, even with her wobbly legs and booming chest. Finally, when she thought he would never stop, he rested at a spot about three feet from the edge. She had to admit the view was breathtaking.

Maggie nodded fiercely, holding her breath. "It's beautiful," she managed and then shut her eyes tight.

"Enough torture for Maggie Field today. I want to show you something." She opened her eyes as R.J.'s face lit up.

"What are you doing?" Maggie watched as R.J. removed a Swiss Army Knife from the back pocket of his jeans.

Funny, she wasn't aware that he carried a knife with him.

"What are you doing with that, R.J.?" Maggie repeated, her eyes fixed on his every move.

Naomi

TRUE TO HIS word, Bryce was at her house early the next morning. Naomi took a last sip of her coffee and grabbed her coat.

"Ready?" Bryce rinsed out his coffee mug.

"I'm ready. I feel good about this. It feels like I'm finally on the right track."

"I'm glad." Bryce leaned over and kissed her gently.

"And I'm glad you're part of this now."

"I wouldn't have it any other way." He squeezed her hands. "Come on, let's do this."

The chilly air hit her as she opened the door. It would be a cold day ahead of them, but she was glad to have Bryce beside her to keep her warm.

Neither spoke as they took the short drive to the cliffs by the Hudson River. A few times, Naomi peeked over at Bryce while he was driving. His boyish good looks were only enhanced by the fact he hadn't shaved that morning. She kind of liked his stubble, it made him even sexier.

"This is it." Bryce pulled his truck into a parking spot by the woods.

Naomi practically jumped out of her side of the car and rushed forward toward the woods.

"Someone had too much coffee this morning," Bryce teased.

"It's not the caffeine." Her eyes were straight ahead on

the clearing in the woods. "Come on."

Hand in hand, they made their way up the path. Naomi led the way, but she wasn't sure where she was even headed. This was the setting of all her dreams, but the problem was, it all looked the same.

Think, Naomi. Think.

There were clues.

The boulder, the heart etching in the tree, the cliffs.

"Shoot, Bryce. I don't know where to begin."

"Then we keep on walking. Calm down, Naomi."

He was right. Getting herself all worked up wouldn't serve any purpose. Keep walking.

An eerie feeling crept over her as they made their way up the path closer to the top of the mountain. In her sleep, she had been terrified in these woods. Here now, in the light of day with Bryce, it was safer, of course, but still ominous.

"You okay?"

"Yes, thank you." Naomi grabbed his hand as they made their way to the edge of the cliff.

Where was that spot with the boulder? Nothing looked right up here except for the fact that they were on the top of the mountain, looking down at the river below. Her legs shook slightly as she peered down.

"What are you thinking?"

"I don't know. I'm trying to see if I can spot anything familiar." Scanning the area, she frowned.

"Let's move around." He took her hand and led her to another area overlooking the river.

Together, they scouted the area, walking several miles before sitting down in a grassy clearing further down the path.

"We've been at this for hours. I'm done." Naomi rested her head on Bryce's shoulder. He wrapped his arms around her and sighed. The cold air bit at her cheeks as she warmed up in Bryce's embrace.

"Too bad we don't have any wine."

"Wine?"

"Sure, this would be a great spot for a picnic," Bryce said.

"I guess." She wasn't in the mood to think about picnics or anything else.

"Holly would love this place. She's all about the outdoors, that kid."

"How is she doing with the move and all?"

"She's resilient, I think most kids are. She loves you, by the way." He kissed the top of her head.

"She's at her aunt's house today?"

"Yup. She had a sleepover at my sister's last night. She loves spending time with her cousins."

"That's nice. It must be difficult for her to be away from her mother."

"It's for the best, believe me. Genna is a piece of work, to put it politely." He shook his head. Naomi recalled that he never got around to telling her what had happened with his ex. With all the chaos going on around her, she had forgotten to ask him about Holly's mother.

"I'm so sorry. You never did get to tell me about Genna."

Bryce frowned as he moved his eyes to the ground. "I guess there's not much to tell. She took off, after having an affair, that is. Seems she met some guy at work and it was going on right under my nose. I was too blind to see it. Last thing I knew, she had moved down South with the guy."

"Oh, Bryce. I'm sorry. I can't imagine how you must feel."

"Heck, like I said, it's for the best. She was a crappy wife and a worse mother. She did us both a favor."

"You're an amazing father. Holly will be fine, I know it."

"Thank you. What do you say we head back? Holly's due to come home soon and it's getting pretty cold."

Bryce stood and then helped Naomi to her feet. She was glad to have this time with Bryce but felt defeated that she hadn't discovered any clues to the murder. Maggie would just have to understand. Perhaps she would even give her some more help if she decided to come back around the house, that is.

CHAPTER THIRTY-FOUR

Naomi

SHE SAW HIS face, his startling blue eyes caught her breath. She was dreaming again, part of her knew it was a dream, but like it goes with being in a dream state, her lucidity was fleeting. *Ryan,* she cried out, touching his cheek.

He lifted a glass of wine to toast her. She felt an odd sensation as she pointed and then placed her hand over her chest. Her heart had opened to him. Then, the warmth had vanished.

Spinning around frantically, she took in her surroundings. It was the grassy spot she and Bryce had been resting at that day. Everything was muddled around her and then she heard a distinctive crunching sound coming from the woods. If she could only make out what it was…

Fear spread though her, taking hold until her chest thundered wildly. They had to leave, but Ryan wouldn't budge.

Let's go, she screamed in his face, pulling him, but he sat firmly on the ground, smiling and shaking his head over and over.

A sudden flash of Nick's face popped into her mind before she woke, sweat sticking to her pajama top. Her hand shook as she reached for her cell phone on the nightstand.

"Come on, answer the phone, dammit!" Visions of her dream came flashing back, taking hold of her.

"Holly!" The little girl's voice forced her back to reality.

"Who's this?"

"Holly. It's Naomi, from next door."

"I know where you live, silly Nomi. Are you coming over today to play?"

"I… I don't know, sweetie. I would love to, though. Is your daddy there?"

She could hear Holly's voice calling for Bryce. She chattered about a play date with Naomi.

"Like I said, my daughter is smitten with you."

"Hey, Bryce. She's adorable. Tell her I would love to play with her." The idea of simply going over to Bryce's and taking a break from all of this heartache that surrounded her held such appeal. But first, she had business to attend to.

Bryce relayed the message to a squealing Holly. Biting her lip, she forced herself to breathe deeply as she waited for him to return to the phone.

"Listen, Bryce. I had another dream. She's telling me more. I have a new clue."

"I'm listening."

"That spot we were at yesterday, the one where you said we should picnic?" She took a breath. "They had a picnic there, Ryan and Maggie. I'm sure of it. He was raising a wine glass, toasting to Maggie. She heard a noise in the woods, Bryce. Someone was there, watching from the edge of the woods."

"You're kidding?"

"No, Bryce. I wish I was. And there's more. I think it was Nick."

"Are you sure?"

"If I were to imagine that Maggie was giving me a message through these dreams, then yes, I'm sure."

"And Ryan? Do you think this clears him?"

Hell, no. "I don't think so. He is somehow involved in this. I just have to figure out how deeply." She shivered at the memory of Ryan in her dream. The way he just continued to smile, the fact that he wouldn't help her must mean something.

"What are you going to do now?" he asked. She could hear Holly speaking to Bryce in the background.

"I'm going back."

"Whoa. Slow down. When?"

"This morning, as soon as I get myself dressed."

"Hell, Naomi. You can't go up there by yourself. I have Holly here and I can't go with you today."

"Bryce, I'm fine. I'll be careful, promise."

"Naomi. I have a bad feeling about this. If you just wait until tomorrow when Holly is in school, I'll see if I can go up there with you early, before I head to work for the day."

"That's ridiculous. I'm not going to ask you to be late for work, and besides, I'm a grown woman. I can handle it."

She heard his resigned sigh through her phone. "Don't you have someone who can go with you?"

Amy would have a million questions, and she wouldn't bother Maggie's parents with this right now. "I said I'll be fine."

"What about that police officer? Call her and tell her what's happening. Maybe she'll go with you."

"Oh yeah, right. I could just picture Officer Marty and me, going on a hike together. One of us would most likely throw the other off the cliff before the day was over." She laughed bitterly.

"That's not funny. Listen, Ryan is on the loose. You know what they say about how criminals often revisit the scene of the crime."

He wasn't going to let up. "Okay, if it makes you feel better, I'll leave a message with Officer Marty telling her about the dream, and I'll let her know I'm heading up there."

"I wish you would wait."

Naomi considered his request, but Maggie had waited long enough for closure, and Naomi knew she would go crazy sitting around the house.

"I'm sorry, Bryce. I can't."

"Promise you'll make the call, and keep your cell on you. Call me the second you get to the woods. I want to be on the phone with you every step of the way."

It was sweet that he cared. "Yes, Bryce. Don't worry."

"Famous last words."

"Don't say that, even in joking."

Naomi hung up her cell and pondered over the dream once more. She needed a plan of action before heading up to the cliffs again. She would start in the grassy clearing and head up the path once more. This time she had some frame of reference. If she could find the tree with the carving, that would be incredible.

Placing the call to the police station, she simply asked for Miriam's voice mail. She wasn't in the mood for Miriam's crap today. Hell, she wouldn't have made the call at all if it weren't for the fact that she had promised Bryce.

Her mind was on one thing only as she made the trip to the river once more.

Maggie.

It seemed that Maggie had placed the responsibility of solving this crime on her, and she wouldn't disappoint.

Naomi sped into the nearly empty parking area, finding a spot and then slamming her car into park. The day was a bit milder than yesterday, so that was a plus at least. If Bryce were by her side again today, it would be even better.

The sun warmed her cheeks as Naomi found the clearing and then headed further into the thick woods. A chill raced through her body as she experienced a strange sense of déjà vu. It was like it had appeared in her dreams. She was so close she could taste it.

Naomi unbuttoned the top of her coat and quickened her pace until she stood in the center of the clearing. She gazed out at the surrounding woods where Nick most surely had been standing that day.

"Maggie. I'm here. What happened that day? What are

you trying to tell me?"

Spinning her head to the side, she clutched her chest at the sound of a bird overhead. Thoughts that Ryan could be following her up here spooked her. Now she was overreacting to the natural sounds of the woods.

"Damn you, Ryan. You were a wolf in sheep's clothing the entire time, weren't you?" she cried out.

Her anger towards Ryan kept her motivated. She trudged her way up the path with tunnel vision. She would find the clues she was destined to discover. She had to. Any other option was unacceptable.

Walking off the path, she found oak tree after oak tree, each one naked of the heart carving she sought out. She knew Ryan well; if she were him, where would she take a romantic date?

One that he might just want to kill?

Fear prickled her scalp as she was hit with an idea. Yes, it had to be. More determined than ever, she walked back to the path and sprinted up the mountain despite her burning thighs.

The sound of her cell ringing startled her as she cringed. She had forgotten to call Bryce. Sure enough, it was him.

"Sorry."

"Damn, Naomi. I was worried. Stay on the phone with me."

"Bryce, I'm okay. I have to get off for just a bit, but I promise to call you soon."

"I don't know what I'm going to do with you. Are you sure you're not in any danger?"

"Yes," she answered. Whether or not that was true, was not yet determined, but she was in a zone and needed to focus. "Talk to you soon."

Back on track, she reached the top of the mountain and caught her breath. She rested her hands on her thighs as she steadied her breathing. Yes, this is where Ryan would want to be if he were going to kill Maggie.

Right on the edge of the cliff.

Probably in the most scenic spot he could find, to lure poor Maggie to the edge.

Heading over to an area that exposed the river below, she sucked in her breath and stumbled backwards, losing her footing in some small rocks.

"Damn," she cried out, falling to the ground.

Her eyes came into contact with a large oak tree. Slowly, her gaze wandered up the length of the tree. It was there she found what she was looking for.

Rising to her feet, she brushed the dirt from her pants and brought her hands up to touch the etching. Her chest pounded as her fingers traced over R.J.'s and Maggie's initials again and again. It was hard to imagine the two of them together, up here. It was even more difficult to picture Ryan harming her.

"Oh, Ryan, What did you do?" she whispered into the deserted woods.

Her throat ached as the tears came. For Maggie and for Ryan's betrayal. She had grown to love him in such a special way. The thought of Ryan teaming up with Nick made him a monster in her mind.

Sobbing, she sank to the cold ground and gave in to her complex emotions. How would she tell Maggie's parents all that she would discover? It was only a matter of time before the truth was exposed, and it wouldn't be pretty.

Ryan's warm smile and blue eyes filled her mind. He was a master manipulator of the worst kind. "Damn you!" she cried out into the vast woods.

And if all of her clues added up to the grisly truth she feared, Ryan had his sights on her next.

It wasn't safe for her to be alone in these woods. Bryce was right. Rising to her feet, Naomi wiped her eyes. It would help to have a picture of this. She reached for her cell and snapped a few photos of the heart carving.

As she promised earlier, she called Bryce to let him

know she was okay and would be heading home.

CHAPTER THIRTY-FIVE

Maggie

"ARE YOU GOING to answer me? Why do you have that knife?"

R.J. chuckled, moving toward her. "Relax. I want to show you something."

Guiding her toward a large oak tree, he then released her hand. "Watch."

R.J. carefully carved into the tree. He was making a large heart. She studied him as she saw their initials being etched inside of the shape. He was clever, and he was romantic.

"Wow. That looks amazing." She crossed her arms over her chest, smiling. Men like him didn't come around very often. Thinking of how lucky she had been to find him, she moved closer, placing a soft kiss on his lips.

"How did I find such a catch?" Her mother's words echoed in her mind.

"How did I?" He kissed her this time. "I love you."

She giggled and pointed to her chest. "And I love you."

Lost in his kiss, she barely heard the approaching footsteps. When it registered in her mind that someone was near, it was too late.

"Well, well, well. What do we have here?" A sick, menacing laugh caused her to step back.

"What-what are you doing here?" She felt her stomach lurch. R.J. grabbed her hand, pulling her to his side.

"You have no right to be here. Leave us alone," R.J. demanded.

"I was about to ask you the very same question." Nick zeroed *in on Maggie, ignoring R.J, dismissing his words.*

"Nick, don't move a step closer." Maggie edged backward, away from Nick's reach.

"Stop right there, Nick. What do you want from her?" R.J. stepped forward, blocking Maggie from Nick.

"You have no business butting in here. This is between me and Maggie. Step to the side."

"Like hell." R.J. moved closer to Nick.

"Stop it, would you just stop! Nick, what do you want?" Maggie cried out, moving out from behind R.J. Her stomach lurched, her head dizzy from the wine.

"Looks like the two of you are pretty close, Maggie. Tell me, how exactly do you go from telling one man you love him and then, POW, break his heart and move right on to another?" Tears glistened in his eyes.

"It wasn't like that, Nick." she muttered.

"Like hell it wasn't. I heard you tell this loser here that you loved him, too. How could you, Maggie? How could you?" He poked her chest, backing her away from the oak tree.

"I've heard enough. Maggie and I are together now, and you'll just have to accept it. I love her and I won't allow you to hurt her anymore."

"See, Maggie?" Nick's voice rose in anger. "That's just what I'm talking about. All this talk of love, what do you do? Jump in bed with man after man and tell them you love them all? You're a cold, heartless—"

"Leave her alone!" R.J.'s voice boomed as he stepped in front of Maggie. He stood face to face with Nick, jabbing his arm with his finger.

"Don't you touch me!" Nick backed up, looking up at R.J.'s full height.

They were close to the edge of the cliff.

Too close.

Maggie opened her mouth to warn them, watching the men move closer to the edge. Didn't R.J. see where he was headed?

"R.J.! Stop, you're too close to the edge!"

"You leave her alone, you hear? Leave her alone! Get out of here!" R.J. advanced further on Nick.

There was no time. Maggie rushed over to the men. "Oh my God, R.J.! He's going to fall! Stop it!" She tried to clear her foggy mind.

"You're nothing to her. Nothing! She'll use you just like she did me and then leave you. Just like that, she'll be sleeping with another piece of crap just like you."

Maggie grabbed R.J's arm from behind just as he was reaching to punch Nick. Caught in the middle, she flinched as Nick's fist made contact with her face instead of the intended target. Stumbling, her body smashed to the cold, hard ground. She hit her head on a rock. Glancing at the men, she tried to stand, but then another wave of dizziness swept over her.

R.J.'s mouth opened wide, screaming her name. "Maggie! Maggie, no!"

Closing her eyes, she fell and tumbled back. R.J's hand reached for her, but it was too late as she fell deeper into the darkness. His howling scream was the last thing she heard before her world changed forever.

Naomi

Satisfied that she had found the carving, Naomi soon realized that she was no closer to solving the mystery. In her mind, she pictured Ryan luring Maggie up to the top of the mountain and then pushing her off. It would be consistent with the autopsy findings. But why would he do that? Were he and Nick some kind of twisted tag team killers?

Besides the fact that she had no evidence, except that her dreams were leading her to exposing the truth, Naomi knew without Ryan, none of this could be proven. She needed to find him. There was no chance in hell Nick would talk. Knowing Nick, he would keep his mouth shut until the bitter end.

"Nomi? Don't you like to play with Miss Tratt?" A dark haired doll sat before her. Miss Tratt was Holly's kindergarten teacher, and Holly delighted in playing school with her dolls.

"Yes, I do. I'm sorry." Naomi couldn't think of anything else but Ryan right now. Even when she was here on her "play date" with Holly.

"You need to pay better attention." Holly enunciated the word attention perfectly. This must be a phrase her teacher used often.

"You're right. I will." Hearing Bryce's chuckle from across the room, she turned her head and smiled at him. A warm feeling came over her.

She and Bryce had plans to go to dinner and a movie next weekend, when Holly would be visiting her grandmother. Life was good, except for the unsolved mystery looming over her.

"Okay, Holly. It has been a pleasure playing with you today. I have to head home and get some work done, but I'll see you later." She rubbed the top of Holly's head and sucked in her breath as Holly slammed her with a hug.

"Wow." Naomi laughed, hugging her back.

"Okay, Naomi needs to breathe, sweetheart. We'll see her later tonight, right?" Bryce asked.

"Yes. I'm bringing dessert. Your favorite, Holly."

"Cannoli?"

"Yes, and I know a place that makes the most delicious ones around."

Naomi waved good-bye as Bryce followed her outside. He reached over and placed a quick kiss on the tip of her nose. "You're a natural with kids."

"Oh, please. It's so easy with Holly."

"Still." He moved a piece of hair from her eyes. "I'm looking forward to dinner with you tonight."

"Me, too. I'll see you guys around six."

"Stay out of trouble, you."

"Of course." Naomi winked. Heading back to her house, her mind was focused on finding Ryan.

Instead of heading for her front door, she veered off in the direction of the cemetery beyond. Maggie's body had been returned to her resting spot. The spunk that Maggie showed as a spirit got Naomi thinking about how much she would have liked to have known her in life. They could have been great friends if their paths had crossed.

Naomi bent down to touch Maggie's headstone. "I miss you, Maggie. A lot."

Turning to look back at her house, she spied Zelda sitting near the window. No more manic pacing or howling. She never thought there would be a time when she longed for the spirit of a ghost to haunt her home.

"I'm trying to help you, Maggie. I won't rest until I do." A lone tear slid down Naomi's cheek as she whispered the words.

With her head down, Naomi made her way back to her house.

It was a sickness of sorts, she supposed. Being obsessed with Maggie and Ryan left her little time to focus on anything else. Glaring at her laptop, she frowned. Forget about writing. There would be no writing until she had finished figuring out this mess. Then she would write a hell of a story about Maggie and all she had been through. She would write about the good and the bad. She would write what made Maggie smile and what made her cry.

Ultimately, she would write what made Maggie die.

Needing to feel close to Maggie, she did the only thing she could think of to pass the time. Naomi placed a call to Maggie's parents asking if she could stop by for some coffee.

CHAPTER THIRTY-SIX

Naomi

"WE KNOW YOU'VE been up to something, dear, so spill. Where have you been?" Mr. Field narrowed his gaze on her.

"Yes, Naomi. We've stopped by several times to see you, and you weren't home. Aren't writers supposed to be working on their books?" Virginia chuckled.

They both knew her too well. "Yes, you've got that right, Virginia. I actually was working on my book, but just not in the way you would imagine."

"Your research. Tell us, is there anything new?" Tom lifted his head from his mug of coffee.

"Yes and no. Ryan is still missing, but I finally got some more clues. You see, these dreams I've been having, I realized that it's Maggie. She's been sending me clues all along."

"What kind of clues?" Virginia studied her.

"Flashes of the woods near the river. A spot where she and Ryan had a picnic."

"I still can't picture him going by the name Ryan. He was always R.J. to us."

"I know, Virginia. This can't be easy on you." Naomi reached out and touched Virginia's hand.

"And I still can't believe in my heart that he's a cold-blooded murderer." Virginia turned away so Naomi wouldn't see her tears.

"Oh, come on. It's clear as day. Why else would he run?"

Tom interjected his own opinion.

"Tom, did you see his tortured face at the police station? I've been thinking a lot over the past few days. He's hiding something all right, but a murderer? I find that very hard to accept."

Naomi had been over this in her mind a thousand times as well and didn't feel as confident that Ryan was innocent. He was all tangled up in this mess. What his role was exactly was yet to be determined.

"Oh, dear. I keep forgetting how devastating this must be for you, too. He was your boyfriend. I can't even imagine the betrayal you must feel right now," Virginia said.

"Honestly? I'm not sure what our relationship was, especially toward the end. As we became less involved romantically, it seemed we became closer. Does that make any sense?"

In her own mind, she still hadn't come to terms with their close friendship and swift deception. It stung so badly.

"Listen. When they were having their picnic, there was a noise in the woods." Naomi attempted to recall the specifics of her dream.

"Oh my God. Why didn't I pick up on this before? She pointed to her chest, she told him she loved him that day. It was such a special day for her."

Turning her head away from Maggie's parents, she realized her words were bittersweet. It was a special day, and it was the worst day.

"I'm sorry." She lifted her gaze to meet their distraught faces.

"It's okay, sweetie. You're just trying to remember." Tom moved to her side and placed a hand on her shoulder, urging her to continue.

Naomi shut her eyes tight, fighting the impending tears. "I… She was happy. So happy at that moment leading up to the sound coming from the edge of the woods." Tears slid down her cheeks as Naomi swallowed.

At this moment, she couldn't bear to see their faces. She continued on, with her eyes closed, so that she could escape the pain and focus on the memory of the dream.

"He told her it was nothing. He acted as if she were imagining the sound. That was it, but I saw a flash of Nick's face before I woke. And I knew where to look for the etching."

"Whoa. Slow down. What etching?"

"Tom, there was a heart with Maggie's and Ryan's initials carved into it. I went back up there and found exactly where that tree was. Thanks to the dream, I had a point of reference."

Naomi grabbed her cell phone from her bag on the kitchen table. "Here, I took a picture of it." Naomi found the photo and showed it to them.

"Oh my God, you have to go the police." Virginia covered her mouth. "It might mean something."

"Where was this tree exactly?" Tom asked.

Naomi hesitated as she glanced back and forth between Maggie's parents.

"It was right at the edge of the cliff." She barely got the words out. Hanging her head, she struggled for her next breath.

"What? She... Maggie was deathly afraid of heights," Virginia whispered.

Tom sunk down to his chair, covering his head with his hands. Holding on to Virginia's quaking hands steadied her. The soft sobs were almost too much to bear.

Through her own tears, Naomi guided Virginia to her seat. Nobody spoke—there was nothing left to say. Naomi knew her next step would be to sit down and talk with Officer Marty. For now, she stayed right where she needed to be.

Beside the two people who loved Maggie most in this world.

Naomi

WAITING FOR HER appointment with Officer Marty, she reviewed all of the details she wanted to bring forth to their discussion. She wasn't even sure that Miriam Marty would believe a word she said. Knowing their relationship, the officer might just dismiss the current information.

Swearing under her breath, Naomi figured Miriam Marty was purposely making her sweat out the meeting. It wasn't as if there was a line of people waiting to see the officer.

Naomi thumbed through the only available reading material: a hot rod car magazine. After a minute, she threw it back on the table. This was getting ridiculous. She had been waiting for over a half hour.

"Excuse me?" Naomi spoke to the officer covering the front desk area. "Do you know how much longer it will be?"

Pushing her glasses up further on her nose, the woman scowled at Naomi. "Officer Marty will be with you as soon as she can. Like I said before, she's aware that you're waiting."

"I'm sure she's getting a big kick out of it, too," Naomi mumbled.

"What was that?"

"Nothing. I'm going to go back and sit down to read that fascinating car magazine."

Her comment earned a smirk from the officer. Boredom was setting in. What did one expect to happen in these circumstances? Normally Naomi wouldn't consider herself to be a wiseass, but this place seemed to bring out the worst in her.

Minutes later, Miriam Marty walked through the main door, a red scarf wrapped tightly around her neck.

Reaching to take her scarf off, Miriam nodded in Naomi's direction. She leaned over to whisper to the officer behind the desk before making her way over to Naomi.

"Sorry about that. I got held up in town."

"No problem," Naomi responded. "I was enjoying this fine magazine." Naomi lifted it in the air with saccharine smile.

Miriam smirked. "Come with me."

Following in the officer's path, Naomi was led to the familiar office. It was just as cold and unappealing as the last time she was here. She took a seat in the hard chair across from Miriam Marty. She stared at the gray walls, devoid of decorations of any kind.

"I was talking to some people in town, showing Ryan's picture around. The last time anyone had seen him, before he disappeared, was with you. I have issued an all-points bulletin for him across the country as a person of interest. So far, it's as if he's vanished. Nothing has come up to alert us to his whereabouts."

Naomi blew out the breath she had been holding. "Wonderful. Somehow that doesn't surprise me."

"What is it that you wanted to speak with me about?" Miriam chewed on her pen.

Sighing, Naomi figured she should tell it as it is. "I know you're not going to believe this, but Maggie has been communicating with me through my dreams."

Miriam locked eyes with Naomi. "Go on."

Did she actually believe her? "I was doing a little investigating of my own the past few days."

Miriam shook her head firmly but smiled. "Of course you were. Continue, please. I'm dying to hear this."

Naomi told her story, from the picnic area, right up to the heart carving on the oak tree. "Here. I took some pictures." Handing her cell phone over the Miriam, she waited for her response.

Studying the photograph intently, Miriam tilted her

head and zoomed in on the image. "It looks as if this carving is several years old."

"Yes, that would be correct."

"Of course we'll go up there with our forensics team and sweep the area. You said it was near the cliff?"

"Right near the edge, yes." Naomi swallowed hard as that familiar feeling returned to her gut. It didn't get any easier to imagine Maggie falling from that height. She supposed it never would.

Miriam lifted the pen to her mouth once more, narrowing her gaze on Naomi. "You do realize I'm going to ask you to come with us? You'll need to show us the exact location."

Naomi straightened her back. "I'd be more than happy to assist. Just say when, and I'm there."

"Give me some time to get the team together. Expect to hear back from me within the hour, and we'll meet you up there. Is it the parking area near the golf course?"

"Yes, just past it. That's the one."

"Fine." Miriam nodded. "Speak to you soon."

Rising to her feet, Naomi turned to walk away.

"Naomi?"

"Yes?"

"Thank you. We could use any clues we can get with this case. Even from you."

Naomi grinned widely at the comment. It was probably the closest she would ever come to receiving a compliment from Miriam. The officer returned her smile. Sometimes, it was the little things that made it all worthwhile.

CHAPTER THIRTY-SEVEN

Naomi

WITH BRYCE BY her side, they led the police team up to the grassy clearing. She was happy that Bryce could be there with her. His friend John had stopped by with his wife and daughter. They had graciously offered to watch Holly for an hour or so while he accompanied Naomi to the cliffs.

"This is the spot that was in my dream." Her arms swept the area. Pointing to the woods beyond, she continued. "Over there is where the noise came from. I believe that would have been Nick, spying on Maggie and Ryan."

Miriam scribbled down some notes as the forensics team took some pictures and walked to survey the woods. Miriam had explained that, most likely, any evidence would have been long gone at this point, but it helped to get a picture of the suspected crime scene.

Still, Naomi couldn't come to terms with the fact that the police believed in her theory. She supposed it was due to the fact that they were coming up cold in every other area they had investigated thus far.

When the team had finished looking around, she and Bryce led them up the path to the oak tree. They stopped a few times to venture off the path, hoping to find evidence, but so far there was nothing concrete to go on, besides Naomi's story, that is.

"This is it." Naomi averted her gaze from the view of the Hudson River below. Knowing now how Maggie had feared heights, it made her sick to her stomach.

"You okay?" Bryce leaned over.

"Yes, I'm fine." Knowing it was not exactly the truth, she lifted her head. She was here to help Maggie. She needed to keep a clear head.

The team snapped picture after picture. They had determined that the carving was, indeed, several years old.

"It makes sense. Findings are consistent with the pathology reports. Damn Officer Frank and his pathetic friend," Officer Marty cursed as she huddled with the team. Naomi could hear the hushed voices speaking of the possibility that Maggie could have fallen to her death at that precise spot.

"Naomi? Thank you. It's not proven, but heck, this is the best we have to go on. You can go back home."

"Oh. Aren't you guys leaving, too?" she asked Miriam Marty.

The officer shook her head. "We've got a lot of work to do. You've been a help, thank you."

"But I could stay. It wouldn't be a problem."

"Police business, Naomi. Surely you understand."

"Come on, Naomi. It's time to get back," Bryce urged.

"Please let me know if you find anything."

"Of course." Miriam Marty huddled with her team once more. Naomi could hear plans of going down by the river, looking for a spot where Maggie's body could have possibly landed.

"Naomi. You don't need to hear this. Time to go." Bryce pulled her to his side, leading her down the mountain in silence.

Descending further along the path, they finally reached Bryce's truck. He walked over to her side of the vehicle and opened the door for her. Glancing up at him, her heart broke.

"Oh, honey. I'm so sorry this is all turning out so awful."

"I-I didn't even know her." Naomi sobbed into his

shoulder. Her body wracked with the sadness and tension of the past weeks.

"That's where you're wrong. You may know her better than most people. You've made a connection with her."

She hadn't thought of it that way before. He was right. Of course he was. The connection she and Maggie shared was a powerful one, and it always would be. Maggie had saved her butt when Nick was stalking around outside and when he had almost strangled her. Naomi would return the favor by giving Maggie peace.

"There's no easy way here. To think of her having a boating accident was incredibly sad, but *this?* This is unbearable."

"I know it is. Just think, if you hadn't come along, no one would have ever known there was foul play involved. Maggie would have haunted your home for an eternity. She's lucky you moved in."

"I'm lucky to have met her," she stated quietly.

Naomi stepped up into the truck and rested her mind for a moment. For now, she decided she had experienced enough horror for one day. "Are we still on for dinner?"

Bryce chuckled as he drove out of the parking lot, past the golf course. "Are you kidding me? Holly hasn't stopped talking about you since you left."

"Good." She smiled at the thought of Holly's sweet face. She could stand a little innocence in her life. "Bryce? Can we lay off the Maggie talk? Just for tonight?" Thinking of Officer Marty and her crew combing the woods directly below the cliff for clues, she sighed. Taking a break from all the heartache for the night wasn't a bad idea.

"I'm very happy to hear you ask. I wouldn't have it any other way." He rubbed her thigh as they hit the main road, on their way home.

ALTHOUGH IT WAS at her request that any talk of Maggie was prohibited that evening, Naomi's mind never wandered far from her. Bryce could tell. She was sure of it. From the way he would glance at her from across the room while she played with Holly, to the way he mouthed the words she needed to hear, she knew he was tuned into her emotions. Seeing his lips whisper *I'm crazy about you* made her feel better. She was ready for more with Bryce. After all the deception and lies from men in her past, she couldn't be more positive that, in Bryce, she had found what she was looking for all along.

Love wasn't something to rush into, she found. It came slow and steady. This thing she and Bryce were experiencing deserved the time it took for true love to happen. Once everything with Maggie and Ryan settled down, she would make it a priority to show him how much she cared for him. Of course, she would also be very busy writing Maggie's story once things had settled.

Bryce was worth making time for, though. He was more than worth it.

Lost in her thoughts of Bryce, Zelda snuck up on her, meowing. "What is it, sweetie?" She scooped the cat into her arms.

She continued to speak her own special feline language. Something was up; she could sense it as Zelda's meowing had turned to howling. Jumping from her arms, Zelda led her to the bay window overlooking the graveyard beyond.

"Well, I'll be," she whispered, her hands pressed on the cold window pane. Shivering, Naomi stepped to the side so that he wouldn't spot her. Once her heartbeat had settled down, she crept past the window on her knees.

Grabbing her cell phone, she dialed Officer Marty's number. Shoot. Her voicemail came through.

"Miriam. Ryan's here, he's at my house, walking around the cemetery. As I speak, he's leaning over Maggie's grave. Come quickly."

Sinking to the floor with her cell phone in hand, she waited for Officer Marty. She could call Bryce, but didn't want to put him and Holly in any danger. Praying silently, she hoped Miriam Marty would put their differences aside and hurry for once in her life.

CHAPTER THIRTY-EIGHT

Naomi

MIRIAM MARTY DIDN'T disappoint. Within minutes of Naomi placing the call, she had called Naomi back, telling her she was on the way. Every noise she heard, each creak the house made, Naomi imagined it was Ryan, trying to break in.

As much as she longed to see him, speak with him, the thought of an interaction with Ryan alone, in the cold dark night, terrified her. Her best friend had become her worst nightmare. It had happened so quickly that she hadn't seen it coming until it was too late.

He had gall, coming back here to her house, to Maggie's grave. Criminals often messed up, though and it was those times that they were most likely to be caught.

The sharp rap on her door sent Zelda shrieking up the stairs. Hurrying to the door, she nearly opened it before realizing it could be Ryan on the other side.

"Who is it?"

"Let me in," Miriam Marty commanded from outside. She had never been so relieved to see that woman's face as she was at this moment.

"Thank God." Naomi almost hugged her. Almost.

"I need to ask you something. You're going to have to concentrate."

Naomi nodded as she led Miriam into the kitchen.

"In that dream you had, the last one in which you saw Ryan carving the initials in the tree, what was he wearing?"

"What was he wearing? What the heck kind of question is that? I have no idea. He's out there, aren't you going to look for him?"

"Think, Naomi. Think. It's important."

Naomi struggled to recall the specifics of her dream. Ryan's face had been the focus of her dreams, not his clothing. "I-I don't know. I can't remember. Why is this so important?"

"Damn, Naomi. I can't say, but think about it. Promise me."

"I will. Are you going to look for him?" She repeated her question.

"I have my partner out there searching the grounds. Tell me what you saw. Don't leave anything out."

"Zelda, my cat, started behaving strangely, as she often did when Maggie was around. She led me to this window here." Naomi walked over to the window and parted the curtains.

"Don't! He could see us."

She should have known better, what was she thinking? "Sorry. It's been a long day. Anyway, I saw him out there, bending over her grave."

"So wait. You're telling me that from here, you could make a positive identification? You're sure it was Ryan? Even in the darkness?"

"I... well, I think so. The man appeared to be around his height and weight, and he was wearing a white shirt." But could she be a hundred percent correct? "Who else could it have possibly been?"

"I don't know. My partner is sneaking around out there. We'll see what he finds. Got any coffee while we wait?"

"Sure. Of course."

Naomi led Miriam back into the kitchen and prepared some decaf for herself and regular coffee for the officer.

"So you really believe all this ghost business?" Miriam's eyes peeked at her from over her coffee mug.

"Yes, absolutely. But you doubt me, don't you?"

Miriam leaned forward, close to Naomi. "If you ever tell anyone this, I'll deny it, you hear?"

"Go ahead." Naomi couldn't wait to hear this.

"I was eighteen. My mom had passed away a year or so earlier." Miriam hesitated. Now it clicked why Miriam was such a tough woman. It had to have been so difficult to lose a mother at such an early age.

Naomi nodded for Miriam to continue. "She was on my mind all the time, as you could imagine. Funnily enough, my mom had always promised that if there was any way, any way at all that she could communicate with me if she were ever to pass, she would. I was so angry that she hadn't kept her promise to me. I was so young back then, I actually believed that she was holding back on me, punishing me in some way." Miriam sniffled, wiping at her eyes. Naomi could see Miriam's rough exterior breaking down. If Naomi didn't think the officer would pull away, she would have reached for her hand.

Oh, what the heck. Naomi leaned over and took hold of Miriam's hand. Amazingly enough, Miriam squeezed Naomi's hand and continued.

"I tried to imagine what I could have possibly done for my mother to break that promise. Was I a disappointment to her? It was one of the darkest times of my life. I sobbed myself to sleep and then, in the middle of the night, something unbelievable happened. I smelled her vanilla-scented perfume before I opened my eyes to find her sitting on the bed beside me. She was stunning in the moonlight." Her eyes had a faraway look.

The story Miriam told was so powerful that Naomi could imagine the scene, could almost see Miriam as a teen.

"Go on," Naomi urged, holding Miriam's hand steady.

"She told me… she told me that she loved me and that she had tried so hard to see me. She said that I should never doubt her love and that she would be beside me, watching me grow into the young woman she was already so proud of." Miriam pulled her hand away, choking back her tears.

"Oh my God, Miriam. You do believe. That was such a beautiful story," Naomi whispered. "Thank you."

As quickly as her wall went down, it snapped back up. "It was nothing." Miriam stood, all business.

Naomi would allow her some distance. She had a strong feeling that she and the officer would relate to each other differently now. There was a complexity to Miriam that she now understood and could accept. Knowing that the officer's attitude had nothing to do with her personally put Naomi at ease.

Before Naomi could say anything else, a knock on the door broke the moment.

"That would be Harry." Miriam hustled to let her partner in. He stood in the doorway, stretching out his hand to Naomi.

"Nice to meet you, I'm Harry. I'm afraid I have to report that nothing seems amiss out there."

"But he was there. I saw him with my own eyes," Naomi exclaimed.

"I'm not saying that he wasn't. What I am telling you is that I couldn't find evidence to prove it."

"Damn," Miriam cursed.

"I… What do I do now?" Naomi wouldn't be able to close her eyes, knowing that Ryan had been right outside her home.

"We can't leave her here alone tonight, Harry. She could be in danger."

Harry shook his head. "You heard what Chief Olsen said, we're understaffed tonight."

"That's not acceptable. There's a murder suspect roaming the property. There's no chance in hell that I'm leaving Naomi here alone, defenseless." Miriam paced the small kitchen.

Naomi considered speaking up, saying that she would

be fine, but then reconsidered. A fact was a fact. Ryan was, indeed, a murder suspect and he had just been near her house, so no, she didn't feel comfortable sleeping here tonight.

"I'm staying."

Her head turned upon hearing Miriam's words.

"Really? Didn't you pull an all-nighter just yesterday?" Harry asked.

"You don't need to stay with me. I can always stay with my friend Amy."

"It's not negotiable. Besides, I want you to stay put here tonight. Your presence may just bring Ryan lurking around here again. And if I see him, he's mine." Miriam clenched her fists.

"Oh." So now she was bait for luring Ryan in. What was the difference anyhow? Naomi wanted him caught more than anyone. Anyone besides Maggie's parents, that is.

Harry bit his lip, flushing. "I don't know about this. I can't stay tonight, and you shouldn't be here without back-up."

"Well, if you're so concerned, then break your date tonight. If not, zip it. This is between us, by the way. I'm officially clocked out in an hour."

"Miriam, I'm going to say that I don't think this is a good idea. Let her go to her friend's house."

"Mind your business, Harry, and stay out of it."

There was some satisfaction is seeing that Naomi wasn't the only one to be on the receiving end of Miriam's sharp tongue.

"Get settled in. I'm going to leave, park my car up the road, and head back. Don't answer the door for anyone. I'll need your keys so I can get back in."

Handing her house keys over to Miriam, she silently pleaded for the officer to return quickly.

CHAPTER THIRTY-NINE

Naomi

SLEEP WOULDN'T COME easily that night. Not with Ryan out there. Again, her mind considered all she knew about Ryan, the good and the bad. Something made her focus on the very first time she had welcomed him into her home. There was a piece that was important about that day, she knew it, but it was somehow out of her reach.

Besides his obvious obsession with the house and the cemetery beyond, she was forgetting a crucial bit of information.

Think. Think.

She recalled answering the door, showing him around. Zelda had even been smitten with him from the start.

That was it. That was it! It was Zelda, or, more so, her reaction to Ryan. Zelda was enamored with him. In Naomi's experience, she had never found her cat to be a poor judge of character. Coupled with Maggie touching her chest, signaling the love that had been between the two of them, Naomi was stumped.

Maggie could be emptying her emotions, good or bad. If she still had love in her heart for him, she may have been trying to convey her feelings. Or, on the other hand, if he had performed the ultimate betrayal, she may have been acting out the pieces of her torn, confused soul.

Miriam was downstairs, settled on the couch, ready for Ryan. She should try to get some sleep, because God only knew what tomorrow would bring. Bryce was on her mind as well, and though she longed to call him to say good night, she knew her voice would give away her emotions. It was best to avoid speaking with him until the light of day tomorrow. Placing Bryce and Holly in danger was not even a consideration.

Naomi drifted in and out of sleep, seeing a compilation of events, of faces. She was in the woods, then she was at Bryce's house. One face became the focus as she struggled to grasp what was happening. It was Ryan's face that now became clear, and he was smiling. Those intense eyes were cast upon her, seeing through her. She saw him from a distance now, carving his initials into the oak tree. Turning back, he smiled at her, making her heart thump wildly.

A vivid green streamed through her thoughts; what was she even looking at? Green, what was green? He spun his head around, grinning widely at her.

He wore green.

His T-shirt was green.

Gasping for air, Naomi jolted upright in her bed. Waiting out her pounding heart, she blinked her eyes in the darkness.

"Miriam!" Racing down the stairs with Zelda weaving in and out of her path, she nearly stumbled.

Within seconds, the officer appeared at the bottom of the steps. "What's the matter, what's wrong?" She grabbed hold of Naomi's shoulders to steady her.

"He wore green! Ryan wore a green T-shirt." Naomi managed to slow down her breathing to speak clearly.

Miriam released Naomi and turned away.

"What is it? What?"

It was bad, that much was evident. "Miriam, tell me."

"We need to talk. Sit down." Miriam led her to the couch, which was surrounded by coffee cups, napkins, and a used paper plate. It appeared that Miriam had been in the middle of a midnight snack.

"I don't understand. Why is the color of the shirt he wore so important?" Her eyes scanned Miriam's strained face.

Placing her head in her hands, Miriam cried out, "None of this makes any sense, not even to me. I have to admit that I'm out of my element here. Naomi, I don't know how to tell you this other than to just come right out and say it."

She wished Miriam would just spit it out. She sat on the edge of the couch, waiting for the words she knew would be difficult to hear. "Tell me, I can handle it." What information could Miriam share that would shock her or upset her any more at this point?

Miriam grabbed hold of Naomi's hands and faced her directly. "Naomi. I need you to breathe."

"I'm breathing, I'm breathing, Miriam." She closed her eyes, protecting herself from the certain blow.

"Look at me." Miriam held her hands steady. "We found a body down at the bottom of the cliff."

A body? But what did this have to do with anything pertaining to Maggie or Ryan?

"It's badly decomposed at this point. Most likely, this person died several years ago." Miriam noticeably swallowed.

Naomi shut her eyes tight, attempting to block out the words she knew were coming. The words she would give anything to change.

Her chest heaved as she breathed in and out until she could hear her own ragged breaths. "The body that was found, it... he was wearing a green T-shirt, Naomi."

As if her body had already processed what her mind hadn't a chance to, Naomi sprinted to the kitchen, heading for the sink. She held her head low and vomited as Miriam stood behind her.

"I'm sorry," Miriam mumbled, rubbing her back. "I'm so sorry."

Trembling, Naomi turned to face Miriam. The officer's

face was as white as a sheet. Possibilities raced through her mind as she considered this new information. It could only mean the unbelievable. The inconceivable.

There was no other explanation. In a world filled with layers of unknown phenomenon, she had to consider the chance that it could be possible.

"When will you know for sure?" Naomi managed, wiping her mouth.

"Hopefully sometime tomorrow. Given the circumstances, they're making this their top priority in pathology. We already know he's a male, and his age fits. We need to check the dental records against him."

"I need to sit down." Naomi's quivering legs guided her way to the kitchen table. Black spots floated in and out of her line of vision.

"With a positive identification from Maggie's parents, it rules out the chance that someone is posing as Ryan, that someone has stolen his identity."

Naomi had already sorted that thorough in her head. Evidence pointed in one direction. If the body truly belonged to Ryan, then there was no other explanation.

"He's-he could be-" Naomi started. Once she said the words aloud, it would become a fact. She couldn't bear to think of it.

"A ghost," Miriam finished.

EVEN BRYCE COULDN'T console her today. The sole thing, the only thing that gave her any peace, was to think that if Ryan had been a ghost all along, he may be innocent. It was no wonder he couldn't remember his relationship with Maggie until clues were practically thrown in his face. It could also explain why he pulled back more the closer he got to finding out the truth about Maggie.

But why had his mind blocked out Maggie and everything leading up to her demise?

To his demise?

Something so awful must have happened to cause the lapse in memory.

Naomi was itching to write this story, to get all of her conflicted, painful emotions out of her head and onto the paper.

Waiting out Miriam's phone call was pure hell. Torture beyond anything she had experienced before. Before she allowed herself to speculate about what it might mean if the body was, indeed, Ryan's, she should quiet her mind and try to focus on other things. There was no point in figuring out something that may or may not even be true.

Truth was a funny thing. In the deepest part of her soul, she knew what the outcome was going to be. Crying out in the middle of the living room, she fell to the floor, wrapping her arms around her knees. Zelda scooted to her side, purring against her. How was she going to make it without him? She already missed him with all of her heart.

Along with knowing the body found near the Hudson River belonged to Ryan, she also now found peace in the knowledge that Ryan wouldn't harm her or Maggie, not if his life depended on it.

Memories and flashbacks consumed her soul as she replayed each and every moment she spent with him, starting with that fateful day she had met him at the restaurant to the last time she had spoken with him. If she had never left him alone with Maggie's spirit, maybe he would still be here by her side today.

Who was she kidding? Time was fleeting for both Maggie and Ryan. It couldn't be coincidence that after they had finally found each other, they had disappeared from her life.

Buzzing sounded from her cell phone. It was Bryce again. Bless his heart, the man certainly tried. After placing the ringing cell down on the table, she sat watching it.

"Hi, Bryce," she finally answered.

"I've been so worried about you. Can I stop by for a minute?"

"Like I told you before, Bryce, this is so difficult for me. I think it's best for me to be alone right now." As much as she would love his kind words and tender touch, she wasn't in the mood for company.

"I'm sorry but that's not acceptable. I'm at your front door. Let me in."

Sighing, Naomi trudged to the kitchen and peeked through the curtains by the sink. He had perseverance, she had to give him that.

Face-to-face with Bryce, her heart melted a bit at the sight of him standing there in jeans and a red-checked flannel. And there was that sexy stubble again.

"Hi."

"Come here," Bryce said, opening his arms wide.

In his embrace, she was more relaxed. Allowing herself to breathe deeply into his shoulder, she felt warm tears cascade down her cheeks as she spilled everything she had experienced in the past few hours.

"Sweetie, let's wait until you hear from Officer Marty before speculating. Can you do that for me?"

Looking up into his warm eyes, Naomi's tears continued to flow. "I already know the outcome. I don't need to wait for her call," she sobbed.

"I'm sorry. I don't know what else to say. I feel helpless standing here, watching you in so much pain." He lifted her chin. "What can I do for you? How can I make this better?"

"Oh, Bryce. Nothing in the world can make this go away. You can continue to be here for me, though." She laid her cheek against his chest, feeling his hands smooth her messy locks of hair. Now that he was here, she was glad he hadn't listened to her pleas to leave her alone. Naomi was learning that she needed Bryce, and hell, it felt pretty good to need someone.

"I wouldn't leave you for a minute," he whispered. He pulled her closer, kissing the top of her head. Naomi breathed in his fresh, clean scent.

Naomi wasn't sure how long they had been standing there, but when she heard the knock on her door, all of the tension that had recently dissipated quickly returned.

Bryce held her steady from behind as Officer Marty approached. The grim set to her jaw told Naomi everything she needed to know.

Miriam stood at her door in her blue jeans and dark sweater. "I'm so sorry, Naomi. I wish I had better news for you." The fact that she kept returning off duty wasn't lost on Naomi. Like her, Miriam was getting caught up in this case. Once you knew the players, it was so hard not to get sucked in.

"Don't…" Naomi's voice broke as she covered her face in Bryce's chest.

"She just needs a minute, please." Bryce held on to Naomi as Miriam stood back, giving Naomi and Bryce the space they needed.

"Oh, how could this be? I knew it was true, though. From the start, there was always something off about him. He was so full of love, energy, kindness…" Naomi's words faded as she cried openly.

Glancing at Miriam, she gulped as she saw tears well in the officer's eyes. "Naomi. We need to figure out what all of this means. This connection you have to the paranormal is the key to solving this whole mess."

"I know, Miriam."

"They trust you, and they need your help to find peace. Is there any way possible that you can attempt communication with either one of them again?"

His face. His beautiful kind heart.

How could he be dead?

"He was so full of life. He had an appetite for knowledge."

Heck, for food, too. His thirst for history, the obsession with the cemetery, it all made sense to her now. His boundless energy had never ceased to amaze her.

One of her very best friends was a ghost.

A ghost.

How could she wrap her brain around the fact that she would never see him again, grab a cup of coffee with him, touch him? Both he and Maggie sought closure and counted on her to bring it to them. She would do anything for either of them, but knowing the price it would cost broke her heart.

Closure would mean that they would be at peace, at rest. It also meant she would have to say good-bye to them forever. Was it selfish to even think along those lines? It was human nature to miss them, but it was also human nature to help them. And so she would. Nothing else would matter until she saw them both at rest.

"What do we need to do? Tell me and I'll do it." She directed her question to Miriam. "I want to do this. Now."

"That's my girl." Bryce rubbed her back.

"Okay, so listen. Do what you feel will bring you closer to them. Go to sleep. Have some more dreams. Heck, visit the graveyard in the middle of the night."

"Miriam, I think both you and I know that it doesn't quite work that way. If it did, this mystery would have been solved weeks ago."

"I know, I know. There's got to be something we can do, though."

"It's odd the way information seems to filter in, in bits and fragments. It's as if they can't fully communicate with me. They give clues, then they pull away. I'm at a loss right now."

"Think like a writer, Naomi. You've done it before. What would your characters do next?" Bryce rubbed her shoulders as he encouraged her to think.

"It's not working this time, Bryce. I'm trying so hard to think, to piece the clues together."

Pacing the floor, Miriam bit down hard on her lip. "I've been doing some thinking. Something has made Ryan block out not only Maggie's death, but his own. What if something happened to make him feel as if he couldn't move on and accept the truth until that horrible event was exposed?"

Interesting theory, but what could have happened that was more horrific than both of them dying that day near the river? It must be connected to his love for Maggie. Knowing Ryan, he would put his own needs to the side for the sake of his love for Maggie. "It would have to involve Maggie. Why would he forget? Was it just too traumatic to remember?"

"No, my gut tells me there's more."

She would have to agree with Miriam there. "If it were just the fact that he had witnessed her, say, being pushed off the cliff by Nick, then by finding her they would have already found peace."

"Yes. Good thinking, Naomi. And if Maggie is gone now and Ryan is still wandering around in the cemetery on his own, it's not finished. There's still something missing."

Visions of running away from Nick and Ryan came back to haunt her thoughts. "But then why was I dreaming that Ryan was after me?"

"They were Maggie's thoughts most likely, that brought forth that dream. If I were to speculate here, and that's a big *if*, I would say that dreams aren't always easy to interpret. Maggie's emotions must be all over the place here and we know communicating with the real world is tricky for her. I wouldn't discount the idea that she's just mixing up her memories of that day or that by allowing him into that dream, it could mean something else entirely."

Miriam's train of thought made sense. In the world of speculation, any scenario could be entirely possible.

"I'm following you." An idea struck Naomi as she stood there, glancing back and forth between Bryce and Miriam.

"I'm going to start writing. I know the beginning of their story anyway, right? Nothing gets me thinking more than writing."

Bryce looked at Miriam and shrugged. She should have done this long ago. It might give her some much needed answers. Sorting through the timeline of events certainly couldn't hurt. There was another thing she needed to do as well, but she wasn't entirely confident Miriam would feel the same.

"Miriam?" It was worth a shot. "I need to ask you a rather large favor. All I ask is that you keep an open mind."

Miriam's eyes scanned Naomi's face. "Oh, no. I told you before, no way."

Bryce tried to follow their conversation, but his face gave away the fact that he was clueless as to what was going on.

"He's the only other one besides Ryan and Maggie that knows exactly what went down that day. He's involved in this conundrum; otherwise why the grand cover-up, the threats?"

"Listen. We already know that he's involved, but it would be sheer stupidity to allow you to speak with him, and like I said last time, he's not talking."

"He's still at the station, I hope."

"Absolutely. The judge considered him a flight risk, so bail was set so high, his sorry butt won't see the light of day in quite a while, if ever."

"Naomi," Bryce interjected. He touched her arm. "I don't want you within a hundred feet of Nick. What are you thinking?"

"Don't you both see how important this is? I have to see him, Miriam, please."

She could see Miriam working it through, from the way she shook her head to eventually making eye contact with Naomi. "He's refusing his public defender. He's a stubborn guy, Naomi, I'll tell you that."

"So that means he isn't bound to any privacy issues as of now. That if he agrees to see me as a visitor, I could technically get in to see him?"

"First of all, why would he ever agree to see you? A guy like that isn't going to help you, Naomi. He's guilty as sin, probably due to the fact that he not only murdered Maggie, but now Ryan as well. That's two people, Naomi, two. Let's not make it three." He held three fingers in the air.

"I can count," Naomi grumbled. "Still, it's essential that I speak with him. If he refuses, I'll drop it. Fair enough?"

"Oh, heck, Naomi. As much as I hate to admit it, you make a good point. He is the only witness—uh, make that suspect."

"Miriam, with all due respect, are you nuts?" Bryce cried out. His face flushed a deep red, causing Naomi to wince.

"Trust us on this one, Bryce. The sooner we can move on from this case, the better off we'll all be, including Maggie and Ryan."

"Let's do this." Naomi rushed toward the small closet near the stairs. Miriam shrugged and avoided making eye contact with Bryce.

"What? Well, then I'm going, too."

"You can come along, Bryce, but you can't come in when I speak with Nick. He won't talk in front of anyone else. I'm sure of it."

He glanced at his watch and cursed. "Shoot, Naomi. I'm going to be late for work. I don't like this."

"She's safe with me. Promise." Miriam hooked her arm around Naomi's shoulder and plastered on a smile.

"It's not like I have any choice. Please be careful, Naomi." Naomi stood on her tiptoes and leaned over to kiss him quickly.

"Promise."

CHAPTER FORTY

Naomi

WHAT WAS HE going to do? Checking the time on her cell phone, Naomi sighed. She hoped he would agree to see her. He had kept warning her away from Ryan the last time she saw him. Funny, he had nearly helped to convince her that Ryan was a threat. She pushed the image of Ryan from her mind. It was too painful and she would require all of her strength to get through a conversation with Nick. If he even agreed to see her, that is.

"Ma'am? This way, please." An officer came out to the waiting area where she had signed in. She walked past hushed conversations.

"He's coming out to see me?"

"Looks that way, ma'am. That is why I called you."

Sarcasm didn't sit well with Naomi right now. She mumbled under her breath as the officer led her into a narrow, well lit room. The bland walls and lack of décor did not ease her nerves any.

The buzz of chatter could be heard as she passed inmate after inmate. The last seat was empty. That would be hers. Nick's chair on the opposite side of the stained, foggy plexiglass was empty. She still wasn't sure he would show until she saw him appear from the opposite side of the room behind the divider. His orange suit only exaggerated the shadows beneath his eyes.

He threw himself down on the hard, plastic chair, and

Naomi silently prayed she would get some cooperation and answers from him. He sat, eyes scanning her face. It looked as if she would be the first to speak. A wave of nausea came over her. Not sure if it was due to the stench of sweat in the air or her nerves, she swallowed and lifted her head. Picking up the black phone on the wall, she tried to steady her shaking hands.

"Nick."

He snatched the phone from his side of the glass. "What do you want from me, Naomi? What could you possibly want now?"

Naomi fidgeted in her chair. Miriam was across the room, her eyes peeled on Naomi, nodding for her to continue.

"I want the truth, Nick. For once in your life, I want you to put aside your issues and try to help someone else. What happened that day? How did Maggie and Ryan die?"

The mention of Ryan's name caught his attention. His eyebrow lifted as a sneer set upon his face. "I warned you about him, didn't I?"

He did. My God, what must he have thought after he saw Ryan? If she were to guess, Nick was involved in Ryan's death as well as Maggie's. No wonder Nick had behaved as if he was losing his mind.

"Yes. But you knew he was dead, didn't you, Nick?"

His face was inches from the plastic divider between them. Spittle covered the plexiglass before her. "I had no freaking idea what the hell happened to him. How would I have known? I wasn't even there."

"Nick, you're lying. You were there, in the woods when they were picnicking. She was frightened. At first I thought Ryan was working with you, that you were both murderers, but then his body was found. That kind of dispelled that theory, wouldn't you say?"

He glanced around the room, his eyes on Miriam in the far corner. "He... his body was found?"

"Yup. Now are you going to tell me what happened and

why you and your uncle covered up Maggie's death?"

"I don't have to talk to you. I owe you nothing." He sat back on his chair, his eyes cold.

Now it was Naomi's turn to lean in to the glass. "Excuse me?" From the corner of her eye, she could see Miriam tapping her watch. She knew her time with Nick wasn't unlimited. "Of course you owe me answers. A man and a woman are dead and you're responsible."

"I'm not. I'm not responsible! He did it, it was all his fault."

"Bull, and it's not nice to speak ill of the dead, Nick. How did they die?"

"I'm going to get a lawyer. I am not going down for what Ryan did."

"Ryan is dead! Dead! You were there, he told me."

"He told you? I thought…" His brows scrunched as he fidgeted in his chair. "I thought at first that maybe somehow he had survived, but he couldn't possibly have."

"Oh? And why is that?"

"No you don't. You're trying to get me to talk and I won't."

"Listen to me good, Nick. Ryan is a ghost, he's been by my side for weeks and now he's in my dreams, along with Maggie. They won't stop until they see justice. If you're as innocent as you claim, spare everyone the time and cost of a trial and come clean. What happened that day at the cliffs?"

He bit his lip, eyes boring into hers. She counted to ten silently, waiting for his resolve to slip. She was close, and it seemed that above all, he disliked any talk of Ryan.

"They're haunting my every waking thought and don't give me peace, not even in my dreams. I doubt you'd be able to handle the agony I've witnessed firsthand if they decide to zero in on you." She narrowed her gaze on him, baiting him.

He spun his head around the room, as if searching for the ghosts of Maggie and Ryan. "No."

"You bet." Smugly, Naomi silently cheered her ingenious plan.

"I don't believe you. You're full of crap, Naomi. Always have been," he spat.

"Oh? Well then, how would I have known about the picnic, the heart etching near where they fell to their deaths?" It was a wild card, but she decided to play it. Miriam had shared that autopsy results were conclusive for Ryan falling from a great height.

"I didn't push them over, I swear. It was Ryan's fault. If it weren't for him getting up in my face, she would have never tried to save me. She wouldn't have stumbled..." Tears welled in his eyes, and he was distraught. Miriam edged closer to them, doing her best to stay out of Nick's line of vision.

"Is everything okay here?" One of the officers approached, his eyes wide. Miriam grabbed hold of the man's arm, leading him away from Naomi and Nick. Nick's emotions were so high, he didn't seem to notice the interaction.

"Wait a minute. Did you just say that Maggie tried to save you?" Her heart pounded wildly.

"She did. Oh my God, Naomi. I would have never killed her. I was in love with her. Heartbroken, yes, but I would have never pushed her. She died trying to save me. He died trying to reach for her. It was a horrible accident, Naomi." His mouth turned down.

An accident? Could she afford to believe a word he was saying? It was Ryan's indirect argument with Nick that had caused the fall? Looking at Nick's strained face, she knew he was telling the truth. My God, no wonder Ryan couldn't come to terms with what had happened that day years ago. Although it had been a horrific accident, she knew the guilt he must be facing was unbearable.

"Nick, how could you have kept this a secret? Why didn't you just explain what happened?" Tears for Ryan,

Maggie, and even Nick fell freely down her face.

"Who would believe me? I didn't even know for sure where Ryan's body was. My uncle Frank and I searched endlessly for the bodies. Maggie, she was easy to find, but him? We never did find him."

"The police discovered his remains in the woods below where he fell. Why the cover up? Couldn't your uncle have helped you?"

"He claimed no one would believe me. I was guilty of following her around, Naomi. I *stalked her*. Hell, there were probably witnesses. I never thought anybody would look into it any further. She haunted me, though. She did. She was in my dreams, taunting me over and over to turn myself in. I couldn't. I just couldn't do it. When you got close, I panicked. I didn't mean to hurt you, either, Naomi. I was scared, just so scared."

"That's no excuse, Nick, and you know it. You may not be guilty of murder, but you're sure as hell guilty of plenty of criminal offenses. What the heck were you and Frank thinking? My God, the amount of pain you caused her family? There's no excuse." She ran her hands through her dark, tangled hair, unable to fathom the events that were unfolding before her.

"I'm sorry, Naomi. I truly am."

Standing to her feet, she shook her head in disgust. "Save it, Nick." She pushed her chair back. This kept getting worse and worse.

Poor Maggie. Poor Ryan.

And Maggie's parents? It was unfathomable what had occurred.

Seconds later, Miriam nodded toward Naomi. She watched as Miriam followed Nick and the other officer to the back room. Figuring the interrogation would last for hours, she decided to go home and call Bryce. Heck, she could definitely start her story now. Now that all of the major pieces of the puzzle were in place, she would begin to unfold a tale that would help to bring Maggie and Ryan some justice.

Half an hour after she had discovered the cold, honest truth, she found herself sitting alone in the diner that she and Ryan had frequented so often. When the waitress had asked if she would like her usual coffee and platter of cookies, she had almost broken down. Ryan wouldn't be here anymore. He wouldn't laugh with her, talk with her, eat an offensive amount of food. Nothing.

His absence was deafening.

Sipping at her coffee, she stared out the café window. Couples walked past, hand in hand. Bryce. She still hadn't called Bryce. She needed this time of solitude to get herself together. So many of the finer details would have to be sorted out. Where would they lay him to rest? Did he have any family close by?

Funny, they had never gotten past the fact that his mother had passed years ago, and his father had been an absentee parent. She did know that he had a brother who lived out West, but had nothing other than that to go on. Miriam would surely make the necessary connections, so that they could lay him to rest properly.

In her heart, Naomi knew instinctively where he should be buried, but the choice wasn't hers to make. He would want to be by Maggie's side, just as he had been in life. They were kindred spirits, meant to be joined together in the afterlife. Naomi could only hope that Ryan's brother would understand. If not, well, Maggie wouldn't be very pleased. To say the least.

"Any more coffee?" The familiar young waitress walked over with a pot of regular coffee.

"I'm good, thanks." She looked down at her half empty cup of coffee.

"Will your friend be joining you today?" The blonde girl couldn't disguise her interest in Ryan. She sensed that the waitress had harbored a little crush on Ryan the past few times they had been in the café.

"No," Naomi whispered. She dropped her chin down. "No, he won't." Biting back her tears, she had to turn her head away.

"Oh. I didn't mean…"

"It's-it's fine." Naomi waved her hand to dismiss the rest of the conversation. What could she possibly even say? Oh, and by the way, that handsome man I know you're crushing on, he's a ghost?

She needed to get the heck out of there. First though, she would call Bryce and tell him about her discovery. Next, well, next would be the most difficult part. Telling Maggie's parents was something she knew she must do, before the police had a chance to. After getting into her car, she closed the door and reached for her phone.

"Bryce." She waited a beat before continuing. "I have so much to tell you."

"How did it go?"

"Well, it was awful, but I learned a lot. Bryce, it was all a horrible accident. Apparently Nick had followed Ryan and Maggie up to the cliff, and then an argument ensued between Nick and Ryan. They were near the edge of the cliff when Ryan and Nick became physical. Maggie intervened to warn Nick he was too close to the edge. Nick says she stumbled and fell."

"And Ryan went after her, trying to save her," Bryce finished her sentence.

"Yes. So Nick said."

"And do you believe him?"

She sighed. "Yes, I do. I don't think he was lying."

"Well then that means Ryan isn't a murderer. That clears him."

Guilt rushed through her. "You know, I'm ashamed to admit that I ever considered it. What kind of friend was I to doubt him?"

"Don't do that. Don't tear yourself apart—you couldn't

have known. All the evidence certainly pointed to both Ryan and Nick being guilty."

"Yeah, well, neither one of them is a murderer, but somehow I don't feel any better about all of this. How could Nick have covered this up?"

And what kind of person was she to ever have dated him? The question had run through her mind a hundred times over the past few weeks. Now that she was sure he wasn't a murderer, she still doubted herself. Murderer or elaborate schemer, he was the worst kind of person. Selfish didn't begin to describe his actions. He and his uncle had better pay the price for their horrific decisions and the cruel injustice of the legal system.

"I have to go, Bryce. I have to speak to Maggie's parents now." She lowered her voice.

"Oh, man. Are you sure you want to do this alone?"

"Thank you for asking, but it's the only way I would want to handle this. I'll call you later, okay?"

"Yes, and I'll be thinking of you. This is tough, Naomi, but they deserve to hear it from you. You'll give them the closure they need."

"Thank you. Talk to you soon."

"Naomi?" he asked. "I think you're an amazing person, and I'm so lucky to have met you."

His words gave her courage. "Thank you, and I'm lucky to have you in my life."

Gently, she placed her cell phone down on the console and then started the car for her trip across town. What would be the best way to approach them? Tell them everything or just the basics?

Once she stood on the front porch, and she saw their vulnerable faces, she knew that she would spare the harsh details and just give the bare facts. If they wished to know more, they could ask Miriam.

"Come in. My God, what's happened?" Virginia scooted her through the front entrance. She sucked in her breath, preparing to tell them what she had uncovered about Maggie's accident.

"Sit down, please."

Tom sat first, then Virginia and Naomi followed suit. The sound of the grandfather clock ticked and ticked.

Tick, tock.

Tick, tock.

"It was an accident. Neither Nick nor Ryan is a murderer."

"What? How do you know this? What did you find out?" Tom stood, moving closer.

"I spoke with Nick, and everything he said makes sense. Basically, he and Ryan were in the middle of a fight near the edge, and Maggie stepped forward to try to stop Nick from backing up to the cliff."

"And you believe him? What about Ryan? Has he been found?" Virginia exclaimed.

"Virginia, Tom? I think you need to keep an open mind here for what I'm about to tell you." Her gaze wavered between Maggie's parents. If they believed Maggie was a ghost, they might believe the news she was about to tell them.

"Ryan died that day on the cliff with Maggie. He was killed trying to save her."

Clenching her teeth, she waited out the inevitable questions and the shock that would follow. She could still hardly believe that Ryan was a ghost herself.

"What did you just say?" Tom moved in, his eyes wide.

"I said that Ryan died ..."

"But that's ludicrous!"

"Tom, I agree with you, but unfortunately it's a fact. Officer Marty found his body in the woods at the bottom of the cliffs."

Virginia placed her hand on her chest and sat on the couch. "I don't feel very well." She placed her pale face in her hands.

"I'm so sorry to have to tell you all of this. It was a positive ID. Nick and his uncle covered everything up to save Nick's butt."

Tom sat down beside his wife and wrapped his arms around her. Naomi stared at the couple she had grown to care for so much. They needed some time to be alone, some time to start the healing process. Shaking her head, Naomi quietly backed up and turned to walk toward the door. Her throat ached as her eyes filled with tears.

"Naomi, where are you going?" Virginia lifted her hand, motioning for Naomi to come join them. "Come here. Don't you dare leave us right now."

Virginia and Tom opened their arms to her, and she sank into them. This cathartic release of emotions took a toll on her. All she had wanted in the past few weeks were answers and closure for Maggie.

Now she had her answers and somehow she felt worse, if anything. Worse, no doubt, because she would never see Ryan again, never sit with him for hours at time. Whom would she roam the graveyard with? Have dinner with?

Bryce, of course, was the obvious answer, and as much as she was growing to care for him, there would always be a hole in her heart where Ryan belonged. *Damn you, Ryan. Why did you have to leave me?*

CHAPTER FORTY-ONE

Naomi

DARKNESS SETTLED OVER the cold, damp cemetery. It had been two days since Naomi discovered the truth about Maggie and Ryan. She had opened herself up to the spirits of Maggie and Ryan, she had tried everything she could think of to bring them back to her, just one last time, so she could say good-bye.

Strange how things worked out; she had risked everything to bring closure for two of her favorite people, and now she needed them to return the favor. Without the final piece in place, she would be forever haunted by the memory of a beautiful woman named Maggie and one of the sweetest men she had ever known.

So now, she stood before Maggie's grave, crying out for her to come forward, to make a sound, to touch her, anything. Where had they gone? And were they happy together at last?

Ryan's brother Phil was proving to be a pill. He claimed it wasn't wise to bury Ryan in a place so far from his own home. Naomi had practically screamed that he was acting selfishly. Explaining how he and Maggie had such a special bond, in life and in death, only made him more upset. Obviously he wasn't one of the believers.

Phil was due to arrive the next day from out West. Naomi had asked for him to stop by when he had a chance. Her plan involved getting him in a room with both herself and Miriam. If he didn't take her word for the fact that Ryan was now a ghost, maybe he would believe a police officer.

Maggie was characteristically silent. A harsh wind swept through the air, messing with Naomi's hair. Shivering, Naomi wrapped her arms tightly around herself and said good night to Maggie's grave. Crunching on the dried leaves, Naomi relaxed as she listened to the hooting of an owl nearby.

Moonlight lit the narrow path leading back to her house. Bryce had said he would call to say good night to her soon. She had made a promise to Bryce that as soon as this mystery had come to an end, she would focus on other things. Things like their relationship, her book and above all, the real world. Living among the spirits didn't do much to brighten her mood.

But, she had come to find that living without them was far worse.

She opened the door to find Zelda waiting for her. Peering down at her cat's cute little face, she sighed. "Looks like it's just you and me now, Zelda. You okay with that?"

She knew Zelda was just as affected as she was by Maggie's absence. Reaching down to grab her cat, Naomi cuddled her before placing her on the counter top. Normally, she never allowed Zelda to jump up on the counter, but tonight her melancholy mood overrode her silly rules.

"That's right, don't get used to being up here, Zelda," Naomi responded to Zelda's content purring.

Tonight, she would write. Over the past several days, she had knocked out a few chapters. The first chapters set the stage for the plot of the story, and in turn, evoked varied emotions from Naomi. It would get more distressing the deeper she got into weaving Maggie and Ryan's tale.

Was this what they wanted from her? If so, would they appear before her one last time? Either way, she had promised to write the story and she was intent on keeping her word. Flowing from her fingertips came the words that needed to be said. She barely noticed the time that slipped by while she was writing. It was always like that once she got into the groove.

Stretching her legs, she padded into the kitchen to grab some decaf tea. She noticed her cell phone on the table. Shoot, Bryce had said he would call. She must have been at her desk for at least two hours.

Sure enough, there was a missed call and a text from Bryce. *Tried calling. Wanted to say goodnight. It's late, I'll talk to you in the morning. XOXO B*

Holding her phone to her chest, she swayed slightly. "Forgive me, Bryce. My head is so wrapped up in them. I promise you I'll make it up to you." She said the words aloud, even knowing Bryce couldn't hear her plea.

EARLY THE NEXT morning, Naomi rose before her bedside alarm sounded. Sleep still evaded her, and she guessed that it would for some time to come. She didn't want to miss Phil's visit. Since he claimed that he only had a few minutes to spend with her, she needed to make the most of her time.

After a quick shower, Naomi ran to the store and purchased some bagels for them. Hopefully the smell of fresh coffee and warm bagels would be enough to entice him to stay for a while. The longer he stayed, the better her chances were at getting him to agree to lay Ryan to rest outside in the cemetery next to his soul mate.

Miriam had texted that she was on her way, due to arrive without her partner again. Naomi couldn't ignore the fact that she and Miriam were growing closer. Hell, they might even consider each other friends at this point.

The table was set, and the unmistakable aroma of coffee drifted through the air. She paced the floor, trying to keep calm while waiting. Spying a car pulling up in the driveway, she walked over to the window and saw Miriam approaching. Good, it would be best if they presented a united front from the start.

"Hey, good morning."

"Hi, Miriam. He should be arriving any minute. Come in, I have some fresh coffee on."

Miriam smiled at the sight of the bagels and coffee in the kitchen. "You sure know how to charm someone. Works for me." She grabbed a cup and poured herself a piping hot cup of coffee. "Bagels, too?"

"I go all out," Naomi chuckled as she watched Miriam grab a poppy seed bagel. Naomi was too nervous to eat right now. She felt like pulling her hair out as she fixated on the clock.

"He's late," Naomi commented.

"He'll come."

"How do you know that?" Naomi squinted her eyes at Miriam.

"I don't. Just trying to make you feel better." She bit into her bagel. A smear of cream cheese stayed on her lip. Just as she was about to say something, memories of Ryan came flooding in. The way he would eat, oblivious to everything else around him.

"He's here." Miriam leaned over the windowsill, watching a red Jeep pull up. "Not bad on the eyes, either," Miriam whistled.

She had never heard Miriam comment on a man in all the time she had known her. As a matter of fact, she realized right then that she had no idea what the officer's romantic status was.

"Here." Naomi leaned over, dabbing at Miriam's mouth with a napkin. "You've got a little cream cheese on your mouth."

Before Phil had a chance to knock on the door, Naomi and Miriam greeted him.

Sucking in her breath, Naomi felt her knees buckle

at the sight of Phil. Except for his shorter stature, he and Ryan could pass as twins. He looked a few years older than Ryan, as well. A few laugh lines did nothing to diminish his attractiveness.

"Hi, I'm Naomi. It's nice to meet you." She extended her hand to him. Waiting for Miriam to introduce herself, she noticed the look in Phil's eyes. He scanned Miriam up and down, his eyes finally resting on her face.

Miriam, too, stood speechless. Naomi knocked her hip into Miriam, clearing her throat. "Oh. Nice to meet you. I'm Officer Marty. Call me Miriam." Miriam blushed a deep red. *So she is human*, Naomi thought to herself with a grin.

"Miriam. Nice to meet you." Phil's gaze remained fixed on her.

"Come on. I have coffee and bagels inside." Leading him to the table, Naomi watched as Miriam excused herself to the restroom. She was probably splashing cold water on her face as Naomi prepared Phil's coffee.

"So, Phil. I want to tell you that I was a good friend of your brother's."

"Oh? How long ago did you meet him?"

"I met him a few months ago," Naomi managed. His direct gaze challenged her.

"Really? So then you didn't know him." It wasn't a question.

"No, like I said, we became close friends." It suddenly felt warm in here. Naomi pulled at the collar of her sweater.

"When he was dead."

She gulped. "Yes." Where the hell was Miriam?

"I can't believe I'm listening to this garbage. So Ryan's ghost and you became fast friends?" He was mocking her. Damn, where was Miriam?

"Yes. That's right."

"And his ghostly form came to you and told you where to bury his body?"

She glanced impatiently at the empty staircase. "It wasn't exactly like
that…"

"I'm going to call this as I see it. It's bull." He leaned forward, never breaking eye contact. Miriam may just have met her match with this guy. Sighing loudly, she turned her head at the sound of Miriam's voice.

"What's bull?" She approached the table, looking a bit blotchy but less red than she had been minutes earlier.

"This story. I'm not being sucked into it. What do you guys want? What's your hidden agenda?"

Miriam laughed wickedly. "Hidden agenda?" She edged closer to him. "Just what might our agenda be? Do you know how ridiculous you sound? What could we possibly have to gain from wanting Ryan's body on this property?"

"Well… I…"

"Exactly." Miriam placed a fist on the table in front of Phil. They sat, face-to-face.

"Coffee anyone?" Naomi stood as she whistled.

"No." They stated the response in unison. *Wow.* Tension hung thickly in the air.

"Please just try to have an open mind. Now that you know why Ryan disappeared, just open your mind a bit. Clearly he and Maggie were dating. I'm not making any of this up."

"Hey, hold on there a second." Miriam placed her hand on her chin and squinted at Phil. "Why the heck didn't you report your brother as a missing person?"

"Excellent question," Naomi commented.

"If you knew anything at all about my brother, you would know that he was a free spirit. Sometimes I went up to a year without hearing from him. He did email me a few times, though, over the past few years. Why would I think anything was amiss? Heck, you hung out with the guy and had no clue he was a ghost."

"He does have a point," Miriam raised her brows at

Naomi.

"Well, yes. I suppose he wasn't exactly what I'd call a missing person." It baffled her that Maggie's spirit was so different in form and that her communication was so stunted compared to Ryan. Her only theory was that since her body had been laid to rest, she wasn't able to wander about the human world like her friend. Ryan had been in complete denial about his own death, so that had most likely been a huge factor as well.

"There's no point in arguing, Phil. Don't waste our time, and we won't waste yours. We're coming together because both you and Naomi cared deeply for Ryan. But don't forget who held his heart."

"Maggie," Phil whispered, his head hung low.

"Yes." Miriam reached over and placed her hand over his. "If I didn't say it before, I'm so sorry about your brother."

"Thank you." Phil's eyes misted over.

It was working. But Naomi sensed sincerity in Miriam. This wasn't part of the plan to persuade Phil over to their side of thinking. This was genuine empathy coming from Miriam. Interesting.

"Fine, ladies. You get your way. Can I have some coffee, please?"

"Thank you!" Miriam impulsively jumped from her chair and wrapped her arms around him.

Naomi looked on, smiling. Something was definitely up with Miriam. It was rare for her to show anyone her soft side. That took trust and time.

Phil finished up his cup of coffee and excused himself. He asked Miriam if she wouldn't mind walking him out to discuss some of the details of the case.

"Sure. Hey, there's a small park around the corner if you want to take a walk," Miriam suggested.

"That sounds good, but I have to grab my gloves from the back of my car. Do you have gloves?"

"Nah. I'm fine," Miriam shrugged. Naomi watched

in fascination as they walked to his car and he grabbed his gloves. After some discussion, he placed the gloves in Miriam's hands.

"Well, I'll be." Naomi grinned as she witnessed them together. She couldn't blame Miriam for being smitten. He was Ryan's brother, after all.

Closing the main door to her house, Naomi leaned against it as her mind wandered to her own romance with Bryce. She owed him a phone call and hoped he wasn't angry with her for not calling him back last night.

"Hey."

She smiled at the sound of his deep voice. All male, very sexy.

"Hey. I wanted to apologize for last night. I was caught up writing and didn't hear the phone ring."

"No worries. Did you get much accomplished?"

"I think so. It's so emotional for me, though. I feel as if it's taken longer than any other book I've written."

"That makes sense, Naomi. Think about it. You're emotionally invested in this story, and you're technically one of the main characters."

"Hm. I suppose I am." She hadn't thought of it that way. Nor had she considered how she would write herself into the story.

"Are you free tonight for dinner? I have a sitter available, and I'd really like to spend some time with you."

It sounded amazing. "Yes, Bryce. I'd like that."

"Good. Get some writing done, and I'd love to hear all about your book when I see you later."

He was too good to be true, but he was proving to be genuine.

Sighing, she walked into the living room, drawn to the window overlooking the cemetery. *Where are you, Ryan? Where have you gone?*

"Thank you."

Spinning around at the sound of his voice, she knocked

into the lamp next to the window. He stood in plain view right in front of her.

His arms opened wide for her. He smelled fresh, clean and alive. He broke the embrace to look her in the eyes.

"Naomi."

His bloodshot eyes told of his sorrow. They told the tale of his travels over his absence.

"Don't go. Don't leave me," Naomi whispered as she clung to him.

"Naomi, don't. Don't make this any harder for me. Don't make me choose."

"Choose?" She didn't understand.

"She needs me. Maggie needs me and I need her."

"What are you saying? You can stay?"

His bitter laugh filled the air. "Like this, not like before. I can stay like she did. In a state of unrest, searching for closure."

But no, that wasn't at all what she wished for him. "Where is she, Ryan? Where's Maggie?"

"She's waiting for me." He gazed out the window, out at the graveyard beyond. "I won't leave her alone out there. It's too dark, too cold, without someone you love by your side."

She couldn't stop the tears from falling. "Oh, Ryan. I don't want it to end like this. You and her, you're soul mates. Go to her."

"You'll be fine. You have Bryce by your side. Heck, you'd be fine anyway. It was your strength that drew me toward you, you know." Tears flowed down from his eyes, and he didn't try to hide them.

"Thank you for talking sense into my brother. If you hadn't, I would have made his life miserable for all eternity."

They both laughed at his comment. He was here, standing by her side, and she couldn't think how she was going to say good-bye to him. "This is it, isn't it?"

"I'm afraid it is." His hands smoothed her cheeks. There

was nothing either could say at this moment. She wanted him to stay here forever. She knew, instinctively, his heart was torn. Torn between his soulmate and his best friend.

"So I guess you've figured it all out by now. It was my fault. If I hadn't pushed her to overcome her fears, given her the wine, argued with Nick…" His voice trailed off as he brought his hand up to cover his face.

"Don't you do that to yourself, Ryan. I won't allow it. You loved her. It was an accident. A tragic accident," she exclaimed.

"It shouldn't have happened."

"But it did and there's nothing you can do except face the fact that she loves you so much, forgives you." Naomi cried at the sight of his distraught eyes.

"It's just too much to bear."

"I know." She held him until she felt his deep, wracking sobs to her core. "But she loves you, and at this point, not much else is important."

He pulled away from her, as if preparing to leave.

"Will I see you again?" she asked, desperate to keep him there beside her.

"God, I hope not for a very long time." He kissed the top of her head and grabbed her closer once more.

"I love you." he mouthed, studying her eyes, her face. "You're one of the most precious things in the world to me."

Wracking sobs shook her body. "I love you, too."

In a moment of high emotion, she melted into him as he tilted her head up to face him. He placed his lips on hers and she kissed him. For all the good times, bad times, sweetness and sorrow. For all they had been through and meant to one another.

"Don't go yet. Just stay for a few minutes more," she cried.

"I have to, or I'll never be able to turn my back on you." He walked, his form fading through the window.

"No!" Her hands spread out on the window, sobbing as

she watched him walk to Maggie's grave.

"Naomi."

It was Bryce, standing there, his mouth open, eyes wide with disbelief.

"Bryce. It's not what it looked like."

"Don't, Naomi. Don't. "He backed away, into the kitchen. She heard the slam of the door that signaled his disappointment and hurt.

CHAPTER FORTY-TWO

Naomi

THE SERVICE was small; not many people attended. As a matter of fact, it was only Naomi, Miriam, Phil and Maggie's parents, besides a few of his former co-workers from the college on the hill. Naomi felt as if a piece of her was missing. Not only had she lost Ryan, but Bryce had slipped from her fingers as well. Miriam swore he would come around, with time.

Naomi, on the other hand, wasn't so sure.

She couldn't bear to watch as Ryan's body was laid to rest beside Maggie's grave. Not now; the hurt was too raw. Later, she would come back here when she was alone and say her good-byes. She wasn't as strong as Ryan thought she was. She needed him so much after all.

She turned to leave and head back to her house alone, head tilted down. Her only hope of getting her mind off of Ryan and Bryce was to write tonight. All night, if that's what it took.

"Where are you going?"

Naomi jumped at the sound of Bryce's voice. "Bryce. What are you doing here?" She tried to keep her cool as her heart raced.

"I needed to see you. We have to talk."

Exactly what she feared most. "Now really isn't a great time." She turned back to stare at Ryan's grave.

"You look like hell."

Lifting her head to face him, she stared him right in the eye. "Thanks, Bryce, I needed to hear that right about now."

"That's not what I meant. You look like you've been up crying for days." He came closer, his mouth in a frown.

"I can't hide the fact that I'm upset, that I feel like a hole has been ripped out of my chest." She felt anger, and it was a welcome emotion. Anything but the pain she had been experiencing since she had discovered Ryan was gone. "Despite what you think, Ryan and I don't have those kind of feelings for each other. We never really did. Ours was a deep friendship, and I wouldn't expect anyone else to understand."

"Stop it, Naomi. Relax. I came here to tell you I'm an idiot. A fool. How could I have been jealous of a ghost? Even if he were still alive, I trust you."

This wasn't what she had been expecting. She was ready to fight him, to let him know how pissed she was that he wasn't speaking to her. Not sure how to respond now, she held back.

"Is there any chance you'll forgive me?"

His brown eyes pleaded with her. Her heart melted a tiny bit. "I... Oh, Bryce. How can I stay mad at you?" She opened her arms to him.

It felt good. It felt right.

She was home.

Home in his arms, in his life. She belonged here with him and his little girl. Call it fate, call it destiny, she had been thrown into his path for a reason.

"I have something I've been trying to tell you the past few days—heck, probably longer than that." He smiled down at her, moving a lock of hair out of her eyes.

"What is it, Bryce?" she whispered as her heart opened to him.

"I love you."

Tears sprang from her eyes. "I don't know what to say," she cried. "I'm an emotional, happy wreck right now."

Laughter bubbled up inside her.

"Say you love me too." he muttered in her ear.

Warmth spread through her. "I love you too, Bryce."

He leaned down and kissed her. She just might be all right, after all. Ryan was correct about Bryce. He was one of the good ones.

And maybe she was as strong as Ryan had believed.

BRYCE HAD LEFT a few minutes earlier. So much for getting any writing done today. Wrapped in his arms for the remainder of that afternoon, she had never felt so content, but Bryce had to get back home. Holly's aunt was dropping off Holly after a day with her cousins.

Tomorrow, Naomi would go over and visit Holly. Just she and Holly. They would have another "play date." Smiling at the thought, she grabbed her heavy coat before she chickened out and changed her mind.

It was time for a proper good-bye.

Whistling wind snapped at her cheeks as she made her way out to his grave. Cold, misting rain had started to fall lightly from the sky. She pictured Ryan crying from the heavens. As quickly as the thought registered, she dismissed it. Ryan wouldn't symbolize the pouring rain. He represented the bright sunshine instead, just as he had been in life, bright and full of life.

The grave stood straight ahead, faint moonlight lighting the way. Sucking in a deep breath, she closed her eyes. Counting to ten, she then opened them, calling forth every ounce of her courage.

Brushing the wet stone off with the sleeve of her coat, she sat down on the wet ground. "Ryan."

He was gone, though. Happy with the woman he had called his soulmate. She couldn't have picked a better person for him if she searched for miles. "You two are long overdue for some happiness, you know."

From behind, someone tapped her shoulder. Gasping, she spun around to find Ryan. He stood, surreal in the foggy night.

"Ryan." Her jaw dropped. She didn't want to break the spell she was under. She couldn't move.

"I knew you would come, I couldn't stand it if you stayed away. But now, Naomi, is the time for our last good-bye. Seeing you like this is breaking my heart." He reached out and touched her, and instead of coldness, she felt his warmth. Seemed that even death couldn't take that from him.

"Ryan," she cried out.

"Enough of the tears, Naomi. Be at peace, we finally are. Be happy for us."

"I am. I miss you, though. Why did you have to go and die on me? Why did you leave me when I needed you most?"

Even as the words spilled from her, she knew she was wrong. How the hell could it be his fault that he was taken? He was dead before she had even known him. "I'm sorry. I shouldn't have said that."

"You're human. It's okay, sweetheart. It's okay."

"Where is she, Ryan? I need to see her, too. I have to say good-bye to Maggie."

His silence unnerved her. What did it mean?

"I've been here all along, right beside you, Naomi." It was a voice she had only heard in a different way.

Humming, moaning, and crying, but never like this—this was the side of Maggie that showed what she had been in life.

If she thought Maggie was beautiful before, she positively glowed right now. Being with Ryan had a supernatural effect on her. Maggie radiated warmth and love. Gone was the bitter, agonized soul.

"Maggie."

The spirit opened her arms wide, pulling Naomi inside the light and warmth. Naomi felt an overwhelming sense of peace and happiness. She didn't want to leave.

"I can't even begin to know how to thank you for everything you've done. Your interest from the start has been incredible. You saved my soul, Naomi. I'll forever be grateful to you for that. "

"I wouldn't change a thing, Maggie. You were so loved, you're still so loved. Your parents love you more than their hearts can hold. Not many people can claim that type of love in this world, Maggie."

A tender touch descended upon her. "They love you, too. Take good care of them for me, will you? You mean the world to them.'

"They mean so much to me, too, Maggie. I can't even begin to tell you how close we've become."

Maggie's eyes filled with tears. "I know," she whispered. Her fingertips grazed Naomi's cheek. "I told you, I've been by your side all along. I knew you could do it. Knew you were smart enough to piece together the clues to free Ryan and me. I've been waiting for you to come along, all these years."

Howling wind picked up, and Naomi felt her time with Ryan and Maggie was coming to an end. Warmth faded as a cold chill increased. Is this how the ending of her story would play out? She struggled to be heard over the pounding rain and increasing wind.

"You need to let go, Naomi. If you don't, you'll be trapped forever with hatred in your heart. Your heart will turn cold and you'll become bitter in the end."

"What are you saying? I have closure now, I feel it." But she was lying to herself. One crucial piece of the puzzle was missing, and she suddenly realized what it was and the devastating impact it could have upon her.

"Be strong, be brave," Maggie called out as she placed a gently kiss on Naomi's cheek. "Forgive him."

"I don't know if I can," Naomi sobbed freely, reaching out for Ryan and Maggie. They slipped further away with each word she spoke.

"Ryan!"

"Be brave. Be happy," he called out, his voice diminishing, fading as quickly as his ghostly form.

She was soaking wet, and her heart cried for him, for all he had been through. "I will, Ryan. I will." The last thing she noticed was the tears falling from Ryan's eyes as he and Maggie disappeared from sight. "You be happy, too," Naomi whispered. She held her hand out, but no one reached out in return. Knowing it was the last time she would lay eyes on them, she sat back down on the cold, wet earth, not wanting to be anywhere else but beside Maggie and Ryan.

She had no idea how long she had been sitting there, in the cold, icy rain. Time didn't matter; it was irrelevant. She forgot that someone else loved her every bit as much as Ryan did.

She heard him approaching, saw his confusion at finding her here, alone in the cemetery in the stormy, black night.

It was a moment that she would play back for a long time to come. The moment that she knew for certain, that she, too, had found her soulmate.

He didn't ask questions, simply scooped her up in his arms and carried her back to her house. Up the stairs, he gently placed her down on the floor to her room and stripped her sticky, wet clothes from her body. He rummaged through her dresser, finding a pair of cotton pajamas, which he gently clothed her in.

Guiding her to her bed, he turned down the sheets and placed a pillow under her head. Lastly, he leaned over, without a word, and kissed her forehead before turning to leave.

Watching him go, she felt tears of happiness this time. "I love you," she whispered as he disappeared down the stairs.

CHAPTER FORTY-THREE

Naomi

SITTING IN THE waiting area, once again, she recalled how nervous she had been last time she was here, days ago. This felt different, though.

This felt like the closure she had been desperately seeking.

Nick had been an ass, to put it mildly, but he had also told the truth in the end. Who was she to throw stones? She had never walked a mile in his shoes.

Shoes that had been lonely and neglected since childhood.

There was a fine line between empathy and tolerance. She teetered on the edge. Cringing at the metaphor, she dismissed the thought.

She heard a man calling her name, then she was led down a path to a plastic chair in the middle of the room this time. She swallowed hard at the sight of him. His color was off, and a slight beard had started to grow on his boyish face.

As if in a standoff, they hesitated to see who would pick up the phone first. She grabbed it and waited for him to pick up on his side.

"What is it now, Naomi?" Instead of the usual hostility, his stature seemed smaller, his voice weaker. Half determined to turn around and walk the heck out of there, she recalled Ryan's last wish.

288

"I-I need to say something to you."

"Save it, I get enough abuse around here." He scoffed as he shook his head.

"Let me finish. I came to say that I appreciate you telling me the truth. I thank you for not dragging this deeper than it already was. I will never understand or condone your poor decisions, but I'm going to let it go." She maintained eye contact, unsure of what he was feeling. "If Maggie could save you that day, I guess I can forgive you."

"Oh, wow, Naomi. That's mighty big of you. So glad you forgive me. Maybe I can get some sleep around here for a change."

"I knew this was a bad idea. I should have never come here." Naomi smacked her phone down and stood, grabbing her bag from the floor.

A rapping sounded on the glass. He waved his hand, motioning for her to sit back down.

Begrudgingly, she took a seat and waited a moment before picking up the black phone.

"What?"

"I'm sorry. This whole thing sucks so badly, Naomi." His head sunk down to his chin.

"Listen up, Nick. I'm not here to pacify you or to be your friend. What happened between us, with Maggie and Ryan? All of it, that's what sucks, Nick. I came to say my piece, and now I'm leaving."

"Naomi, wait. Will I see you again?"

"Not if I can help it, Nick, but if we do cross paths, respect my request for you to stay away. You've hurt us all enough."

Was this what Maggie had meant when she wished she would forgive Nick? Probably not quite, but it was a start. In time, the pain would lessen, and then she could let go a tiny piece more until all the heartache was gone. Like she said, it was the beginning.

Without looking back at his pitiful face, she held her

head high and exited the prison. Only when she walked out into the chilly, damp air did she smile. Turning around to take in the stark prison in front of her, she nodded her head.

"How was that, Maggie? I hope you approve." She walked over to her car and sat for a moment, stilling her shaking hands.

As she was about to start the ignition, a text sounded from her bag. Reaching in, Naomi opened the message and grinned widely. Just when she thought nothing else could surprise her. It seemed Phil would be hanging around for a few extra days before heading back home.

Naomi responded to Miriam's text, stating she would love to meet up with her and Phil for dinner tomorrow night, and yes, she would see if Bryce was available as well.

She placed her cell down on the console and drove home, happy to be heading back to Bryce and Holly.

She had promised Bryce's daughter some time alone, just the two of them. Bryce had suggested they go out for some hot cocoa, or to a matinee. She was so out of touch with what children watched in the movies nowadays, but she trusted Bryce's suggestion for the new animated princess movie Holly had wanted to see so badly.

Spying the little girl peeking out the door waiting for her, her heart filled with warmth. She already had her jacket on, ready to go. Bryce opened the door as she pulled up further into the driveway. Holly spilled out, rushing toward her with an expression that only children can pull off.

"Nomi!" Holly squealed, jumping up at her as she walked from the car. Naomi squeezed her back with every bit of her strength.

"You sure you guys don't want me tagging along?" He squinted in the bright sunlight.

"Girls day out!" Holly shouted, giving Naomi a solid high five.

"Okay, I see when I'm not wanted." He backed up, feigning hurt, but winked at Naomi as she buckled Holly into the booster seat Bryce had handed over. Once Holly was secure in the back seat of the car, Naomi closed the door, allowing her and Bryce to have a private moment before heading out.

He placed his hands on either side of her hips and leaned in. "I love you." He bit down gently on her lower lip. Kissing him back, she whispered to him.

"I love you, too."

Backing out of the driveway, she waved good-bye to Bryce from her rear view mirror.

"Nomi?"

"Yes, sweetie?"

"Does girls' day out mean popcorn, too?"

"Sure, Holly. Why not?"

"Good. It's our little secret."

Naomi caught Holly's smile from the rear view and returned it.

Laughing out loud, Naomi finally knew what it meant to feel complete.

EPILOGUE

Six Months Later

Naomi

WITH HER FINGERS pounding on the keyboard, Naomi kept at it until the day darkened around her. Zelda was lying contentedly at her feet. She was so close, only minutes away from the ending of Maggie's story.

The last scene developed before her. After saying her good-byes to Maggie and Ryan, after visiting Nick in prison to start the healing process, Naomi ended the final chapter with her day at the movies with Holly.

Realizing something amazing, her fingertips came to a rest at last. She typed the words that felt so good to every author: "The End." Cleansing tears signaled the closing of her book. She hadn't known until the very last chapter that this was not entirely Maggie's story after all. As a matter of fact, several people shared in the tale. Maggie and Ryan, of course, but also Maggie's parents, Miriam, Phil, and lastly, Bryce and Holly.

"I suppose that does it." She knew she would miss writing this story. It already felt bittersweet, concluding this book.

Tomorrow she would reread her entire story, from start to finish, even backwards at parts, just to ensure she had gotten the story perfect. She hadn't yet given her story a title, but an idea was brewing.

Needing just a bit more time to be a hundred percent sure this was a deserving title to such an important book, she would sit tight for now.

She picked up her cell phone to glance at the time. Shoot. Bryce would be here any minute. As usual, she lost track of time when she was writing. He had said prepare for a day outside. Thankfully, the day was mild and sunny, so opposite of the cool, autumn weather in which her life changed forever.

Bryce refused to tell her where they were headed, but the mystery was certainly enticing. Grabbing her bag, she headed into the kitchen to peek out the window. Sure enough, he pulled in the driveway as she watched. Guessing that he didn't just walk over meant the surprise destination wouldn't be within driving distance, she grinned. What was he up to?

"Okay, Bryce," she called as he stepped out to his truck, "are you going to tell me where you're taking me, or are you going to let the suspense do me in?"

He laughed heartily, but stood his ground. "Oh no, you don't. You'll find out when we get there. You're just going to have to practice some patience. But trust me, it'll be worth the wait."

"Hm. I guess I'm going to have to take your word for it, but it sounds like trouble to me." Naomi grabbed him playfully, smacking a kiss on his lips for a moment longer than necessary.

"Hey, save that for later, Naomi, or you're going to ruin my whole plan." He winked at her.

"Fine, let's go. I can barely wait to find out what you're up to."

He led her to her side of his truck, jumped in himself, and then pulled out of the driveway in silence. Normally chatty, Bryce kept his focus on the road ahead. The familiar road up ahead stretched past the golf course and into the parking area near the mountains.

At first, she thought this must be a joke, bringing her here, but Bryce wasn't a cruel person.

"What?" Her eyes fixed on Bryce's face.

He parked the truck and turned to Naomi. Placing his hand on her chin, he guided her eyes up to face.

"It's okay. Do you trust me?"

She realized that coming to terms with the events of the past few months included experiencing the cliffs in a different light. For this was the place that Ryan and Maggie lost their lives. It was also a place they had grown to love and enjoy so much prior to the accident.

Without this day trip, the cliffs would forever signify horror and despair. With this outing, they could represent another form of closure for her.

"Come. Help me grab some things from the back."

He reached into the back of the truck, pulling out some bags, a bottle of wine, and two wineglasses.

"A picnic?" Her eyes went wide. An image of her visions in the woods crashed back. But since Maggie and Ryan had discovered peace, the terrifying nightmares had ceased. Actually, come to think of it, the picnic in the mountain had been one of Maggie and Ryan's most favorite memories.

Until Maggie had heard movement from the woods, that is.

Let it go. She could almost hear Ryan's voice saying the gentle words. He was just out of reach.

"You up for this, honey?" Concern etched his face.

Bryce had gone through a lot of trouble planning this day out, and she didn't wish to hurt his feelings.

"I-I'm fine." Naomi managed.

"Naomi? I think you're the strongest person I've ever known." She listened to him as she nodded her head. "It's because of your determination, your unique will, that I brought you back here. I want this place to be special to us, just like it was to them. Does that make sense?"

It made perfect sense. And that was why she loved him so much.

He got her. Understood what made her tick.

Grabbing his hand, they made the hike up the mountain. Reaching the grassy clearing, Naomi stopped, prepared to stay a while.

"No, this isn't it."

He led her further up the mountain until her stomach was in a tight knot. *What was this tough love or something, Bryce?*

She could stop him, head back to the safer clearing. But she knew there was a purpose to his madness, and she was curious to find out what he had planned.

"We can go back if you're not comfortable, but something tells me you're going to be happy if you decide to head up there."

Scanning the wooded area, she bit her lip, determined to trudge forward. She had Bryce by her side, she could do this. Once they were standing on the top of the mountain, he led her further until they reached their destination.

"It's just a little bit further," he whispered into her ear as she stayed by his side. Her quaking legs gave away her brave façade.

"I know where it is, Bryce," she breathed in. Eyes wide, she swallowed, seeing Ryan's face encouraging her.

"Stop. We're here." Bryce released her hand. She breathed deeply to steady her raw nerves. As she stood silently, he uncorked the bottle of wine and poured the deep red liquid into a glass for her.

Accepting the wine with a shaking hand, she welcomed the beverage as it slid down, warming her belly.

"Just a second, I brought something else with me." Rummaging through his bag, he produced a small knife.

Instantly, a smile formed as she knew what he would do next. "Should I do the honors? Or would you like to?" He held the knife within arm's reach.

"This is your idea, you go ahead." Mesmerized, she watched as he carved a small heart next to the etching made years earlier by Ryan for his Maggie.

Tears rolled down her face as he carved their initials. Their own heart was now complete, resting right beside the original. N and B.

"What do you think?"

"I think it's beautiful and I think you're amazing."

He released a breath, chuckling softly. "You have no idea how relieved I am to hear you say that." Turning for a moment, he reached down into the bag on the ground once more. "Close your eyes."

Wondering what he had in store next, she acquiesced, a smile forming on her face.

"Keep them closed."

She nodded, savoring the moment.

"I brought you here for more than one reason, Naomi. First, I wanted to give you closure, help you to remember that although this place held bad memories, it also included wonderful ones. Next, I wanted to honor Ryan and Maggie's love. I also know you're just the one, the *only* one who could write their love story. Heck, I'm really nervous, Naomi."

Tempted to open her eyes to see his face as he spoke, she used every bit of restraint to keep her eyes shut tight.

"Naomi. I want our love story to be just as meaningful. In my mind, it deserves its place right here next to Maggie and Ryan. What I'm trying to say, Naomi…"

She nodded, not sure if she could keep her eyes closed for one second more.

"You can open your eyes now," he laughed.

Peering up at him, his eyes held hers, connecting with her. Her heart tugged as she attempted to hold back the tears.

Kneeling down on one knee, he fumbled with the small box he had held behind his back until that moment.

"Naomi? Will you marry me and make me and Holly the two happiest people ever?" His eyes softened as he gazed up at her.

"Yes, Bryce. Yes!" She had forgotten that the two of

them were standing near the edge of the cliff. All of her fear subsided. He stood, and she leapt up to kiss him, seeing Maggie's face in her mind, smiling warmly.

She knew one thing. If she had to do it all over again, she wouldn't change a thing. Maggie had opened up Naomi's eyes, made her see how important her connection with love, with Bryce, was, and how much of a journey it could be to find the one person in this big world you were meant to stand beside.

She also realized another thing. She had one more chapter left to write. And she also knew for certain now that she had the perfect title for her book.

It would be called *Maggie*.

ACKNOWLEDGEMENTS

WHERE DO I start? There are so many people to thank. Maggie will always have a special place in my heart since it was the first novel that I published on my own, but with a ton of love and support from so many amazing people.

Alexandra, as I always say, your love for the paranormal continues to rub off on me. The books, the movies and the discussions all inspire me to write my own paranormal novels. So thank you again.

Mom, Dad, Alan, Jimmer, Damian, Amanda and Siobhan, thank you for your love and support. Mom, thanks for reading Maggie and all your valuable feedback. Siobhan, I hope the fact that I was inspired by your house and property while creating Maggie doesn't freak you out. (laughs) Thanks for the countless times I wandered around your yard and beyond for inspiration.

I wanted to thank my oldest friends for their ongoing support. Kim, Janine, Karen, Jen and Diann- thank you for reading my books, and for listening and just being there.

I can't thank my street team enough. Seriously. This group of amazing women have been my support team throughout writing this story and many others.

My editor, Dawn Yacovetta has got to be one of the sweetest women out there. Thank you so much for all your help and feedback while editing Maggie. I can't tell you how much I appreciate your hard work.

Sara Meadows, what can I say? As proofreader for Maggie and my amazing PA, thank you for everything, including giving me the nudge (push- haha) to finally give self-publishing a try. Also, thank you for your help throughout the entire process of publishing Maggie. Your friendship and support have been amazing. And your patience too! (Keep calm- format on.)

Thank you to my team of beta readers for Maggie. Kim DiMauro, Lauren Gebhardt, Maari Hammond, Kallie Kennon, Tabatha Marsh, Cindy Mathis, Sara Meadows, Kelly McMullen Lowe, Jessica Sroga, Dawn Yacovetta and Jemimah Zafoune, your feedback was very helpful. I also wanted to thank all the members of my street team for their ongoing support. We have lots of laughs and I appreciate you all. Char Webster and Kelly McMullen Lowe, I wanted to thank you for helping me out with the uploading process and answering all of my questions. Megan Travers, thank you for your help and support with so many of my books.

I love the cover for Maggie. It's absolutely perfect for the story. Thank you to my cover artist and member of my street team, Jena Brignola. Jena created the most amazing teasers and promo posts for Maggie as well. Jill Sava, thank you for your help formatting Maggie.

To my readers, thank you for your support. It makes my day when I hear that people enjoy my books. There's nothing like having someone tell you how much they liked reading your story, so thank you.

So yes, they say it takes a village. Whew!

You can follow me on Instagram @myaomalley and Facebook.com/myaomalley.

XOXO Mya